He rocked her in his arms, murmuring quiet words until her tears began to subside. "Tell me what happened, sweetheart."

With that her weeping started anew. "Oh, Shane, he . . . he . . ."

"He what?" Shane demanded, his grip tightening.

When she failed to respond, he put his large, strong hands on either side of her face and forced her to look into his eyes. "Caroline," he said, the word a gentle command. "Tell me what happened."

"He . . . hit me . . ."

Fury surged through him. "Who did this?"

"I don't know," she stammered through her tears. "It was too dark to see." She took a deep shaky breath. "He said some redskin was my . . . my lover."

He leaned down to kiss her tears away—a gentle kiss on either cheek. She turned her head, ever so slightly, until his lips pressed against hers.

The touch sent a shiver of longing through his body, bringing painfully to the surface all the desire he felt for her, all he had suppressed. He pressed her body to his, tighter, closer, as if to become one. One life. Flesh of his flesh. Together.

But that was impossible . . .

✳

DIAMOND WILDFLOWER ROMANCE

A breathtaking line of searing romance novels . . .
where destiny meets desire
in the untamed fury of the American West.

TEXAS ANGEL

LINDA FRANCIS LEE

DIAMOND BOOKS, NEW YORK

This book is a Diamond original edition,
and has never been previously published.

TEXAS ANGEL

A Diamond Book / published by arrangement with
the author

PRINTING HISTORY
Diamond edition / May 1994

All rights reserved.
Copyright © 1994 by Linda Francis Lee.
This book may not be reproduced in whole or in part,
by mimeograph or any other means, without permission.
For information address: The Berkley Publishing Group,
200 Madison Avenue, New York, NY 10016.

ISBN: 0-7865-0007-7

Diamond Books are published by The Berkley Publishing Group,
200 Madison Avenue, New York, NY 10016.
DIAMOND and the "D" design
are trademarks belonging to Charter Communications, Inc.

PRINTED IN THE UNITED STATES OF AMERICA

10 9 8 7 6 5 4 3 2 1

For Michael

CHAPTER

✳

1

San Antonio, Texas
1860

"HURRY, SHANE!"

Long rays of late-afternoon sun spilled through a high-mullioned window, catching motes of dust in a timeless dance.

"Hurry!" the woman called again, her eyes filled with mischief as she gathered her skirts, then hurried down the long, wood-paneled hall.

Shane Rivers stood at the top of the stairs, cast in light, his dark hair swept back from his forehead. Standing there, so quiet and still, his tall form sculpted with such flawless precision, he seemed hard and formidable. His slate-gray eyes were deep and dark, forbidding, giving no clue to the smile that played just beneath the surface.

He was happy, he realized. Happier, that is, than he had been in a long time. Everything was perfect—almost. But almost was good enough, he reminded himself when thoughts of sunshine and laughter tried to push their way into his mind. Yes, almost would have to do.

1

He took a deep breath, letting it out slowly, clearing his mind. And then the smile that had only threatened before surfaced, easing the chiseled planes of his face, lightening his features until some would have said he was nearly beautiful, and he followed his betrothed.

He caught her outside the door of one of the many guest bedrooms in the huge, sprawling home at the center of town. Picking her up, he twirled her around, voluminous skirts billowing about her. He lowered her slowly, her body sliding against his. Her mischievous laugh gave way to a languorous smile as her fingers slowly trailed down his hard-muscled chest. The palms of her hands came to rest on the pressed front of his black waistcoat, her delicately laced French gloves looking like splashes of light against a midnight sky.

"Careful, Henrietta, or I'm going to think you've brought me up here to have your way with me."

Her eyelids fluttered closed when his mouth brushed the curve of her neck, barely, softly. She slipped her arms around him, pressing closer. "I *have* brought you up here to have my way with you."

His body stilled, a slight, tense hesitation, before he forced a smile, unwound her arms from around him, and put her at arm's length. "Not yet, Henrietta. And not under your father's roof. Especially when in no more than a few minutes he will be holding a party to announce our betrothal."

"Oh, pooh! Father's having this party to raise money to help him become the next governor of Texas. Our announcement is only an excuse." She ducked out from beneath his grip and came up behind him, wrapping her arms around his waist.

Long moments ticked by in silence. He ran his hand through his hair. "Regardless of his intent," he finally said, "we should return downstairs."

She only pressed closer, resting her cheek against his back.

"Henrietta, you're not making this easy."

"That's the point," she purred. "I want you, Shane Rivers. Not in two months when we're husband and wife. I want you now." She kissed a fiery trail along his spine. "Besides, we'll be married soon. What's the harm?" She ran her palms up his abdomen to his chest and then slowly, carefully, maddeningly brought them back down, not stopping at his waist.

Shane's brow furrowed with frustration. "Henrietta," he repeated, his tone warning.

"Yes, love?" She pulled her lip between pearl-white teeth then lowered her hand even farther.

He sucked in his breath, closed his eyes, and groaned. But just as had been happening to him over the last several months, visions of wild red hair and deep green eyes flitted through his mind. He thought of sunshine and the smell of spring—and as always, love and laughter.

And that made him angry. Henrietta was to be his wife.

So when his betrothed's tiny hand descended even farther to press against him, he turned in her arms, lifted her quickly, carried her across the threshold, and kicked the thick wooden door shut behind them, as if in doing so he could banish thoughts of the other completely from his mind.

Music started up in the ballroom of Henrietta Whitley's family home. French doors, swathed in golden silk with braided ropes and tassels, stood open, letting the late-afternoon breeze float through the room to mingle with the crowd like a welcome guest.

Shane stood amid the crowd, and had for some forty-five minutes, waiting. He smiled and laughed as the people he had come to know during the last nine months he had lived in San Antonio sought his company and asked his advice. He was an important man—a status he had worked hard for. And now, after his return to Texas following years in the nation's capital, he planned to make his way in the politics of his home state.

But this day he had little interest in diplomacy or the people around him. Not even the old man, Rupert Bromley, who despite the age difference had become such a good friend, could interest Shane in conversation. His mind was on other things.

The good humor he had fought to maintain slowly began to evaporate as he waited for Henrietta to appear, thoughts of their earlier interlude circling in his mind. Never in his twenty-eight years had he seen a woman of virtue behave in the manner she had in the guest bedroom. In very different kinds of bedroom altogether he had experienced such behavior—in brothels, bordellos, even finely furnished boudoirs of wealthy matrons—but never with a woman he intended to make his wife. The thought left him cold.

Tension shimmered down his spine. And suddenly he found he wanted no part of this—he wanted no part of her. Nearly nine months ago he set out to win her hand, and win her hand he had. He had pursued her with the calm determination that characterized all of his dealings. She was beautiful, had a sense of humor, and being the daughter of a politician, she understood the life they would have to lead.

With that thought, Henrietta appeared at the top of the stairs. Her golden-blond tresses, that less than an hour before had tumbled in wild disarray about her face, were pulled up in an elaborate design of twists and curls. A sweet, innocent smile graced her tiny rosebud mouth.

This was not the smile of a wanton woman, Shane assured himself. Henrietta was going to make the perfect wife. And for a second he wondered if perhaps he had imagined the afternoon liaison.

She came down the steps as regally as a queen, the voluminous blue silk brocade gown flowing around her. Shane stepped forward to meet her. Within seconds the couple was pulled into the festive party, talking and laughing, gliding across the high-polished dance floor until, finally, Shane's unease began to fade.

The only remaining dark spot on the otherwise joyous occasion was the attendance of Dean Fowler, dressed in velvet and lace as if he lived in the gold-gilded salons of Paris instead of the frontier town of San Antonio. Shane knew the man had been traveling from New Orleans to California in search of his fortune when he had stopped in San Antonio. Without explanation, his journey had suddenly ended and the fortune he sought took the shape of Henrietta Whitley.

Shane hadn't liked Fowler since the day he arrived in town and cast his leering eye on Henrietta. As time went by he liked him even less. But Dean had managed to finagle his way into the good graces of Henrietta's father, Lamar Whitley, leaving Shane no choice but to endure the man's company.

The festivities had not long been under way, the gubernatorial campaign fund bursting with contributions, when Lamar called for the crowd's attention.

"Gathered friends, I appreciate you joinin' me and my daughter on this joyous day. Not because you've shown such tremendous support for my bid for the governor's office, but because this afternoon I wish to share with you the announcement of my sweet Henrietta's betrothal to the man who has become such an integral part of my campaign, Mr. Shane Rivers."

Lamar lifted a glass of champagne as the crowd cheered and shouted congratulations. Henrietta smiled, held secure in the crook of Shane's long arm. Toasts were made all around until Dean Fowler stepped forward and raised his glass. He cleared his throat and waited until he had gained everyone's attention.

Shane tensed and Henrietta looked up at him, her eyes questioning. When Shane failed to respond, she turned back to Dean, her delicate brow furrowed with concern.

"Ladies and gentlemen, I, too, would like to make a toast." Dean's lips thinned unnaturally as he surveyed the room, calculating his effect. "To Lamar Whitley, a brave and fair man, who can look beyond a man's heritage and accept him into the bosom of his family."

A low murmur of confusion broke through the crowd. Shane's countenance grew dark and dangerous.

"Perhaps now," Dean continued, feigning ignorance of the uneasy stir he was causing, "Americans and redski— I mean, Indians, can come together in peace since the half-breed son of a full-blooded Comanche warrior is being welcomed into our folds with open arms."

There was a moment of stunned silence before someone cried, "Oh God!"

Disbelief rippled through the room, turning rapidly to indignation and outrage.

"It can't be true!" a man exclaimed. "He doesn't look like a redskin."

"You know I always thought something wasn't quite right about that man."

Henrietta stood as if paralyzed until she spun out of Shane's arm. "No!" she cried, imploring him with wretched eyes to denounce Dean Fowler for a liar. "Tell them it's not true."

Shane stood perfectly still, the tension in his jaw the only sign of his mounting anger. He did not deny the man's words, nor did he confirm them. His silence, however, told the crowd all they needed to know.

Henrietta's shock turned quickly to desperation. "After what we just . . ." Her voice trailed off, the import of the situation sinking in. "What if I become—" Her hand came to her breast, her eyes wild, before she turned on him with the force of ravaged pride urging her on. "You deceived me, you misbegotten heathen beast." She flew at him with teeth bared and nails flaying. She kicked and screamed, the perfect curls of her hair bouncing crazily on her head.

Shane didn't flinch throughout the attack. The word *Indian* filtered through his mind, snagging painfully on old and half-forgotten memories of many years past. When Henrietta's fist struck his jaw, he finally caught her by the wrist and held her at arm's length. Within seconds, a man from the crowd pulled her away and said, "I'll protect you, Miss Henrietta."

Protect her! Protect her from whom? Shane's mind raged. But still he couldn't move.

Other pieces of heated cries filtered to him.

"I didn't know. . . ."

"The deceitful barbarian, he tricked us all. . . ."

"Just imagine what would have happened once they were married! You know how much those heathens covet blond scalps. . . ."

"Thank God we found out in time. . . ."

"Thank goodness Henrietta found out before it was too late. . . ."

And then the voice of Dean Fowler. "I didn't mean to cause such a ruckus," he protested, though he turned his head away so the crowd couldn't see the triumph that flickered in his eyes. "I thought everyone knew he was a half-breed."

With that word, Shane's control snapped. He flew at Dean like a man possessed. He had him by the throat before anyone could move.

"He's killing him!" a woman screamed as Shane tightened his hands around Dean Fowler's neck, choking the life from his body.

Dean's mouth gaped open, his eyes bulged in his head. The pressure Shane exerted turned his knuckles white. The crowd stood by both afraid and fascinated as a life ebbed before them. Only Rupert Bromley had a modicum of sense left and grabbed Shane's arm. "Shane! Son! Don't throw your life away over this self-serving fool," the older man said through clenched teeth as he used every ounce of strength he possessed to pull Shane away from Dean Fowler.

Dean gasped and choked as life surged back into his lungs, his eyes bloodshot and watery, his shoulders slumped and heaving. Shane stood motionless. He stared at his hands as if he didn't recognize them. The voices around him grew louder, coming at him from every direction, making no sense. His mind swam in the murky depths of the past. Dark images tried to pull him under. He clenched his fist as if holding on to some imaginary lifeline, then turned on his heels and walked stiffly from the room.

CHAPTER

✴

2

THE HOOVES OF the black stallion shook the earth as horse and rider galloped furiously down the road. Night was fast approaching, the light drowning on the horizon as the last of the sun's fiery rays were pulled slowly to its blazing breast. Hunched low over the horse's flowing black mane, Shane rode like the devil, as if he could outride the harrowing scene that played over and over in his mind.

He had almost killed a man. The thought hit him like a blow. He had watched as if he were no more than a spectator while his hands wrapped around the neck of another man. Shane closed his eyes, trying to hold at bay the black rage that sought to swallow him. His worst nightmare had nearly played itself out in reality. He had tried to kill a man, proving that everything he had been told was true.

He was a savage.

His thoughts ebbed and flowed, swirled and collided, as he was forced back to another time so long ago. His mother's porcelain features surfaced in his mind. He heard her painful words and the echoing sound of her triumphant laughter. He saw his young stricken face. And he hated himself for the pain he let wash over him.

"No!" he roared into the dusk, the simple word wrenched from his chest.

He hadn't felt the rage in such a long time that he had come to believe he could forget. Then suddenly, in no more than a handful of seconds, the madness seized him. He could still feel the frantic pounding of blood in Dean Fowler's neck. The only thing that had saved them both was Rupert Bromley.

In his mind's eye, Shane saw Rupert's face, the crop of gray hair and clear brown eyes as he had pulled him off Dean Fowler. And Rupert had called him son, causing Shane to tumble back in time to when he was a boy and had longed so desperately for his father. Shane remembered waiting, watching, hoping his father would come for him. But that was decades ago and Rupert Bromley was not his father, though how shamelessly, for a split second, had he wished it were so. He was a grown man now. He no longer wished for things in vain. He simply dealt with possibilities, possibilities that for most men were beyond reach, but somehow over the last eleven years had become stunning and sometimes shocking realities for him.

Shane had accomplished much through hard work and rigid control over his emotions. He had succeeded in a way that made him think he could return to Texas as a civilized man and make a life for himself. And because of that success he had forgotten the truth. Just as his mother had told him all those years ago, he was a savage. The thought seared him anew. He took a deep breath, urging his mount to a faster pace, pressing his eyes shut.

Suddenly the horse careened wildly, rearing on its hind legs, pawing the air in an attempt to come to a bone-jarring halt. Angry shouts rang out in the air. Images of bandits and outlaws filled Shane's mind, shattering the haunting memories of years long past into tiny fragments, like a million shards of glass. His rage exploded, full-blown, consuming him. He no longer tried to hold the deadly emotion at bay. With no more thought for being a civilized man, he pulled a gleaming pistol from the folds of his coat and took aim.

Time stood still. His eyes stared down the shiny barrel of his Colt .45 at the sole bandit who stood in his path. The bandit, however, seeming unimpressed by Shane or his deadly expression and pistol, simply continued the spew of heated words unchecked. Shane's eyes narrowed to slits of flint, and his finger relaxed on the trigger as he tried to make sense of the sight before him.

She stood in the road like a wrathful angel, a hood of dark green cloth slipping to reveal waves of wild red hair. Though her face was obscured by darkness, he could see that all she had to defend herself with was a loosely woven basket full of plants. But then her words penetrated his mind, and he realized her basket was not her only defense. Her words were as stinging as any whip he had ever felt, and it was clear she was giving him a verbal lashing he would not soon forget.

"What's going on here?" Shane demanded, his voice low and ominous.

Her tirade stopped abruptly.

Shane started to berate the girl for her defiance and complete lack of fear in the face of uncertain circumstances, but he was cut short when she stepped closer.

His body jerked back when he made out the deep green eyes that snapped with anger and the long dark lashes that curled slightly at the ends.

"Red," he whispered, a myriad of emotions drifting across his face as he stared down at Rupert Bromley's daughter. He took a deep, calming breath and shook his head. "I should have known."

"Mr. Rivers?" Caroline Bromley asked uncertainly, peering up through the growing darkness, before her lips spread into a huge smile. "Mr. Rivers!" she exclaimed, excitement lacing her words. "I didn't realize it was you."

But then she stopped. Her smile wavered and her lips screwed up with worry before a scowl returned to mar her forehead. "Shane Rivers or not, you can't get away with such depraved riding. You might have killed someone." She didn't mention that the someone might have been her. Instead she simply looked at him with eyebrows raised, clearly expecting something of him.

Shane chuckled as he returned his pistol to its holster, then leaned forward to run a strong hand down his horse's neck. He wasn't sure what she expected, but decided an apology was in order. "I'm sorry if I startled you."

Caroline's eyes opened wide. "Startled me! You nearly ran me down!" She placed her free hand on her hip, and her basket on the other. "And I'm not looking for an apology, Mr. Rivers. I want a promise that you won't ride like that again. What if a young child or small animal had been in your path? Not everyone is as quick and nimble-footed as I am."

Shane's lips quirked up in a crooked smile. "Quick

and nimble-footed, Red? You? If there's a more accident-prone individual in town, I've not met her. And everyone for miles knows it."

Caroline sniffed and waved the unflattering comments away. "All exaggerations I assure you. But we digress. Are you or are you not going to be more careful on that horse? I have enough healing to do without you adding to my list of patients."

She didn't flutter her lashes or throw him a simpering smile in hopes of gaining a favor. She stood before him, her arms akimbo and feet spread wide, demanding he ride with decorum.

Shane rested his forearm on the saddle horn, the other crossed on top. "For you, Red, anything," he replied with a devilish smile. "Now come on. Up with you," he added, before he held out his hand. "I'll take you home. You shouldn't be out here at this time of the evening."

Caroline hesitated as she looked from Shane's proffered hand to the beautiful, but huge, beast on which he rode. "You're going to take me home ... on your horse?" she asked, her nose wrinkling with concern.

"Do you have a better idea?"

"We could walk."

"Don't tell me you're afraid to ride?"

When he received no more of a reply than a careful shrug of her shoulders, he threw back his head and laughed. "How is that possible, Red? Someone who champions the underdog, cares for the sick, teaches young children, doesn't blink an eye in the face of a pistol, is afraid to ride a horse?"

Caroline lifted her chin and took a deep breath before, without another word, she took his hand to allow herself to be pulled up in front of him. "I'm no coward, Mr. Rivers, and I'll not have you saying I am."

"Of course not, Miss Bromley. A thousand pardons."

They rode in silence, Shane's smile still spread on his lips. Whenever he was around her, he found it the same. Somehow Caroline Bromley always managed to make him smile. And it had been that way since the day he met her six months before. But a smile was not all the woman managed to bring about in him, he thought wryly. He remembered all too well the unexpected surge of desire that had coursed through his body when Rupert had introduced them, despite the fact that Shane had been as good as engaged to someone else.

He shook his head. Whether Caroline was interjecting some outrageous comment into one of his and Rupert's many philosophical discussions or tending one of her many invalid beasts, she had the uncanny ability to make Shane laugh then fill his loins with wanting as if he were no more than a boy. Even after Rupert had told him that Caroline was uninterested in marriage, that she had sworn to dedicate her life to healing and to God, Shane hadn't been able to banish her from his mind. With time, he had conceded that such a pure and otherworldly life seemed right for Caroline. But it was still difficult to keep her out of his thoughts. And he was never quite sure why.

She had unruly red hair and wild green eyes that changed with her moods, which was often, he had found. She was tall for a woman, the top of her head coming nearly to his chin despite his six-foot four-inch frame. And he had never seen her in anything but unflattering dresses that gave only a hint of her figure. Still, she intrigued him. But she was Rupert's daughter, and Shane had made a point of not thinking about her as anything else.

"What are you doing out here alone, Red?" he asked as Midnight rocked them gently down the road.

"I was on my way home from the church, and I needed some chamomile for old Hattie Miller. She has hurt her ankle again, and she isn't sleeping well."

"Hopefully, the cure won't take the form of garlic poultices. A person can hardly walk into the post office to get their mail for all the smell."

Caroline wrinkled her nose in thought. "Smell or not, those poultices have helped Hattie a good deal, and I'm pleased."

The horse continued on, the only sounds coming from a barking dog, a door slamming in the distance, and the steady clip-clop of Midnight's hooves echoing in the dark. Caroline reached down and ran her palm against the horse's shiny coat.

"He's beautiful, you know. I've always meant to tell you. You must feed him well?"

Shane glanced down, an amused smile on his lips. "Always looking after everyone's well-being. How did you ever come to this life you lead? I would think someone as pretty as you would spend your days attending parties and leading beaux around by the nose." As always, the idea jarred him. And as usual, he reminded himself that Caroline Bromley was no concern of his.

"Beaux and parties? Me?" Caroline uncharacteristically stammered. "I'm hardly the type. The only male I lead around by the nose is Old Pierre, the three-legged bull!"

Shane laughed out loud, then grabbed her tight when Caroline nearly tumbled off the horse.

"As for healing," she continued, trying as best she could to ignore his less than gentlemanly response and her less than ladylike slip, "I suspect I come by it through necessity. What with Papa constantly blowing things up in his laboratory or feeding some new concoction to himself, we've a great need for a healer in our house."

Shane laughed into the sky, sending a swell of grackles flying from their perch. "How is your father's dung sweeper coming along? Is he ready to show the mayor yet?"

"It's coming along fine. He hoped to have a chance to speak to him about it at the Whitley party. Did you see him there?"

Shane tensed, having managed for a few moments to push the harrowing scenes from his mind. "I'd rather not discuss that particular gathering," he said, his good humor evaporating into the night.

Caroline turned around to peer at him. "Why? What happened?"

"Nothing." He looked straight ahead, his eyes narrowing angrily. The arm that held her tightened its hold.

"Shane?" she persisted.

When he didn't answer, she started to turn around even further, but he held her secure against his chest. With a sigh, she settled back down as Midnight continued down the dirt road.

Both Shane and Caroline were silent then, their easy camaraderie having disappeared among the tiny pinpricks of light that now dotted the night sky.

When they arrived at the Bromley home on the outskirts of town, Shane reined Midnight in and handed

Caroline down to the smooth flagstone path.

"Would you like to come in for a cup of coffee, Mr. Rivers?" she asked, pulling her cloak tight around her, her manners and sense of propriety firmly back in place.

He looked at her for an eternity. Her full red lips parted and her green eyes darkened. He glanced away and saw her father standing in his upstairs laboratory window. When Shane would have raised his hand in greeting, Rupert stepped away, leaving lantern light alone to fill the empty space.

"Thank you, but no, Red. Good night," he said, tipping the broad brim of his hat. He turned his horse around, then pressed the animal into a slow, fluid canter. Without ever looking back, Shane rode down the road, and melted into the inky blackness.

CHAPTER

✳

3

"HAVE YOU FOUND a cure yet?"

Caroline jumped in her seat only to find Mary Jane Williams standing at the door, great anticipation dancing in her soft brown eyes.

"I would've come sooner, but I spent all day making lye soap with Ma," Mary Jane continued. "Ugh! I'm exhausted, and I can't get the smell off my hands."

"Mary Jane, you scared me silly, and no, I haven't found a cure yet. I spent the day washing. I never even made it to town. I just now got to the book. Besides, I doubt there is a cure for freckles."

It was the following evening, and indeed, Caroline had spent the day up to her elbows in work. Mary Jane plopped down at the table, pulling a corner of her coarse apron up to wipe her brow.

"I should've known it was too good to be true," Mary Jane said, her excitement replaced by resignation. "I had only hoped to ensure Henry Simms's notice."

Caroline reached across the well-scrubbed table and patted her friend's hand. "He'll notice you. Show him a bit of your laughter and smiles, and he'll be running circles around you in no time. A good man is not going to love you for your looks. He will love you for yourself."

Mary Jane harrumphed in response. "A lot you know, Caroline Bromley. Men are a fickle bunch, and they're as likely to notice my inner beauty as is that old toad in the pond. You've got to catch a man's eye first with shimmering looks and rose-petal skin, then maybe, down the road a ways, he might notice other things."

"Don't you believe in love?" Caroline asked, resting her jaw on her knuckles, one leg folded beneath her.

"Love? What drivel!" Mary Jane rolled her eyes with disdain. "Caroline, you've had your nose in a book for too long. Men are contrary, mark my words. It does a woman no good to think she's going to find love with a man. And if she knows a man's nature, she's better able to deal with him." Then she snorted. "But I guess you don't have to worry about such things. What with turning your nose up at every man who comes around, not to mention your advancing age, I don't suppose anyone's going to offer for you now anyway. For the life of me, I can't understand why that pa of yours hasn't put his foot down and demanded you choose someone."

"Because he understands that I won't marry without love. He won't force me until I find the right man. Besides, Mary Jane, I'm only a year past twenty."

"Like I said, you're well on your way to becoming a spinster who spends her life teaching other people's children and tending the sick."

Caroline was startled into laughter at her friend's worried look. But if truth be known, in the last year or so, Caroline had begun to worry a bit herself. The thought of a lonely future depressed her, but she refused to settle for the type of empty relationship Mary Jane dreamed about. Caroline wanted deep and abiding love as well as total commitment. And she knew with all her heart she would make some fine man a wonderful wife. But therein lay the problem—her "fine man" had no interest in her as anything other than Rupert Bromley's daughter.

Her mind drifted as she remembered the way Shane had held her in the saddle. Her heart ached with unrequited love. But then again, she thought suddenly with a quick, abandoned rush of hope, he *had* insisted on taking her home. And hadn't she, on more than one occasion, had an uncanny feeling that they shared some inexplicable bond? Perhaps he had more feelings for her than she realized.

A reckless smile broke out on Caroline's full red lips and her green eyes glowed with determination. "There is still hope for me yet. Whether you agree or not, twenty-one is not that old, and a good man will come around." He has to, she added silently to herself.

Caroline turned back to the book that lay before her and began turning the pages. Mary Jane drummed her fingers on the smooth surface of the old polished table and studied her closest friend.

"I saw you ride down the road with Mr. Shane Rivers last evening."

Caroline's hand stilled as she glanced furtively around the kitchen, then leaned forward with excitement dancing in her eyes. "Mary Jane, I nearly swooned. At first I didn't recognize him. I was thinking about Hattie Miller's ankle and her sleepless nights, when he rode out of the darkness like the devil was on his heels and nearly ran me down. After a few words were exchanged," she added, failing to mention the nature of those words, "he insisted he take me home. Well, how could I refuse?"

"By simply saying no," Mary Jane interjected unkindly. "It does your reputation no good to be seen gallivanting around town on a horse with a man holding you tight. You're the schoolteacher, for mercy's sake. No tellin' who all saw you."

Caroline glared at her friend before her eyes went soft and dreamy. "He lifted me into the saddle as if I weighed no more than a grain of salt. And the way he held me—so secure, but gentle. I felt . . . safe." Her words trailed off and she hesitated. "I think perhaps he's partial to me."

At this revelation, Mary Jane sat up in her seat. "Why? What did he say? He's never been particularly partial to you before. In fact, it has not escaped my notice that the man has begun to avoid you whenever possible."

The faraway look in Caroline's eyes evaporated like a tiny spill of water on a blistering hot day. She straightened her spine, pursed her lips, and went back to her book.

Mary Jane, however, was not to be deterred. "Come on, Caroline. What did he say?"

She hesitated for a moment in indecision, before her eyes soften slightly once again. "He said, 'Red. I should have known.' But he said it in such a way that I knew he meant so much more."

" 'Red. I should have known.' That tells you he's partial to you? Good Lord, Caroline. If he *had* known it was you, he probably *would* have run you down after you nearly killed him last week with your wagon. Besides, he's sought after by every female in town. More to the point, do I have to remind you that Shane Rivers is already taken by the very beautiful, not to mention very rich, Henrietta Whitley?"

"The wagon incident was an accident, as well you know. Furthermore, he's not going to marry Henrietta," Caroline stated emphatically.

Mary Jane's eyes narrowed. "What are you talking about? What have you heard?"

"Not much. But Papa got up this morning grumbling about the wedding being off. When I asked what had happened, he grumbled some more and stomped off to his laboratory."

"Really? Too bad neither one of us made it to town. If something happened, it's sure to have spread like wildfire."

Just then Rupert Bromley strode into the kitchen, wearing his best dark vest and trousers with a stiff white shirt beneath. He stopped and scowled when he saw Mary Jane.

"Why, Papa," Caroline said. "Don't you look handsome."

He pulled his hard gaze away from his daughter's friend and looked down at his attire with a shake of his head. "There's no help for it. Can't go to see the mayor in work clothes. I'm going to go and tell him I've completed the dung sweeper. It works perfectly. Now I just need to get him to come over here to have a look." He leaned down and pressed a kiss to the top of Caroline's head before he walked to the door. "With any luck, I'll be back shortly with the mayor in tow."

Rupert glanced back at Mary Jane. "Shouldn't you be gettin' home?"

Mary Jane's eyes narrowed at his sharp tone, but she didn't comment. Instead, she pushed herself up from her seat. "I'd best be going, Caroline. Ma was still finishing up with the soap when I snuck out."

The door closed, leaving Caroline alone in her father's kitchen with her book and her thoughts—a book that no longer seemed so interesting, and thoughts that made her heart flutter like the wings of a hummingbird.

She sat at the table, cast in the hazy glow of a thick flickering candle, her mane of fiery red hair doing its best to escape the confines of her tight chignon. Certainly she'd had gentlemen court her before. But they had always disappeared from her life and she was never quite sure why. Though it hardly mattered since she refused to marry without love, and she had felt nothing more than mild affection for any man until she had met Shane Rivers.

Caroline closed her eyes as a glimpse of reality washed over her. Mary Jane was right. Even if her father was correct and the engagement was off, if she was truthful, she knew Shane thought of her as a friend and nothing more. She was a fool to pretend any differently.

Lost in her thoughts, Caroline jumped in her seat when the door burst open. She spun around, her breath catching in her throat as the candle flame flickered wildly for a moment before it calmed and straightened like a sentinel standing guard.

"Papa, you startled me!" she gasped when she found her father standing at the door.

He stood in the kitchen, clearly disconcerted. "Ah . . . my hat." He grabbed his beaver bowler and disappeared through the doorway without another word.

Caroline watched the door close, muslin curtains that covered the glass-paned window ruffling from the movement. She turned back to the table, closed her eyes, and took a deep breath, filling her lungs. Tears welled up and threatened to spill over. Her life stretched before her, empty of love. At length, she exhaled and opened her eyes. Buck up, girl, she chastened herself. Quit feeling sorry for yourself. Just as Papa always said, she had him to love and care for. Besides, there is Mary Jane, charity work at the church, and a reputation beyond reproach that gives you a great deal of freedom to tend to all the people who need you. Your life is full. You should be thankful for what you have, she added to herself.

With that, she pulled the old book back in front of her and moved her candle closer. She still needed to find a wart remedy for Merle Jenkins. The last one she had tried failed miserably.

She read for a short while, perusing the pages until she heard the click of the door and felt a sudden rush of cool breeze caress her skin. Before she could turn, her candle wavered then flickered out, washing the room in darkness.

"Papa," she called with a chuckle. "What have you forgotten now?"

She received no reply.

"Papa!" she repeated, her voice growing taut. "Papa, stop this nonsense and light the lantern by the door."

The floorboards creaked as someone approached. Her heart began to pound in her chest. She pushed herself up in the dark, her hands clutching the edge of the table. Panic threatened to take hold and she willed herself to remain calm. "Papa? Mary Jane? Stop this—"

She gasped when a clammy hand caught her arm and pulled her away from the table, her eyes opening wide in the dark.

"I've seen that redskin sniffing around here," a man's harsh, muffled voice said, his hand wrapping around her neck. "You been pleasuring him, girl? Is he your lover boy?" he persisted, his grip tightening ever so slightly around the slender column.

"What redskin? What are you talking about?" she gasped, trying to keep the fear from her voice. "What are you doing in here?"

She tried to jerk away, but her skirts tangled with his legs, tripping them both, and they slammed against the wall, knocking her breathless. Fear scrabbled at the edges of her mind. She clawed at him, gasping for air. Then in one almost blinding whoosh, oxygen surged back into her lungs, and with it came a strangled cry.

He flattened his hand across her mouth. "Quiet," he hissed. He grabbed her hair and jerked her head back, bringing tears to her eyes.

The fear that had played with her mind exploded into panic. She had to get away. With a strength she did not know she possessed, she bit down on the hand that covered her mouth and jerked free.

"Damn you," he hissed, yanking his hand to his chest.

She lurched for the door, stumbling when her skirt caught in the legs of an overturned chair. Frantically she tried to pull herself free, but he was on her before she could escape. She lashed out, mumbling in fear, flailing her arms, until her attacker delivered a blow to her face that knocked her to the ground.

"You're gonna listen to me," he said as he pounced on her, covering her mouth again. "Stay away from that damned redskin or you're gonna pay."

She fought against him while at the same time she fought against the tide of pain that racked her body. She kicked and rolled and managed to get to her knees, her hair coming loose.

Suddenly a knock sounded at the front door and he stilled. Before she could scream he pulled a gun from his coat and pressed it to her temple. "You scream and you'll regret it." Very slowly, he stood, the gun still pressed against her head. "Don't move," he whispered, his breath ragged, agitated.

And then he fled, slamming out of the backdoor just as quickly as he came, leaving Caroline on the floor, her body crippled with fear.

CHAPTER

✳

4

SHANE PLANNED TO leave town the next morning at first light. His saddlebags were packed and ready. The only thing left to do was stop by the Bromley home.

He denied he was going there because he wanted to see Caroline one last time, telling himself he simply needed to say farewell to her father and, more importantly, to say thank you. Shane might have become a pariah overnight, but at least he was not sitting in jail, waiting to be strung up for murder. And he owed Rupert for that.

Night surrounded him as he took the front steps of the Bromleys'. Just as Shane raised his hand to knock he heard the crash of furniture falling to the floor. He knocked loudly, and when no one answered he tried the knob. The door swung open into the seemingly empty and now quiet house. A lantern burned in the front parlor, casting the room with an amber glow. As he glanced about he heard the backdoor slam shut before the house grew quiet once again.

"Rupert," he called out.

When no one answered, Shane hurried to the kitchen, threw the door wide, and pressed against the wall to look inside. Light spilled in behind him, slicing the somber blackness in the kitchen. And then he saw her. She knelt on the floor, light washing over her.

"Caroline," he whispered, suddenly hoarse.

She didn't respond.

He crossed the floor to kneel at her side. When he lightly touched her shoulder, she screamed, emitting an anguished sound that seemed to fill every crack and crevice in the room, sending a chill down his spine. Her body jerked into action as she frantically tried to get away.

"Caroline," he repeated, forcibly turning her toward him.

Her eyes were wild, overbright, shimmering with tears. It was a moment before she recognized him, but when she did, she let out an agonizing wail and threw herself into his arms. Clenching her hands in his cambric shirt, she pressed her face into his chest. He could feel her body rack with sobs, her tears wetting his shirt as he held her close, trying to soothe her.

"I'm here, Red," he murmured into the thick mass of her hair.

He rocked her in his arms, murmuring quiet words until her tears began to subside. "Tell me what happened, sweetheart."

With that her weeping started anew. "Oh, Shane, he . . . he . . ."

"He what?" he demanded, his grip tightening.

When she failed to respond, he tenderly put his large, strong hands on either side of her face and forced her to look into his eyes. "Caroline," he said, the word a gentle command. "Tell me what happened."

"He . . . hit me."

Her hand strayed to her cheek, and he noticed the red welt that had begun to form. Anger built.

"He wrapped his . . . hands around my neck. Oh, Shane . . . his hands . . . if you hadn't come—" The words broke off, sobs choking her.

Fury surged through him. "Who did this?" he demanded, his voice seething with anger.

"I don't know," she stammered through her tears. "It was too dark to see." She took a deep shaky breath. "He said some redskin was my . . . my lover."

Moments passed before the meaning of her words registered. When they did, Shane's fingers trailed back, fisting in her hair, pulling her close as he squeezed his eyes shut. "God!" he roared, his head flung back. The word was a curse, wrenched from his chest, filled with fury and pain.

He buried his face in her hair. Would he never be free of his past? Would it always haunt him, sneak up on him when he least expected it, to harm even those who were innocently caught in his world?

They huddled close together on the floor, his hands tangled in her mane of wild hair, the soft light wrapping around them like the fine threads of a silken cocoon, harboring them against the dark.

Long minutes ticked by before he tilted her head back and looked into her eyes. "I'm sorry, Red, so terribly sorry."

She started to question, but stopped when he leaned down to kiss her tears away—a gentle kiss on either cheek. Without thinking, she turned her head, ever so slightly, until his lips pressed against hers.

The touch sent a shiver of longing through his body, leaving him breathless, bringing painfully to the surface all the desire he felt for her, all he had suppressed. For one insane moment he forgot where they were and what had happened. He moaned and pulled her into a crushing embrace, holding her tight, pressing his lips to her hair. He closed his eyes and held her like he would never let her go. He pressed her body to his, tighter, closer, as if to become one. One life. Flesh of his flesh. Together.

But that was impossible.

Sanity returned and he pulled away. The loss left him cold and empty, nearly flattened. "You want kisses, sweet Caroline, without seeming to know where such things lead."

She looked up at him, her green eyes dark and deep, like pools of liquid jade. And then she took a deep breath as if gathering her courage, her ordeal momentarily forgotten, and uttered two simple words. "Show me."

His heart stilled in his chest, her words reverberated in his mind. He searched her eyes for one long interminable space of time. His grip tightened on her shoulders, and he almost pulled her back into his arms when she reached up to touch his lips, her fingers shaking, unsure. But then he saw her worshipful gaze as if he were some kind of a hero. And God, his mind raged, how he wished it were true. But he was not a hero, he reminded himself harshly, never had been. And if almost killing a man wasn't proof enough, lusting after a woman promised to God and healing certainly was.

With a curse, he abruptly pulled away, a feral groan filled with grief rumbling in his chest. "Sweet Jesus, this can't be!"

Her eyes grew wide and haunted. He hated the look,

so filled with hurt and uncertainty. He desperately wanted to turn away, because if he didn't, he knew he would pull her back into his arms and forget her God along with her father's request that Shane leave his daughter alone. And he would forget as well that he was a savage unworthy of her love.

His breath blew hot and moist, but when he would have leaped to his feet, she whispered his name once again, tears shimmering in her luminous eyes.

"I love you, Shane."

The words hung in the air.

"Oh, dear God, don't!" he demanded, his voice ragged as, against all reason, he pulled her back into his arms.

His mind and body fought a fierce battle. He wanted her as he had never wanted anything in his life. And amazingly, as she trembled in his arms, he knew she wanted him, too.

He pressed his lips against her hair, licks of fire spreading through his loins. But reason dampened the flames. Caroline might think she wanted him, and she might say she loved him, but she did so only because she didn't know him, she didn't know his love only destroyed. "Don't love me, Caroline . . . you'll only get hurt."

And as if to prove his words, the backdoor swung open, bringing Rupert into their midst with the mayor and sheriff following close behind. "Rupert, I can't believe you still call that savage friend. He betrayed us all, you worst of all, what with all the time you spent with him. Hell, I wish he had've kilt that Fowler fellow. Then we'd have him swinging by now."

"Sheriff," Rupert said coldly. "We're here to see the dung sweeper not to—"

The small group stopped abruptly as they took in the sight of Caroline locked in the arms of Shane Rivers, the angry red welt clear on her face.

There was a moment of stunned silence before the sheriff drew his gun and trained it on Shane. "Why you filthy scum," he spat. "Ruining *one* of our respectable ladies wasn't enough for you."

Rupert stood stock-still, unable to move, his mouth hanging open as if the sentence left unfinished waited to be spoken. Confusion stretched his features into a hideous mask as he tried to make sense of the situation.

The mayor stepped forward. "Now you've done it, Rivers. Get your hands off Miss Caroline."

Shane noticed Caroline's hair tumbling in disarray and her dress hiked up, revealing petticoats and crinoline. He started to reach down to cover her.

"Whoa there, Rivers." Sheriff Donnelly aimed the barrel at Shane's head. "No fast moves. Just stand up slowly and step away from the lady."

Shane let go of Caroline once she had yanked down her skirt. Then he slowly began to rise, his hands held out at his sides, his face a mask of barely controlled black rage.

Caroline looked from the gun to Shane, panic far greater than that she had experienced earlier beginning to rise like bile in her throat. "You don't understand, Sheriff."

"I understand just fine. The situation is as clear as a hot summer day. You was being mauled by riffraff and I mean to make him pay."

Rupert's face twisted with rage.

Caroline turned to the mayor and then her father. "No! He wasn't attacking me—"

"Now, little lady, ya had a fright," Donnelly said. "But we'll take care of him. He'll never bother you again."

"Papa!" Caroline cried in frustration.

When Rupert failed to respond, the sheriff stepped cautiously next to Shane and quickly reached out and grabbed his wrist. He twisted Shane around and slammed him up against the wall, holstering his weapon, freeing both hands to bind Shane's wrists. "There we go," Donnelly said, his breath coming in rapid gasps. "You been living up there in Washington where they got a lot of unsavory types. Perhaps you was used to gettin' away with triflin' with the ladies. But here in Texas, a man can be shot for botherin' a good woman, and, boy, you been botherin' some of our finest. You ain't gonna get another chance to do it ever again."

"Let him go," Caroline cried, and threw herself at the sheriff. "He didn't attack me!"

Donnelly threw her off with more force than necessary, and she stumbled, almost falling. Rupert reached out and steadied his daughter, his grip angry and tight. Shane growled and lunged back toward the sheriff.

"I wouldn't do that if I were you," the mayor said with deadly calm, aiming his gun at Shane's heart.

Every muscle in Shane's body went rigid. He gazed not at the mayor, but at the sheriff, his eyes blazing with hatred. "Don't touch her again, Donnelly."

Donnelly took a step away, then grumbled under his breath and pulled his shoulders back. "Come on, boy, let's get movin'."

Caroline turned to the mayor. "Are you all insane? How many times do I have to tell you? Shane Rivers didn't attack me!"

Rupert looked at his daughter. His glance found her hair, no longer held by its pins. A flicker of furious accusation crossed his face. Mayor Mackenzie studied Caroline with a scowl before he shifted his weight uncomfortably and sighed.

"I'm not sure, Donnelly," the mayor finally stated. "If Miss Caroline here says he wasn't attacking her, then . . ." Blood surged into the mayor's face at the import of his words.

"You're not sure!" Donnelly exploded. "Hell, Mayor, what are you gonna do? Act like they was a couple of lovebirds and hold a shotgun weddin'? You can see with your own eyes that he roughed her up. She's just trying to protect the scum just like her pa done. Marrying is too good for the likes of him. Hanging's what he deserves."

Caroline gasped, her hand flying to her mouth. "Good God, what are you talking about?" She turned to Shane. "Shane!" she demanded. "Do something! Tell them how you saved me!"

Shane neither moved nor made any attempt to explain. He simply stood as still as stone with murder in his eyes.

Caroline took a deep breath and willed herself to be calm, not understanding the degree of hostility that permeated the room. Shane had been tried and convicted before he had a chance to explain. It made no sense. "I'm going to try to explain this one last time. Someone else attacked me," she stated, her voice determined and taut. "Shane Rivers saved me from a . . . lowlife that the *law* hasn't managed to apprehend! And what happened after that . . . well . . . I—"

"Caroline!" Shane's voice sliced through the kitchen, her name spoken as a command.

Caroline lifted her chin in defiance. "I threw myself at him. Plain and simple. Perhaps you should hang me," she added insolently, trying to cover the mortification that surged at her confession.

She turned away from the sheriff to look at the mayor. "I might not be able to get to Austin to plead my case before you can do something . . . irreversible to Mr. Rivers, but I can get there eventually. And after I have told my story, mark my words, you and the sheriff will have some explaining to do. Now, I suggest you let me speak to Mr. Rivers before something happens that we all regret. He and I have some things to discuss, and afterward, perhaps we can put this whole incident in perspective," Caroline stated in a voice that brooked no argument. She turned toward the door. "And untie that rope, Mr. Donnelly."

The sheriff grumbled.

"I mean it, Sheriff. Besides, how far can he get even if he does try to skip out of here?" Caroline demanded with an authority she didn't feel.

"Hell, Miss Caroline," the sheriff griped. "You're makin' a mistake, I tell ya." But he untied the rope just the same before his hand strayed to his gun.

Shane closed the door behind them and leaned up against the wall. Caroline didn't say anything, merely walked to the window and stared out into the night. For one almost unbearable moment the memory of her attacker's voice loomed in her mind. But, with force, she pushed the sound from her thoughts once and for all, unwilling to think about the attack, just as she had been unwilling earlier when she had thrown herself at Shane. And she *had* thrown herself at him, leaving her with no idea what she could possibly say to put things "in perspective." She had gotten Shane into this mixed-up mess and she had no idea how to clear it up. She hadn't been lying when she said she would travel to Austin to file a complaint, but postmortem investigations wouldn't do Shane Rivers much good.

"What is going on in there, Shane?" she finally asked.

Shane laughed wryly. "They want me dead. The little scene they witnessed merely provides them with an excuse, nothing more."

"You weren't attacking me. We both know that," she said, red singeing her cheeks. "They can't shoot you or hang you for something you didn't do. You need to explain what happened, Shane. They obviously don't believe me."

"Donnelly and Mackenzie aren't going to listen to a word I have to say. They don't like half-breeds being friendly with their kind."

Caroline whirled around and looked at him closely. "Half-breed? You?"

She saw Shane flinch as if he had been struck. Her heart clenched in her chest, and she started to reach out to him but stopped when he stepped away. Her arm fell to her side. Understanding flooded her mind with blinding clarity. The broken engagement, the mayor's and sheriff's unreasonable anger. "So that's what this is all about."

She felt his anguish. She wanted to scream at the unfairness of the world. But that, she knew, wouldn't help him. What she needed was a solution.

And then suddenly it came to her. A trickle of excitement teased her mind. She could solve two problems with one glorious act. She could clear Shane's name and have her perfect man.

"Marry me!" she blurted out. "They can't kill you if they think you're doing right by me."

Shane nearly gaped with astonishment. "Marry you!" Surprise quickly vanished. He pushed away from the wall, angry. He ran his hand through his hair in agitation.

Caroline came to stand before him, her hands clasped to her breast, ignoring his hard glare and forbidding stance. "I'll be a good wife, and I would be proud to have you for a husband."

"You don't know what you're talking about!"

"Of course I do. It's perfect. If what you said is true, those men in there aren't going to change their minds. If we marry, the mayor and sheriff can't do a thing to you."

"I'm not going to marry you to save my hide, Red."

Caroline made a great display of rolling her eyes and sighing. "This is rich! How very noble! You'd rather swing than marry." She tried to hide her concern behind sarcasm as her determination began to turn to panic. She wouldn't be able to live with herself if something happened to this wonderful man because of her. But she had learned during the months she had known him how very *noble* indeed he was.

Then suddenly her eyes opened wide with inspiration. Before she could think twice about the wisdom of such a statement, she hurried on. "Did it ever occur to you that if this incident isn't kept quiet, I'll be ruined?"

She almost cringed at the wounded look that crossed Shane's face. But it was for his own good, or so she told herself as it was only possible for her to press ahead by thinking she was doing it for Shane rather than for herself.

Shane pressed his eyes closed. "Marry you?" he asked aloud, as if speaking the words might cause them to make more sense. "How can I marry you? I only came by to tell your father that I'm leaving at first light. How can I take you with me? I don't even know where I'm going. And I'd think you'd agree I can't stay here." He looked toward the door behind which the sheriff waited. "Though it doesn't look like I'll be given much choice."

As quickly as it had appeared, Caroline's surge of grit ebbed and her shoulders slumped. Defeat and disappointment etched her face. She had proposed to the man, reasoned with him, and still he wouldn't marry her. She refused to beg. "Then run out that door right now, get on your horse, and be away from here before Donnelly knows what happened."

Shane looked at her long and hard. Then he sighed. "If I run out of here, whether I manage to get away or not, you're right about being ruined if the story gets around."

Caroline held her breath.

Shane ran a tired hand across his face as the pendulum in the old clock ticked the minutes away. Neither one spoke, each lost in their thoughts, until Shane drew a deep breath and said, "If we marry, I'll have to take you with me."

Caroline nearly staggered with relief. "I know," she replied, trying to bridle her burgeoning excitement. "But you'll take care of me."

Shane grimaced, deep-seated fatigue etching his brow. "You don't know that."

"Yes, I do. I know you, Shane Rivers."

Shane glanced out the window, pain, anger, and sadness passing through his eyes like storm clouds in a winter sky. "No, Caroline. Don't fool yourself. You hardly know me at all."

The words were bitter, defiant, sending Caroline's pounding heart plummeting into her stomach. Obviously the idea of marriage was repellent to him, at least marriage to her. "If you would rather hang than marry me, fine. I'm not going to beg. I have pride, too, you know."

Despite his anger, his lips tilted at the corners. "I have no doubt you're prideful, Red." His anger faded in measured steps as he gazed at the wild and willful Caroline Bromley. "And if being married to a half-breed doesn't bother you"—he hesitated, the words seeming to stick in his throat—"then consider yourself engaged."

Caroline didn't move as the meaning of his words slowly sank in. She could hardly believe what she was hearing. Marriage. To Shane Rivers.

Her dreams were coming true.

CHAPTER

✳

5

RUPERT BROMLEY STOOD in the same spot he had been standing in for the last fifteen minutes, trying to make sense of the news that Caroline and Shane were to be married. Married. His Caroline. To Shane Rivers.

Rupert was numb.

Shane had been taken away by the mayor, who told Caroline he would release him when the marriage ceremony took place. Caroline stood staring at the door as if she expected Shane to step back through. When the door remained firmly shut, she sighed and turned away, knowing she must face her father.

"I'm sorry about all this, Papa," she said quietly. "But truly what happened was not what it seemed."

A multitude of emotions flashed across Rupert's face, leaving Caroline momentarily confused. Her mind tried to assimilate and make sense of what she saw, it even seemed to catch on some tendril of memory that would lead her to understand. But then her father's face settled back into the paternal gaze she had known her whole life, and the glimpse of comprehension floated away, forgotten.

"Maybe it is, maybe it's not. Either way it all leads to the same place—you being forced to marry."

Caroline sighed. "I want you to know that I couldn't be happier to be marrying Shane Rivers." She reached out to him, laying her hand on his arm. "I love him, Papa."

Rupert moved away.

"I have for a long time." Her steady, level voice grew strangely breathless, and she hesitated. She remembered the feel of Shane's lips pressed against hers, fleetingly, magically, until he had pulled away. There was more feeling there than Shane Rivers was willing to admit—yet.

Her eyes cleared and she looked at her father. "And I know in my heart that one day he will love me, too."

"I'm happy for you, daughter. Rivers is a lucky man. Now go up to your room and get some sleep. Tomorrow is going to be a busy day."

Gathering her skirt, Caroline hurried to her father and threw her arms around him. "Thank you for wishing me well, Papa. It will all turn out for the best. Just you wait and see."

Rupert stood very still in his daughter's embrace. The silence spun out between them like yards of knotty homespun, coarse and uncomfortable, until he patted his daughter on the shoulder, then disengaged himself from her impromptu embrace. "Good night, Caroline."

He leaned down and brushed her forehead with a kiss, then he was gone, leaving Caroline alone in the kitchen, her life, she knew, irrevocably altered. She could only believe it would be for the better.

The white clapboard house on the outskirts of town sat dark and quiet. The moon hung high in the night sky washed milky by stars. Rupert paced the confines of the upstairs bedroom that had years ago been turned into his laboratory. But this night Rupert didn't notice his gadgets or concoctions; he simply paced to and fro, his old, withered face one minute filled with despair, the next filled with rage.

When the moon had journeyed considerably through the heavens, he ran a tired hand across his face then rummaged through corked bottles of clear and colored liquids. Placing a small vial of clear liquid in his pocket, he shrugged into his jacket, grabbed an old cloth, and quietly left the room, his lips set in a resolute line. Determined, he set off toward town.

Rupert came to a long, squat, windowless building on the northern edge of San Antonio. After peering about the quiet, sleeping street, he pulled open the thick, rough-planked wooden door and stepped inside. A dim light glowed through the space. A guard sat in the corner, sleeping.

Rupert poured some of the liquid he had brought along onto the rag and quietly walked over to the guard. He placed the cloth over the guard's mouth and nose. The man's body stiffened then relaxed still further. A quick test of the man's reflexes proved he was in a deep sleep. After that Rupert wasted no time.

In seconds he retrieved a set of keys. He walked to the back of the building, where he came to another thick wooden door. He turned one of the keys in the lock. The door swung open with little effort. Dim light flooded the pitch-dark room. And there, captured by the glowing slice of light, sat Shane, his slate-gray eyes squinting against the intrusion.

Rupert stood in the doorway, taking in the barely

held power of the man who dwarfed the tiny room and looked absurdly out of place half sitting, half lying with one leg drawn up on the grimy old cot. Rupert stood silently, taking in the man who had been his friend, but now had unexpectedly become his enemy.

"So." Rupert let out the word with a heavy sigh. A tired half smile played on his grizzled face as he pulled the door nearly shut behind him as a precaution. "You ended up jailed despite my attempts to save you."

"I'm sorry about all this, Rupert," Shane began, his eyes locked on the older man's. "Let me explain—"

"Explain!" All semblance of friendliness fled from Rupert's voice. "No need for explanations, Rivers. I know all I need to know. I know that you betrayed me! In my very own home!"

Shane slowly pushed himself up until he sat upright on the cot. "Rupert—"

"I saved your hide, damn you," Rupert said tightly, his voice seething. "I saved you from swinging, and what did you do? You . . . you compromised my daughter!"

Every fiber of Shane's being visibly flinched. His eyes filled with a mixture of anger and shame. "Despite what happened or did not happen, I am going to make thing right."

"Make things right! How?" Rupert demanded.

"By marrying Caroline."

"Marrying her!" Rupert bellowed, his barely held rage finally bursting forth. His brown eyes grew crazed. "Marriage is going to save my daughter? Marriage to a . . . a . . . half-breed who's no longer received in polite society is going to help my Caroline?!"

Shane stiffened. His anger flared to white-hot, soul-burning anger.

"What kind of life can you give my Caroline?" Rupert demanded. "Your political prospects are shot, and there's not a soul within a fifty-mile radius that will give you a job. Surely you don't expect Caroline to support you with the chickens and eggs she receives for her healing, or even with her teacher's salary! Mercy, after what the major and sheriff witnessed, she'll be lucky to *keep* her teaching position."

Rupert watched the emotions scud across Shane's face, waiting for just the right moment to continue. "I once thought you were a man of honor," he finally said, his voice lowered. "You gave me your word as a gentleman that you would leave my daughter alone. She's going through a difficult period in her life. And you took advantage of that. You broke your promise. Now, are you going to show total disregard for her well-being by marrying her?"

Shane's sheer physical presence smote the air. "I did not compromise your daughter," he finally said, his voice tight. "The attacker fled when I called out. And you'd do well to remember that in case the man returns."

Rupert's eyes narrowed and he studied Shane. "How do you expect a person to believe that, Rivers, when the mayor, the sheriff, and I all saw you engaged in an . . . an impassioned embrace with my Caroline. Her skirts were up and her hair was down. I saw with my own eyes that you were well on your way to God only knows what. That in itself proves your word is worthless."

Shane's hand clenched convulsively at his side.

"Listen," Rupert continued in a suddenly practical tone. "Problems will only arise if word spreads. I'll speak to the sheriff and the mayor. They can't deny that you didn't actually . . . consummate. I'll make sure they don't say anything about the incident. Caroline can get beyond this." He hesitated. "But she can't get beyond being married to a half-breed."

Long, uncomfortable minutes ticked by as Shane Rivers sat on the narrow cot, his eyes boring into the older man. He did not speak or move, merely sat like granite, cold and hard, as if making some decision. Eventually, he stood, pulling every inch of his hard-chiseled form up straight to tower over the suddenly fidgety older man.

Uncertain what Shane was about to do, Rupert hurriedly held out the set of stolen keys. "I've taken care of the guard. All we have to do is get your horse saddled and you're on your way. Wherever you want to go. It will be hours before anyone knows you're gone."

The dull metal keys jangled slightly in Rupert's hand, but Shane made no attempt to take them. It seemed as though he was going to refuse, as though he was about to sit back down on the cot and wait for the morning to dawn.

Rupert felt the sharp weight of panic. "You can give my daughter nothing she deserves."

Shane pressed his eyes closed. "Let me talk to Caroline first."

Rupert tensed. His mind raced. "There's no time. I'll explain everything to her. She would want you to get away before the sheriff got his hands on you again."

Shane glanced at the keys that still jangled in Rupert's hand. Taking a deep breath, he finally took them and turned to the door. He hesitated on the threshold for an eternity before he pushed the heavy door open and walked boldly out of the tiny cell.

Rupert slumped against the thick mud wall. His heavily lined face sagged. He had done it. He had managed to keep his daughter—no, save his daughter, he corrected himself with a nod of his head. She was innocent of the ways of world and didn't understand what she wanted or what was best for her. He, however, did. He always had. He was her father. Yes, his sweet, sweet Caroline.

Relief washing over him, Rupert pushed himself away from the wall. His relief, however, was short-lived when he realized he had saved Caroline this time, but didn't know if he could continue to do so. His lips narrowed into a thin line.

He could not let something like this happen again.

CHAPTER

✳

6

Five Years Later
1865

THE STAGECOACH BOUNCED and swayed along the rugged trail. The dry summer heat left every passenger in the tiny conveyance parched and miserable. They had been traveling all day and all night for several days, on their way to El Paso, Texas. The wretched journey was only interrupted by brief stops at disreputable wood-and-mud shacks to eat unpalatable meals and change the mules.

The mules! Caroline shook her head ruefully. The sight of the wretched beasts had been the first of many rude awakenings since she had set out on this long and seemingly endless journey. Her first disappointment had come when she learned that the fairly large and relatively new stagecoach pulled by six strong horses didn't travel all the way to her destination. Not two days out of San Antonio, the driver had informed her that they were at the end of the line. Caroline had looked out the window at the dismal shack and wondered what in God's name she was to do!

Perhaps noticing the poorly suppressed panic etched across Caroline's lovely face, the driver had taken pity on her. Leaning down from his perch, spewing an arc of brown spit and tobacco, he had pointed her down the road. And there had been her means of transport to take her the rest of the way—another stagecoach, though one that had seen better days and whose only mode of power was four short, stocky, smelly mules. From the looks of the ramshackle way station and her new transportation, Caroline decided then and there that she had come not only to the end of the line, but to the end of the earth as well. And the trip from that point on had done nothing to disprove her theory.

Her stomach churned with anxiety as she distractedly attempted to smooth her unruly red hair back into its once tight chignon. She would have groaned out loud as she shifted her weight, hopelessly trying to find some comfort during the interminable ride, had not the self-imposed, strict propriety of the last five years forbidden such an unladylike utterance.

Five years of propriety—five years of trying to forget. Had it really been so long since that fateful night when she had forgotten her pride and practically begged Shane Rivers to marry her? Had it really been so long since that fateful hour, the following day, when she found him gone?

Caroline leaned back, suppressing a sigh, her gloved hands folded in her lap, as her mind was forced back to that moment in time.

"Caroline! Wake up!"

Caroline had groaned at the sound of Mary Jane's cheerful and excited voice. She burrowed deeper into the soft folds of her bed, twisting her fine linen night-dress and pantalettes uncomfortably about her legs. "Go away," she grumbled.

For the first time since she could remember, Caroline didn't have the energy to face the day. And she knew it was because she was getting married.

Marriage to Shane Rivers—her most cherished dream of the last six months.

Caroline moaned and pulled the sheet over her head. Of course, a part of her was insanely happy. But another part of her, the saner part, screamed that Shane Rivers had no interest in marrying her. Nothing like the barrel of a revolver and the threat of a noose to prompt a person into saying "I do."

"Curse," Caroline muttered beneath the sheets. How could she allow such a marriage to take place? she wondered, as she had been wondering all through the sleepless night.

"Caroline," Mary Jane repeated, exasperation lacing her voice. "Get up. I have news for you."

When Caroline still did not move, Mary Jane plopped down next to her on the side of the bed. "I went into town early this morning and you'll never guess what I heard!"

"Go away."

"Caroline!" Mary Jane squeaked. "It's all over town. Dean Fowler made an announcement at the Whitley party that caused quite a stir."

Caroline tensed beneath the sheet.

"Shane Rivers is a half-breed!"

Caroline shot up out of the bed coverings in a flash. "Tell me everything."

Mary Jane hunched forward, excitement dancing in

her soft brown eyes. "Well, apparently Mr. Whitley had just made the announcement of Henrietta and Shane's betrothal when Fowler told everyone Shane was the son of a full-blooded Comanche warrior. Imagine—a full-blooded Comanche warrior—one of the most feared Indians in all of Texas. Everyone went crazy. Instead of swooning, Henrietta attacked Shane. Can you imagine! And then suddenly Shane was on Fowler and nearly strangled him to death. Oh!" Mary Jane cried with a shiver of delight. "How I wish I could have seen it."

Caroline's wide-eyed stare narrowed, and she pursed her lips in thought. "Anyone in their right mind would know how a crowd of Texans would react to the news that a Comanche, even a half Comanche, stood in their midst. Not a week goes by without some idiot telling some horrid story, recounting terrible deaths at the hands of Indians. That man obviously told the group about Shane just to get the reaction he did."

"Intentional or not, I wonder what Shane Rivers is going to do now. Everyone's speculating."

Caroline threw back the covers. "He's getting married," she said with purpose, thinking only of the man she loved and how he had been betrayed, forgetting that only moments ago she had lamented her predicament.

"To who?" Mary Jane asked, clearly incredulous.

"To me!"

"You?" Mary Jane gasped, her face stretching into a comical mask of disbelief. "Caroline Bromley, just because he's not marrying Henrietta, don't tell me you think you can convince him to marry you."

"I don't have to. It's already arranged." Caroline went to her wardrobe and pulled the doors open with a bang, ignoring Mary Jane's slack-jawed amazement. Her dear sweet Shane needed her, whether he knew it or not, and she'd not keep him waiting another second longer than necessary.

After a great deal of hurried preparations, the wedding party was nearly ready. The very reverend Reverend Hayes read over his prayer book. The bride, the father of the bride, and the maid of honor stood about, not a single one of whom having anticipated a wedding more than twenty-four hours before. Only the groom was nowhere to be seen.

The hastily assembled group had been waiting a good thirty minutes when the door burst open, bringing the sheriff into the room. "Rivers has escaped!"

The reverend looked bewildered. Mary Jane gasped. Rupert stared straight ahead, silent.

"What are you talking about?" Caroline asked, refusing to believe she heard the man correctly.

"Rivers has skipped town!"

"You must be mistaken, Sheriff," Caroline replied with icy calm, her spine straight, her chin up.

"No mistake about it, Miss Caroline."

Caroline stood perfectly still as the seemingly undeniable news penetrated her mind. She wrapped her arms around herself tightly as if to hold herself together, to make certain the suddenly fragmented pieces of her life did not fall apart. Did this mean that she would never again see Shane walk through the door? she wondered. Impossible. But for all her denials, the truth pressed in on her.

Shane had escaped. Shane had left her.

Despite her attempts to control her thoughts, her mind swam in the clouded depths of misery in an attempt to comprehend. *Shane Rivers was gone.*

Voices rose and fell all around her. But she could make no sense of the words. The cacophony of sound lent the scene a patina of madness. Her mind continued to swim unchecked. She desperately tried to retain control, to deny the truth. But in the end, the thought that had plagued her throughout the sleepless night resurfaced. Without a shred of decency, she had thrown herself shamelessly at Shane Rivers. And God had been watching.

She knew then with mind-paralyzing certainty that she would pay, the first remittance being the loss of Shane.

Then like flakes of dry snow against a surge of wind, the pieces of her life scattered. Losing herself to the long, silky finger of oblivion that beckoned like an old comforting friend, Caroline did something she had never done in the twenty-one years of her careful and practical life. She filled the well-tended white clapboard house on the outskirts of San Antonio, Texas with a soul-wrenching, heart-piercing scream, then fainted dead on the floor.

Caroline was jarred in her seat when the stagecoach hit a deep rut. The heavy leather straps that held the contraption together strained in their effort to keep the coach upright. Once the immediate danger was over, Caroline secured herself back into the corner as best she could, willing her thoughts to other things. But try as she might, a raw primitive grief overwhelmed her. She shuddered as a sharp iciness seeped into her soul, and her eyes glistened with unshed tears for the loss of the man she loved and the life she would never live.

Her throat constricted. She remembered waking in her father's arms, her life forever altered. During the five long and lonely years following her abandonment, her teaching position had been stripped away and her list of patients had dwindled until only her collection of invalid pets remained. All because, in the end, word had spread like wildfire. *Caroline Bromley had been found in the wild embrace of the heathen, Shane Rivers.* And of course the story had grown and been enlarged, taking on a life of its own, depriving Caroline of the life she had so painstakingly built.

But she had been the one who set her life on the path it now took. She had ruined herself. She should have simply demanded that the whole truth come out and not used the incident to trap a man who clearly had no interest in marrying her.

Her father had stood by her, however, never mentioning the incident again. But now he was dead of consumption, the infamous dung sweeper having failed along the way, stripping him of what money they had, leaving Caroline alone and penniless with very few options.

Though she fought it, her chest tightened and her eyes burned as she tried to fight off unbidden memories.

Midnight-black hair. Piercing slate-gray eyes.

How was it possible, she wondered, that after so many years, despite the bitterness, despite the loneliness, unrequited love could still sear her to the core? She closed her eyes against the image of the man. She closed her eyes as if she could blot out the memory of her wantonness. But as happened so often over the last years, the memories would not be held at bay.

How could she have thrown herself at him? she wondered with despair. *Show me*. The words spoken so long ago taunted her. Good God! What had possessed her to say such a thing? But try as she might, Caroline had never been able to forget the simple words or the man. And still, shamefully, she longed to know where his kisses would have led.

But she would never know, she reminded herself harshly. Shane Rivers was gone. He had preferred to be a hunted man than to marry her. And she had finally come to accept the truth that her father had always tried to teach her, the truth that she had always denied—men were traitorous and not to be trusted.

She sighed, gusts of hot, gritty air doing little to cool the perspiration that slid down the front of her once perfectly pressed dress.

El Paso, Texas. Dear heavens! Why did she have to travel to such a distant place? she asked herself for the hundredth time during the bone-jarring, mouth-parching ride.

"Now, now. Don't you cry, dear."

Caroline was momentarily startled by the voice that penetrated her thoughts. Her mind wavered between that time long ago and the present until she remembered that the voice belonged to the kindly older woman she sat next to on the stagecoach to El Paso.

"Oh, I'm terribly sorry." Caroline quickly wiped her eyes and took a deep breath. "I don't know what came over me."

The woman chortled good-naturedly. "This rugged desert, not to mention the ride, is enough to bring a tear to anyone's eye."

Caroline turned to the window and lifted the shade.

She could not have been more surprised by what she saw. Nothing. Absolutely nothing she recognized. She couldn't believe it. Where were the trees and tall grass? The rolling hills covered in green? When she had imagined El Paso, she thought of gunslingers with cow manure covering their boots and a sheriff who wore a big gold star. But never in her wildest imaginings had she envisioned this vast expanse of land marked by cactus and scrub brush.

Deadly thickets of prickly pear stood tall and menacing. Agave crooked and stabbed skeletal fingers up from the earth. A bony-legged, floppy-eared jackrabbit darted from their path to bounce crazily away. The whip cracked overhead, sending the mules into a faster pace. The coach lurched, jarring Caroline and her traveling companions in their seats.

Caroline let the shade drop. As soon as she had received the telegram offering her the teaching position at the hacienda Cielo el Dorado, in El Paso, Texas, she had sighed her relief, even though she hadn't planned to take this particular job. It never occurred to her that out of all the positions she had applied for, every one of them except Cielo el Dorado would reject her. But reject her they did. She'd had no letter of recommendation, after all.

Caroline had learned that her future home was a small town in Texas with the Rio Grande the only thing separating it from Mexico and the *bandidos*. And surely Mexican bandits could swim, she thought with grim humor. She would teach heathen children by day, only to be murdered by night.

Caroline took a deep breath. If she could survive the pain and betrayal of her beloved Shane, she could survive anything. Yes, she would survive. Somehow. She was going to build a new life. And where better than this isolated outpost, where she was needed as a teacher, to live out her spinster life in peace.

As if to confirm her hopes, the harsh landscape gave way to a lush valley, bisected by the murky waters of the Rio Grande. Craggy cottonwoods and silver poplars shimmered in the breeze. Row after row of grapevines pushed toward the water. Fruit trees and an abundance of crops hung heavy with their bounty. And from each side of the river, just past the fields of crops, rose towering mountains with jagged peaks. The sight was breathtaking.

Suddenly the optimism she had longed for filled her. She felt happier than she had in years—in the five years since Shane. Midnight-black hair and piercing slate-gray eyes threatened. Memories flew around her like lightning bugs, burning brightly for a moment, dazzling in their brilliance. But she pushed the memories back, and for the first time it was not so difficult to do.

Her mood suddenly became buoyant. Her porcelain face softened with a beautiful smile as she straightened her hopelessly wrinkled dress and pulled her dusty gloves tight on her hands.

Finally, she vowed, after so many years, she was going to put her past behind her.

CHAPTER

✴

7

DIEGO CERVANTES MASSAGED heavy tallow grease into a newly finished saddle, his strong hands caressing the stiff leather. Long rays of golden sun filtered through splintery gaps in the rough-hewn stable door. The soft nickering of horses sounded from the stalls. The smell of fresh hay drifted along on the late-afternoon breeze. All was calm and as it should be, he thought. But then shouts of greeting sounded from the main courtyard, announcing someone's arrival. His hands stilled. A scowl darkened his handsome face. He leaned over with a sigh, grabbed his shirt, and angrily pulled it on.

The entire rectangular complex of Cielo el Dorado was protected from the dangers of the outside world by thick adobe walls. The rooms of the hacienda were built with the massive wall at their back, each room connecting to the next by a thinner shared wall. Most doors opened directly into the courtyard. The guards used the rooftops as a promenade to watch over the land.

Cielo el Dorado consisted of two connecting court-yards, looking like a squared-off figure eight from the sky. The main courtyard was surrounded by the main living area, while the other courtyard was surrounded by the work areas. The working side held a large storage area and wine-making room, the blacksmith shop, and an additional kitchen that was used by the live-in servants and guards. There was a tannery, a carpentry shop, a butcher block, and a soap-making room. The hacienda was like a town in itself, providing most necessities; anything else could be gotten from El Paso or from across the river in the Mexican town of Paso del Norte.

A stagecoach pulled through the huge front gate of the hacienda just as Diego stepped around the corner. Work ceased as the inhabitants of Cielo el Dorado clamored around the stage to peer inside. Stagecoach arrivals were infrequent and always a welcome diversion—though as far as Diego was concerned, the new arrival he expected was not welcome at all.

His scowl deepened as the driver swung down from his perch and pulled open the coach door. But Diego's brow furrowed with confusion when a young woman with travel-stained clothes stepped from the confines of the stage.

This was not who he expected.

It took a few seconds for him to assimilate the situation, and by the time he had, his grandmother had come up behind him.

"Is he here?" Emma Shelton asked excitedly, her gently lined features filled with hope.

Diego stiffened, his dark countenance darkening even more. "No, Grandmother. If my guess is correct, it would appear our schoolteacher has arrived."

"Oh, the schoolteacher!" she cried, and clasped her hands to her breast. "Thank goodness!" Emma Shelton moved toward the stagecoach with an agility that belied her seventy-nine years.

Diego didn't follow. He stood back to watch, taking in the scene, his bold stance rigid as steel, until the schoolteacher turned and he saw her clearly for the first time. His black-brown eyes narrowed with surprise.

Just then Henry Driver, the hacienda foreman and Emma's longtime friend, came up alongside of him. "The schoolteacher?" he asked simply with a nod in the new arrival's direction.

"It would appear so."

Henry sighed and ran his hand through his graying hair. "Why was I under the impression Miss Caroline Bromley was an ugly old spinster?" he asked, obviously displeased.

Diego couldn't answer him. He couldn't think what had led them to believe such a thing, especially when faced with the fiery beauty of the woman who stood in their midst. "I guess we just assumed," he finally managed, remembering all too well the jolt of feeling that had surged through him when first he took in her beauty.

"Damn." Henry shook his head. "Given that the only women at Cielo el Dorado are old, married, widowed, or some combination of the three, and El Paso's selection not much better, I'd say our Miss Bromley will surely be in demand. We'll be looking for a new schoolteacher within a month. Your grandmother will be crushed."

Henry looked toward Emma, who was welcoming the new teacher. He shrugged his shoulders. "I don't know what we can do about it."

"I do."

Both men turned with dark glares to find that Reina Valdez had suddenly appeared at their sides.

"Send her back." The young woman didn't look at the two men, but focused instead on Emma Shelton and the new schoolteacher as they approached. "Yes. Send her back before Emma becomes attached to her. We wouldn't want dear Emma to be hurt, would we?" she added just as Emma and the new arrival came to stand before them.

No one spoke for a moment, the tail end of Reina's comment heard by everyone. Henry stepped forward into the awkward silence. "Miss Bromley, I am Henry Driver, hacienda foreman. Welcome to Cielo el Dorado."

"Thank you, sir," Caroline replied politely.

Emma turned to Diego just as Reina caught his arm and held it tightly, bringing a slight, almost imperceptible frown to Emma's features. "And this is Reina Valdez," she added with a tight smile.

Reina looked Caroline up and down, her eyes dark, filled with inexplicable loathing, but she said nothing.

Diego stepped away from Reina's clinging hands. "Reina is a ... cousin, let us say," he said. "With no manners. But she has lived with us for many years, and a person becomes accustomed to it."

Reina's face turned red with anger, but she was forestalled from commenting when Diego took Caroline's hand in his. "And I, too, am lacking in manners for not immediately introducing myself. I am Diego Cervantes."

"My grandson," Emma added with a fond smile.

"It's a pleasure to meet you, Mr. Cervantes," Caroline answered, carefully pulling her hand away.

"Now come with me, Miss Bromley," Emma said. "We have plenty of time to get acquainted later. For now, we will get you settled in after your long ride."

Emma took Caroline's arm and led her through the crowd of people. There were wives and mothers, husbands and guards, and the children Caroline would teach, some standing back behind pillars or skirts, others standing out, boldly assessing her. The two women passed through a courtyard filled with cottonwoods and ash trees and a carpet of grass that couldn't have been greener had it grown in San Antonio.

"It has been a long trip for you, and I suspect something of a shock," Emma remarked as they walked along a smooth stone path that took them farther into the hacienda.

Emma smiled with a faraway look. "I remember the first time I traveled west to El Paso from East Texas. It is so very different here. And I also remember the ride."

Caroline nearly laughed out loud, thinking of the words of the woman who had sat next to her in the stagecoach. "Yes, the ride was surely unforgettable, but I suspect not one that was all that unusual."

"If you are black and blue, then you had the usual ride."

"I'm sure by tomorrow I will be," Caroline said as she consciously stopped herself from rubbing a few particularly tender body parts. "For now, I'm just a bit sore and covered in dust."

"You'll feel much better once you have had a chance to freshen up," Emma said.

They stopped at one of the many large wooden doors that opened into the courtyard. Emma turned to Caroline and looked closely at her. "I'm sure you must be filled with uncertainties as you come to this new land with not only its physical differences but, as I am sure you will find, cultural differences as well. Know that we truly are happy you are here and will do anything we can to make your stay, which we hope will be a long one, as joyful as possible."

Was it possible, Caroline wondered, for someone to be so caring when they had only just met? After five years of women crossing the street so as not to walk on the same side as Caroline, these kinds words made her throat tighten with emotion. "Thank you, Mrs. Shelton."

Emma's kind face filled with a smile. "You must call me Emma. Everyone does."

"Only if you'll call me Caroline."

"Caroline it is. Now rest up. We have plenty of time to get to know one another in the weeks before your first day of school."

The first day of school arrived, in Caroline's opinion, much too quickly. Six glorious weeks had passed since her arrival, and she had loved every second. But the thought of venturing back into a schoolroom filled with students had her stomach twisting in nervous knots. She had not been in the classroom in years—in five years to be exact.

She sat on the edge of her bed, having just finished lacing practical black ankle-high boots that had seen a great deal of polish from a great deal of wear. Like her boots, her attire was more practical than fashionable.

A stiff corset covered her chemise and layers of crinoline and petticoats covered no-nonsense drawers. Her dress was practical as well. The cinched-waisted frock was made from old, but perfectly good, striped ticking, livened-up with a black bow at the collar. Her braided hair was wrapped around her head and covered with a chenille net snood, in what she hoped gave her an authoritative air.

When she was ready, Caroline took a deep breath and pushed herself up off the bed. With quick strokes she smoothed imaginary wrinkles in her skirt and automatically checked for stray wisps of hair. After a hesitant glance at herself in the mirror, she smiled. Everything was going to be all right—just as everything else had turned out all right since she arrived at the hacienda. Her smile widened. If the truth be known, everything was better than all right. Life was wonderful. Emma was wonderful. The hacienda was wonderful. El Paso was wonderful. School would be wonderful, too. Surely. Her life was changing—finally—for the better. And with that thought she promised herself she was no longer going to sit by and watch life pass her by. She was going to live—to be adventuresome—and do things she had always been afraid to do.

Making her way toward the kitchen to grab a quick bite to eat before heading for the schoolroom, Caroline still couldn't quite get used to the sight of the free-flowing, loose-fitting Mexican attire that the women of El Paso and Cielo el Dorado wore so easily.

The kitchen was off the main courtyard, as was much of what constituted the main house.

"Good morning, Caroline," Emma chimed from the kitchen table as she chopped green chilies and onions for the midday meal. Tears streamed down her smiling cheeks.

"Things can't be all that bad," Caroline teased.

Emma laughed and set the knife and onion down. "They do this to me every time. Why I don't let someone else do it I'll never know."

"Because you run this kitchen like an army colonel," Caroline replied fondly.

Emma laughed. "What would you like for breakfast, dear?" she asked, starting to get up.

"Sit, sit, sit. I can fend for myself. Besides, I'm much too nervous to eat much."

"Nervous, you? I find that hard to believe."

"Well, believe it," Caroline said, pouring herself a steaming cup of coffee.

After taking a sip of the strong brew, Caroline set her cup aside and sliced a piece of freshly baked bread from the loaf on the counter. She added fluffy eggs mixed with cheese and thick slices of ham to her plate before she joined Emma at the table. Emma eyed the plate that was filled to nearly overflowing, but said nothing, only stifled the smile that threatened.

"Nervous or not," Emma said, expertly dicing a potato, "you are going to do a wonderful job with the children."

"Oh, Emma." Caroline's throat unexpectedly tightened. "I can't tell you how much your faith in me and your friendship has come to mean to me."

Emma reached across the table and squeezed Caroline's hand. "Hopefully as much as your friendship has come to mean to me. Which reminds me," she said as she stood up and wiped her hands on her apron. "I have something for you." She retrieved a heavy leather-bound book. "I meant to give this to you days ago. After seeing the healing you have done around here, I thought you might be interested in this."

Caroline's eyes opened wide. She wiped her hands, then took the tome, setting it down reverently on the table. She ran her hand over the embossed title. *Murphy's Medical Book*. "Oh, Emma! How wonderful!"

"I know you will put it to good use."

Suddenly the door burst open and in came Beth Parker, a twelve-year-old who had very nearly been Caroline's shadow for the past six weeks. She had long brown hair and huge brown eyes, and a smile that Caroline had rarely seen missing from her heart-shaped face.

"What do you think?" Beth practically sang as she held her arms out and twirled around to show off her new skirt and blouse.

"You look lovely, Beth," Emma replied with a fond smile. "I'm pleased that you're so excited about school."

"School, nothin'! I must look my very best if I want to catch Esteban Gonzalez!"

Caroline grinned. "I'm crushed. I thought you wanted to impress me. And who is this Esteban Gonzalez you're so eager to impress?"

Beth sighed dramatically. "He is the most magnificent man I have ever met. Tall, dark, and handsome. And I'm madly and passionately in love with him. One day we'll marry."

Caroline looked surprised.

Emma shook her head. "A twelve-year-old boy hardly makes a man. And a twelve-year-old girl shouldn't be talking of love and marriage—to Esteban Gonzalez, at that!"

Beth put her chin in the air and turned to Caroline. "What do you think of love, Miss Caroline?"

"Men are a contrary lot, mark my words," she answered with enough heat to bring a surprised look from Emma.

Caroline blushed. She realized that she sounded just like Mary Jane. Her heart tightened. Mary Jane, who had withdrawn from her life after her fall from grace. Caroline wanted to close her eyes against the hurt.

"You know, that's just what Missy Surlock says," Beth stated pensively.

Caroline looked up just in time to see Emma's renewed scowl turn on Beth. "Who is Missy Surlock?" she asked.

Before Emma could stop her, Beth leaned forward. "She's the lady who got herself pregnant without having a husband," she whispered.

"Hush, Beth Parker," Emma reprimanded with a sharp chop to an onion. "Girls your age shouldn't be talking about such things."

Beth merely sat back and rolled her eyes.

"Morning, ladies," Henry called as he entered the kitchen.

"Good morning," they replied in unison.

Henry's hand came to his cheek and pressed his jaw experimentally. "My tooth is feeling a good bit better, Miss Caroline. I thank you for seeing to it."

"You're welcome," Caroline replied with a smile, knowing that while he made it sound so easy, it had been anything but. Caroline had been forced to browbeat and corner just about every single known and rumored sick or injured man, woman, and child in the area to see to their ailments. Henry had simply been the first that hadn't kicked and screamed and carried on the whole time.

"Well, I'd best be on my way so I won't be late for my first day of school," Caroline said. She glanced at Beth and smiled. "You'd best be thinking about hurrying, too."

Leaving the kitchen, Caroline headed straight for the schoolroom in the late-summer heat. Thankfully, she arrived before any of her students. Though after she had stood for no more than a few minutes at the front of a long room filled with wooden tables and benches, her thankfulness began to wear thin as beads of sweat gathered in the most unladylike places despite the early-morning hour. But that was the least of her worries. Within seconds, ten students of varying shapes and sizes entered with all the grace and order of a herd of buffalo. Once in their new seats, the children shifted and squirmed. It was going to be a long day, she mused.

The day started with roll call.

"Graciela Barrientos," Caroline called.

The room was silent. Caroline looked out over the faces. Not one child appeared to recognize the name.

"Is there no Graciela Barrientos here?"

"Sure," came the reply from a young boy who, Caroline learned, was named Pepe. "Right there," he said, pointing a finger at the girl in question.

The sought-after Graciela sat quietly.

"Graciela? You must say 'present' when your name is called. That way I know you are here." Caroline spoke kindly and patiently to the small girl, but Graciela's eyes remained fixed on her feet.

"Lady," called Pepe. "She don't speak no English."

Don't, or rather, doesn't speak any English! Caroline thought with a start as her eyes widened then narrowed in turn. With a thud, she sat down in her chair—hard. "How many of you do speak English?"

About half the class raised their hands; the others merely looked at her or their feet with what Caroline interpreted as embarrassment.

Caroline Bromley had a lot to learn.

"Oh, my God," Caroline mumbled, wondering what she was going to do. Failing to recognize the snickers that came from the children for what they were, her eyes clouded with concern.

How was she supposed to teach these children if she could not speak their language? Surely she would have to leave. She couldn't possibly teach them anything. Then she remembered her fruitless attempts to secure any other teaching position. She was stuck. She couldn't speak Spanish, but she couldn't leave either. So, with an obstinate nod of her head, she pushed up from her chair. "All right then, I will just have to learn Spanish so I can teach the rest of you English."

Fortified by renewed conviction, Caroline pulled back her shoulders and quickly formulated a new plan. With the help of Pepe as translator, she slowly began to explain schoolroom procedures.

"Now, children," Caroline said, her hands clasped together. "In addition to roll call we will begin each day with a discussion of current events." She turned to Pepe for the translation.

Pepe smiled, much like Caroline had, looking like

a dark-headed little angel. *"Albondigas, mis amigos. No te deje."*

The class burst out laughing, leaving Caroline with little doubt that the translation had been less than accurate. Groaning inwardly, though with a smile fixed on her face, she sent her translator back to his seat and proceeded alone, deciding she stood a better chance of conveying her instructions through pantomime than through little Pepe.

Her pantomime had not been long under way when Caroline noticed the perspiration that slid down her students' tiny faces and the light-colored shirts that were fast becoming dark. Things were going from bad to worse. Something drastic had to be done.

In a fit of what she felt was pure inspiration, she decided to hold class out-of-doors. She pictured her students sitting under the shade of a sprawling cottonwood tree, their rosy faces upturned with awe and the dawning light of understanding for the new concepts she would teach.

"I know how hot it is in here," Caroline said with a glowing smile. "So today we will go outside—"

But before Caroline had a chance to finish her sentence and reveal her glorious plan, her ten students let out a whooping cry of victory and trampled over one another in their haste to be gone. Even the ones who supposedly didn't speak English! The little scoundrels!

"Wait! Children!" But her words went unheeded. School was over before it had begun.

Caroline was left standing alone in the classroom, frustrated beyond belief. Then, in another fit, though this time of temper, she kicked her desk. Screeching in pain, she hopped about, holding one foot until her agonized dance was interrupted.

"Hello!" Diego called out from the doorway.

Caroline looked up at him warily, hastily releasing her injured appendage. "Hello."

"School's out early."

"Well, yes." Caroline scowled.

"They got the better of you, did they?" Diego asked, his dark eyes sparkling with amusement.

Caroline groaned. "How did you guess?"

Diego strode to the front of the room and perched one hip on the corner of her desk. He crossed his arms and cast a knowing smile. "Perhaps it was the slump of your shoulders, or the look of defeat on your face. Or maybe, it was the mass exodus of young schoolchildren no more than twenty minutes after they arrived." He shrugged his shoulders. "But who's to say."

Caroline shook her head and a reluctant smile crossed her face. "Yes, who's to say."

She walked to the window to check if any of her students were waiting expectantly under the tree. There were none. She sighed, defeated.

Diego followed. "You shouldn't let anyone see you look so dejected by your . . . early dismissal. You should act as though you intended for the little hellions to leave when they did. You must regain the upper hand," he stated with an infuriating chuckle.

Caroline stared at him in surprise, uncertain if she should be insulted or thankful for his unsolicited advice. But then she noticed young Pepe, peeking out from the side of the building with three other boys behind him.

Diego nodded meaningfully. "Come, we will stroll about the hacienda to show them your feathers are not so easily ruffled." Then, without asking, he simply took her hand and pulled her toward the door.

Caroline's reluctant smile disappeared. She pulled her hand away much as she had when first they met. "Thank you, but I have to make preparations for tomorrow."

And then she slipped past him to escape out the door, not far behind her truant students.

Despite the rough start, subsequent schooldays passed with definite signs of hope. During the day, Caroline spent her time coaxing and cajoling her reluctant students into coming to and staying at school. Reading, writing, and arithmetic had not yet been returned to the list of priorities. Simple attendance and language barriers dominated her concerns.

At night Caroline sat with Emma and her family, talking and laughing and eating into the late hours. Diego was gone much of the time, and when he was around, she managed to avoid finding herself alone with him. Only Reina marred her happiness with her looks of hatred and disparaging remarks. But Caroline ignored her as best she could, determined that Cielo el Dorado would be the place where she would spend the rest of her days in peace.

But then one night tension filled the *sala* as the family sat down for the evening meal. Emma's eyes darted to the door whenever someone entered. At the sight of a servant, she sighed and turned away. Caroline glanced around the table. Henry ran a frustrated hand through his gray hair. Diego was unusually quiet. Even Reina didn't offer her usual biting remarks.

The door opened again and Emma started from her

seat, only to sigh when she found yet again it was only
a servant.

Henry growled. "Enough! Serve the meal. We can't
wait forever, *mi querida*." His tone softened. "He may
not come."

Emma nodded solemnly. "Of course, you're right. Let
us begin. Carmen," she said to a serving girl. "We're
ready."

And then it happened, just when Caroline was about
to ask what was wrong. A shout of hello sounded and
the door banged open. Everyone turned in their seats.
Caroline turned as well, and when she did, her breath
caught in her throat. Her world closed around her, and
she found it hard to breathe. The room grew smaller,
hemming her in, her life once again tumbling before
her. She was unaware of anyone else in the room, of
Diego and Reina, who had turned to her at the sound
of her ragged intake of breath. Her mind staggered as
she was forced to another time, so long ago.

Midnight-black hair that had so intrigued her.
Piercing slate-gray eyes stared at her, hard, in bewil-
derment. A glimmer of uncertainty flickered through
his eyes. She saw the look, recognized it for what it
was, and hated herself for the pain she allowed to
engulf her. His confusion was additional evidence that
she had meant nothing to him, that it had all been a lie—
as if she had needed further proof. But in her flights of
fancy, Caroline had always held on to the dream that
there was a reason for his desertion, that one day he
would find her.

Deep down inside she had always known how
absurd her dreams were. He had used her, at her
own prompting no less, to escape the sheriff's noose,

then discarded her like old clothes. Just as her father had always told her men would do.

She floundered in an agonizing maelstrom as her mind tried to understand the unimaginable. Her world grew dark and dim, for this man, this person standing at the door of what she had thought had become her new home, was none other than Shane Rivers, the man who had destroyed her life.

CHAPTER

✴

8

NO ONE SPOKE. Silence.

The weight of recognition. And for a moment his mind froze, throwing him off balance.

"Red," he finally said, his voice barely a whisper, not understood.

Shane Rivers stood on the threshold of the *sala*, his form large and imposing. The hardness of his face gave way, and his eyes filled with a world weariness and pain that contrasted sharply with the vitality and power that emanated from his body. His mind pitched back and forth between San Antonio so many years before and El Paso this night as he tried to make sense of where he was and who sat before him. He could hardly assimilate the information. For a second he thought he was caught up in a dream, as he had been so often over the last five years. But this dream, he knew, was all too real—a reality that made no sense.

It didn't matter that El Paso and San Antonio had been connected for decades by trade and mail routes, that El Paso was a gateway for thousands of wayfarers traveling from east to west. Shane could only think how impossible it was for Caroline to have found him.

He looked at her, as she looked at him. Each mesmerized. Remembering, he was certain, though her delicate brow was marred.

Then it came to him with sharp certainty, as he took in her startled eyes, that she had not found him on purpose. This was simply some kind of bizarre twist of fate—nothing more. His face darkened as if a curtain had fallen to quickly conceal the painful realization.

The strained silence had finally broken, and conversation swirled in the dimly lit room, wrapping around him, a word caught here, perhaps one there, but generally unintelligible. His grandmother's loving greetings mixed with disapproving admonitions went unheard.

"Red," he whispered, taking a step inside.

But it was his grandmother who came to him.

"Oh, Shane, you're finally here," Emma said, reaching up to take his face between her trembling hands.

Shane forced his eyes away from Caroline, down to his grandmother. He touched her hand with the tips of his fingers. And he smiled. His face was transformed. The smile lightened his forbidding appearance, hinting at the beauty it once held.

Metal clattered on china, and Shane's head jerked up. Their eyes met. Slate-gray clashing with disbelieving green.

The murmurs of conversation ceased. Everyone in the room turned from Shane to Caroline. Though before they could make out the shock in her eyes or the blood that drained from her cheeks, Caroline staggered up from her seat. The wooden chair caught on the woven rug, wobbled precariously, then tumbled to the ground with a crash.

"Excuse me, please," Caroline said desperately to

Emma. "I find that I'm not feeling well."

Without waiting for a response, she started for the door, hesitating momentarily when she came face-to-face with Emma—and Shane. But she hesitated only a second. When she passed him by, Shane started to reach out, to keep her there, but she flinched as if struck, and he quickly dropped his hand away.

The strain of silence was heavy in the room.

Emma watched Caroline go and then slowly turned her gaze on Shane, her eyes narrowed in question. But then she smiled. "You're here," was all she said.

Shane didn't respond, merely stared at the empty doorway.

"Cousin!"

Shane turned. "Diego," he stated, his voice unreadable.

"It's been a long time. What? Six, seven years since last you visited us?" Diego shrugged his shoulders and leaned back in the high-backed chair. "You remember everyone, don't you? Henry? Reina?" His voice grew overloud. "But of course you do. And surely they remember you, too. Yes, everyone remembers my cousin Shane. Even after all this time. And like always, everything will stop for you. Eh?"

Shane took a deep breath then sighed. He stared across the richly appointed room. The thick red velvet curtains and dark wood furniture only added to the weight. "I would have been disappointed had things changed, I suppose."

Diego laughed, a short burst of sound, as he leaned the chair back until it rested on two hind legs. "Things never change, cousin, never."

"Enough," Emma stated, leading Shane to the table.

"It's time to celebrate. Sit here, Shane, and fill your plate. I will return shortly. I must check on Caroline."

She turned to go, but Henry stopped her. "Emma," he said with a quick questioning look at Shane. "Let her go. She's been working hard. I'm sure she's just tired. Let her sleep. You can check on her in the morning."

Emma glanced from Henry to the now vacant door. "Yes, you're probably right. The dear woman has worked herself to the bone these last weeks."

Shane opened his mouth to question Emma about Caroline, but snapped it shut, not certain how he felt, not certain what he wanted to know.

Emma moved to sit back down, and Shane held her chair, Henry standing politely. Diego simply lounged in his seat while Reina stared at her plate.

"Maria," Emma called to the serving girl. "Now we are truly ready."

They ate *salpicón*—seasoned shredded beef with tortillas. A heavy earthenware bowl held beans in a thin sauce with chilies, onions, and tomatoes. Shane ate with relish, the Mexican dishes extremely welcome after the hardtack he had been treated to for so long.

"So tell me, Shane," Henry began, "what brings you to El Paso?"

"Yes, cousin, tell us all." Diego's tone was harsh as he clutched the stem of his wineglass. "We are dying to know."

Shane hesitated. "As Diego pointed out, it's been a long time since last I saw my family."

Diego snorted. "Well, here we are. Look your fill. Then you can get back on your horse, or in a stage, or whatever else might have brought you here, and go on your way as you always do."

"Diego!" Emma stated sharply. "Don't start this."

Shane reached across the table and laid his hand over his grandmother's in an oddly parental gesture. "It doesn't matter, Emma. Let it go."

She started to protest, but the words were curtailed when Diego pushed up from his seat, throwing his napkin down on the table. "Yes, *Emma*," he mimicked. "Let it go." Then he strode from the room with Reina close on his heels.

Emma sighed, and Henry reached over to rest his hand on her shoulder. She tilted her head and smiled at the foreman with a look so filled with love that Shane felt the need to look away. And when he did, Emma blushed.

"I shouldn't be acting like a young miss. I'm an old woman," Emma said, her cheeks still filled with red.

Henry chuckled. "Never old, *mi querida*." He got up to retrieve some of the hacienda's fine brandy and three glasses. He poured a small amount in each. "Our best so far," he said as he handed the glasses around.

"It was the best I had tasted when last I was here."

"It's even better now. Learned a thing or two from a Frenchman who stayed with us several years back," Henry explained.

"I'd like to hear what you learned. Perhaps tomorrow you could take me through the vineyard and winery?" Shane added, trying to make conversation to mask his feelings about seeing Caroline.

"Be happy to. I remember well your fondness for the land and wine-making."

Shane smiled. "Yes. There's something magical in a process that has been handed down through generations—a link that connects us with the past."

Emma eyed her grandson. "It could be handed down to you—if you stayed."

Shane glanced at her, but didn't respond.

Emma looked away and toyed with her napkin. "I was so thankful when the news reached us that the war was over."

Shane took a sip, savoring the burn of the strong drink.

"And your letter was a great relief. I hadn't heard from you in so long that I was afraid—" Emma's words stuck in her throat.

Amusement flickered across Shane's face, and he offered her a crooked smile. "I'm too mean and hardheaded to kill. Though certainly a few tried. I survived the war, dear Emma, and I'm afraid you'll be stuck with me for a very long time."

"Then you do plan to stay!" she stated, hope written clearly in her pale blue eyes.

Shane took another sip and looked toward the empty door through which Caroline had fled. With a shrug he took another sip. "I don't know," he finally answered. "I don't know."

As if reading his thoughts, Emma glanced at the door. "You seemed to know our new schoolteacher?"

Shane looked down into his glass and stared at the amber liquid, swirling it around, watching as it ran down the sides of the crystal. "Yes, I knew her once. But that was a lifetime ago. I imagine she didn't even recognize me."

Henry snorted his disbelief.

Emma stiffened. "My guess is that she did." She stared at Shane as if weighing her words. "Is there anything I should know?"

Setting the brandy down on the table with a heavy sigh, a mark of deep regret and sorrow etched on his face, Shane looked at his grandmother. "No, Emma, there's nothing you should know." Then he pushed himself back from the table, hugged his grandmother in thanks for the meal, and walked out into the dark.

Sounds of the night filled the blackened sky. The moon had just begun to appear. And Shane needed to find a place where he could think. Taking a lantern from its perch on an adobe column, he headed toward the river. He followed a well-traveled path to an *acequia* that brought a thick branch of the Rio Grande to the western fields. When he reached the edge of the water he stopped. He stood there, staring, feeling. But what, he wondered, did he feel?

He thought of the need he had felt to return to the hacienda. In the years since his grandfather had died and his grandmother had come west to El Paso to purchase Cielo el Dorado, Shane had not seen much of Emma or spent much time at the hacienda. But when he had visited he had always loved it—the rugged beauty of the harsh mountain peaks bisected by the green river valley, the awe-inspiring shades of purple cast by the rising sun, and the brilliant shades of red and orange cast when it set. Such contrasts, such beauty—and no memories. He liked that most of all.

He hooked the lantern on a branch of a cottonwood and leaned up against the trunk, losing himself in the shadows. His head fell back, pressing against the craggy bark. He felt so tired, tired unto death.

After five long years of war, he, unlike so many others, had survived. He had gotten caught up in the War

Between the States soon after he fled San Antonio. It had seemed the perfect place for a man who was trying to escape.

He laughed harshly. Fighting had suited him perfectly, fighting in an insane war that he had wished more than once had taken his life.

He ran a large, scarred hand across his face. All he wanted to do now was work the land. And forget. He had planned to do just that in El Paso, even if it meant dealing with Diego. But he hadn't been prepared to find Caroline Bromley. Sweet Caroline.

Emotion washed over him. And just as he had all those years ago, he wanted her.

He jerked away from the tree with a curse, telling himself that just as he had left her before, he must leave her alone now. She could never love him if she knew what he was really like.

And as if his thoughts brought her to him, Caroline appeared, stepping into the moonlight out of the dark.

He stood in the shadows, silently, unable to move. He looked at her. His throat tightened strangely. His brow furrowed and a thick vein stood out on his hard-carved neck.

She was beautiful. Unaware as she was that she was being watched, the terror that he had seen in her eyes earlier was gone. Instead he found hints of the woman he had known before—full of fiery vitality and life, something he hadn't seen in so long.

He shifted his weight and she turned. She peered into the darkness. "Who's there?"

Her quiet, lilting voice was his undoing. He moved out of the shadows, knowing he shouldn't, and took a step toward her. Her eyes opened wide and she clutched one of the roses that lined the hacienda wall carefully to her breast.

"Caroline," he said, her name a caress.

"I've lost my way," she stammered, suddenly frantic, trying to turn and retrace her steps.

He smiled, though the slight curve on his lips held little humor. "So have I, sweet Caroline, so have I."

Her body stilled. She inhaled deeply as if remembering, and her eyes fluttered closed. Her arms pressed tighter to her breast.

"Is it possible that you're the same sweet innocent who so captivated me in San Antonio?"

Her eyes snapped open. "No," she whispered, looking away, though seemingly unable to move.

"Your eyes are still so green," he said, stepping closer. "And your lips still beckon." He took the remaining steps until he stood before her on the sandy banks of the flowing river, the moon now full and high, the black sky a canvas of stars. His mind told him to leave her alone. But some emotion, stronger than intellect, kept him there.

He reached out and touched her cheek. The feel of her skin flooded his mind. "The years have done nothing to lessen your allure. If anything, the passing time has made you more beautiful."

His fingers trailed back to her ear, sweeping a long tendril of hair back, before he traced a path along the line of her jaw. He felt, as much as saw, her intake of breath. He saw as well the wild flutter of her heart in her neck. The simple touch was like wind to a raging fire. But still he knew he should leave her alone. He should turn away and return to the hacienda, and then leave in the morning. Frustration assailed him and his hand clenched at her jaw, the veins in his muscled forearm standing out. But he failed to take his hand away—it simply continued its course, fisted, until it reached her chin. He forced her to turn her head, to look back at him. Tears shimmered in the green depths. And then he was lost, the fire consuming him.

The rose dropped to the sandy bank, and he pulled her into his arms. She clung to him with a fierceness that startled him, left him breathless.

"Caroline," he moaned, stroking her hair.

He felt her tears soak through to his skin. His strong hands seared a path up her arms, over her shoulders, to the delicate curve of her neck. With one thumb he tilted her chin as he lowered his head to hers. He captured her lips in a gentle kiss. One strong hand traced a path down her back, pressing them close as the gentle kiss became a demand—long and slow, deep, unyielding.

"Shane." Her voice was a faint murmur.

But though the sound was faint, he heard his name on her lips, reminding him of the past, bringing him up short. His body tensed. He pressed his eyes closed and held on tight. Flames licked at his loins. But he couldn't. He couldn't hold on to her. He cursed the fates that placed him in such a position, not once but twice, as if he had to be reminded again and again of his unworthiness. And with that thought, he set her at arm's length.

She stared at him just as she had all those years ago, confused, questioning. Shane looked away and found the discarded rose. He reached down and retrieved the flower then handed it to her. "You're still so beautiful. But there's a difference, though a difference that can't be explained away by mere years."

The words brought a gasp to her lips. A quick surge of anger filled her eyes and she staggered back as if something had actually let her go. "Stay away from me, Shane Rivers!"

"Caroline," he whispered hoarsely.

But when he started to reach out to her, she threw the rose in his face, then turned on her heel and ran.

Shane watched her go, wanting desperately to follow, strangely bereft over her departure, strangely sorrowful over the look in her eyes. No longer able to keep the thoughts from his mind, he wondered what had brought her so far from San Antonio and her father. He wondered what had happened during the five intervening years.

His hand strayed to his face, to the sting on his cheek where the rose had struck. When he pulled his hand away, he found a small pinprick of blood. He stared at his hand until the rose on the ground came into focus. Bending his knees, he retrieved the flower, muscles in his back and forearm rippling from the movement. He put his nose to the petals and inhaled, closing his eyes, remembering. *Stay away from me*, she had cried.

He sighed as he thought about the months it had taken to get her out of his mind. He remembered how over the years, something would unexpectedly bring her to mind. Sitting in the dark forest, still as stone, waiting for the enemy, his mind would dredge up her image. The pungent smell of gunpowder forced him to recall the smell of lemons in her hair. But time, and necessity, had made it easier to keep her image distant. He had put his abundant energies into fighting, earning medals and honors he had no use for. Now he would have to purge her from his mind all over again.

And suddenly he didn't know if that was possible—despite Rupert—despite her God.

CHAPTER

✳

9

CAROLINE'S EYES SNAPPED open. Instantly, she was wide-awake. And filled with dread.

"Good God," she moaned to the ceiling. "What am I to do?"

Panic began to creep in, seeping into every pore of her body. What had she done in coming to such a place? she asked herself. She remembered thinking that for the most part El Paso was the perfect place to go. Caroline groaned. Perfect. Ha! El Paso, Texas, had turned out to be the worst place she could have gone.

Rolling over, she buried her face in the pillow and beat her fists against the sturdy mattress. "Stupid, stupid, stupid," she berated herself.

But then she paused.

"No!" she cried, rolling back, swinging her legs over the side to sit at the edge of the bed. "You'll not turn into a featherbrained idiot over this, Caroline Bromley. You've survived before, you'll survive again. How many times do you have to remind yourself of that?"

Her hands fisted against the tangled muslin sheets, her brow furrowed with determination. Over the years of living in a close-knit community that considered her a fallen woman, she had been forced to accept her life as a spinster, or go crazy. Lacking some fundamental mental makeup to go insane, she had learned a practicality and levelheadedness that had served her well.

"You're not some weak, spineless female! You're a chin-up, shoulders-back, straight-spined individual who can take care of herself!" And that was exactly what she planned to do.

It was these qualities that led her to conclude the solution was simple enough. She had four weeks' pay coming to her. She would ask for her money, then leave El Paso just as fast as she could. If she managed to procure a teaching position here, she could get one somewhere else, she told herself, conveniently disregarding the fact that El Paso was the only job offer she had received. There had to be other outposts that needed a teacher. She would find one. Then she would never have to lay eyes on Shane Rivers again.

Her heart clenched and her eyes burned at the thought. She had told herself she had finally put him behind her. But after one fleeting touch, she wondered how she had lived without him all these years. It came crashing in on her—the yearning, the desire. She trembled and she ached. But then she sucked in her breath and cursed herself. The man was a scoundrel and a liar. She'd not fall prey to him again. And she'd come entirely too close to just that last night. No, she had to take action.

After dressing quickly, Caroline hurried to the servants' area to see who might be going into town. It didn't take long before she had secured a ride to the stage depot with Jorge, one of the field hands. Gratefully, she hopped into the wagon, avoiding the quizzical

looks from people not used to her going into town so
early in the morning.

At the depot, a large burly man with wiry hair stood
behind the counter, reading an old San Antonio news-
paper. He didn't look up until she stood before him. As
he lowered the paper first surprise, then admiration lit
his eyes.

"Miss Caroline," he said, tossing the paper aside.
"What brings you into town so early?"

"I've come to inquire after the next stage," she replied,
her hands clutched demurely at her waist.

"You only just got here. What you want to go and
leave for?"

She smiled at him as she would smile at a troublesome student. "Mr. Burke, I don't believe that is any of
your business."

Harold Burke laughed. "That's the truth, ma'am. Not
one bit of my business. So let me see," he said, turning
to a single sheet of paper that lay on the counter. "With
the northern just out of here at sunup, we shouldn't see
another for a good six weeks, maybe more, what with
all the trouble with bandits and soldiers without a war
to fight or a home to go to out on the roads causing a
heap of trouble."

Caroline's eyes grew large and filled with distress.

"Now don't you fret, Miss Caroline. Those stage drivers are armed to the teeth these days. Few people are
actually getting hurt. Just more of a nuisance, is all."

Caroline shook her head, trying to clear her misery.
While certainly she was concerned for the stage drivers,
it was the fact that she had just missed a stagecoach
that caused her upset. How could she possibly survive
six weeks? Emma would surely ask her to leave once

Shane told his grandmother about Caroline's wanton ways. No one in their right mind would allow a fallen woman to mold young minds if they knew the truth.

But there was no help for it, she realized. She had to wait it out. She grimaced when she thought of Emma again, however. The woman had been so kind and wonderful to her. She hated to disappoint her. But what could she do? she asked herself. She couldn't turn back time and do things over again.

"Thank you, Mr. Burke," Caroline said, forcing a smile. "I'll check back later."

Moving out onto the wood-planked walkway, lost in her thoughts, Caroline nearly ran into a young woman who stepped out in front of her. "Goodness," Caroline gasped, her hand flying to her chest. Upon seeing the young and clearly very pregnant woman, she relaxed and chuckled at her jumpiness. "You startled me."

The woman had white-blond hair that had been hastily pulled up in a knot at the back of her head. Her eyes were the color of the midafternoon sky on a cloudless day. But the eyes that should have been considered beautiful were marred by deep, half-moon shadows of fatigue. She stared at Caroline like a frightened doe. She seemed to want to ask her something. But just when she started to speak, the field hand who had brought Caroline to town pulled up in the wagon.

"Señorita Caroline," Jorge called. "If we do not hurry, you will be late for the schooltime."

Caroline glanced from the young woman to Jorge, then back, but before she could speak, the girl twirled awkwardly around and slipped away down the boardwalk. Caroline called after her to no avail.

"Señorita! *Pronto!*" Jorge called again.

After a second of indecision, Caroline sighed, knowing that indeed she must return to the hacienda, then hurried down the few steps to the dirt road. She took Jorge's proffered hand and climbed up onto the wagon seat, wondering what the young woman had wanted to say.

The horse and wagon made good time along the hard-packed sand and dirt road that led to the hacienda. Caroline's heart pounded the whole way in fear of seeing Emma. And no sooner did they career through the front gate than her eyes lighted upon the older woman.

"You're up and about early," Emma said, once Caroline approached.

"Yes, I needed some things from town for . . . a . . . project that I have planned for today," she offered lamely, clutching her bag that thankfully she had thought to take along.

"You always have something exciting going on in that schoolroom. I'm sure the children love it," Emma said with a quick squeeze of Caroline's arm. "I'm glad to see you're feeling better. I was going to check on you last night, but thought perhaps all you needed was a good night's sleep."

"Yes, I'm fine, Emma. Thank you for asking."

Caroline nearly wept with relief. Emma still knew nothing of her past. She was safe, at least for now.

Caroline practically ran to the schoolroom and barely had a chance to take off her bonnet before her students started to arrive.

"Good morning, children," she said as she turned, flushed and smiling, to face them.

The smile, however, froze and the words stuck in her throat when Caroline found a young boy standing at the door, brandishing the largest, most sinister-looking knife she had ever had the misfortune to lay eyes on. Her shock turned quickly to slack-jawed amazement when suddenly, with the quick flick of his wrist, the youth sent the quivering shaft of steel hurtling across the room to stick with a thud in the small desk at the front and center of the floor.

"I am Esteban Gonzalez," the boy announced in heavily accented English, "and I do not need schooling."

It took a moment, but eventually Caroline pulled herself together enough to realize that young Beth's secret love had finally arrived for his first day of class. Her open mouth straightened into a hard line as she studied the boy.

His swarthy good looks stood in stark contrast to his mere twelve years. And as she stared at him, trying to hide the fact that his little display had aged her a good ten years, Caroline was not sure if she should laugh or call the sheriff. Neither act seeming appropriate, she simply walked over to the desk and yanked the blade from the wooden plank.

"Welcome, Esteban Gonzalez. I am Miss Bromley. I'm glad you don't need any schooling, as it will make my job much easier." She eyed the six-inch razor-sharp edge and quelled a shiver. "However, since you're already here, you might as well stay and help us with your expertise."

Caroline gave the boy no opportunity to respond. She turned on her heel, her skirts billowing around her practical boots, and walked back to her desk, opened a drawer, and dropped the knife inside. "This, I believe, is now mine."

"Hey, you cannot do that!" Esteban's thin chest puffed up and his hands fisted on his hips.

Caroline raised a delicate brow in question. "Can't I?"

He glanced about the small room, surveying the curious faces that looked on with great interest.

"We could, of course, ask Mrs. Shelton or Mr. Driver what they think," Caroline suggested.

Esteban glared at Caroline and grumbled, looking as though he would put up a fight. But her worries were not to be realized and her breath came out in a relieved *whoosh* when Esteban grunted, then reluctantly made his way to a desk and folded himself onto the hard chair.

Esteban Gonzalez was not the only surprise Caroline received that morning. With each passing day she invariably found a new child who had slipped in and taken a backseat. Some were young, some were old, but none brought with them anything but themselves, much less a hog. And that is just what the second new student of the day had done. Young Opal White arrived with a big, fat hog at her side, a huge, droopy bow tied around its neck.

"Welcome to our class, Opal," Caroline began with a kind smile. "We're so happy you have joined us. However, this is no place for a . . . hog," she finished with a gentle shrug.

Opal's hazel eyes widened with concern. "Oh, miss, please do not worry your head over such a thing. Hortense won't bother a single soul. I promise," she added as she fell to her knees and attempted to wrap her tiny arms around the snorting animal's pinkish mass. But Hortense had a greater interest in Caroline's boots than Opal's hugs and quickly inched her way over to nuzzle the worn black leather.

"See!" Opal exclaimed. "She likes you. Please let her stay."

The class eyed Caroline speculatively. She had won one battle by dealing with the notorious troublemaker Esteban. She didn't want to lose any points by mucking up this situation. "Hortense can stay for today, but not again, Opal, do you understand?"

Opal smiled to show a sparsely toothed mouth, then led her pet to an empty desk at the side of the room and instructed Hortense to sit politely next to her. Caroline could only watch with amusement. What was she to do?

Though school had gotten off to a less than auspicious beginning, by the time the students streamed out the door in search of their homes at the end of the day, Caroline was convinced that some learning had taken place. She had learned a bit of Spanish and the children were fessing up to the English they knew. The only thing she still had not gotten used to was the heat. Good Lord, was it hot. And it was the beginning of October. The most unladylike beads of perspiration covered her forehead and upper lip. Caroline sighed and took a handkerchief from her pocket to wipe her brow, knowing she still had to finish her lesson plans and straighten the room before she could seek out cooler climes.

She secretly longed to wear the delicious, free-flowing, loose-fitting Mexican garments the other women wore. But despite the heat, Caroline was unwilling to give up the last few trappings of respectability left to her—no matter how much she longed to toss that very equipage, with all its whalebone corsets and stiff horsehair crinolines into the refuse heap. Thankfully, she had never been able to afford the complicated hooped framework that ladies in San Antonio had begun to wear beneath their skirts. Good Lord, what would she have done had she been strapped into such a contraption in this heat? Just the thought caused beads of sweat to well to new proportions.

With a shake of her head, Caroline went back to her lessons for the next day. She had finally managed to concentrate when the door was pushed open. At first, the harsh golden sunlight made it difficult to make out who had entered. But then she saw her. The girl who had started to speak to her that morning in town. Caroline stood and smiled, though the girl came no closer.

"Come in," Caroline said, extending her hand.

The girl looked scared to death and unsure of what exactly she should do. Her hair was still pulled up, though it looked as if she had taken great pains to make it look nice.

"Please, come in," Caroline repeated. "It is perfectly all right."

After a moment's hesitation, the girl moved forward. Her clothes were those of the East, much like Caroline's, rather than those of the area. The hem was ragged and recently washed, not yet completely dry. Caroline noticed the seams that had been opened up and expanded with mismatched pieces of material to accommodate her increasing size. She was not altogether certain, but from the looks of the girl, she suspected she should deliver fairly soon.

"I'm Caroline Bromley," she began, trying to coax the reason for the visit out of her. "What is your name?"

"Missy Surlock, ma'am."

Missy Surlock, "the girl who got herself pregnant without getting herself a husband," Caroline remembered Beth saying. She should have guessed. A sharp pang of sympathy swept through her. A man had done this to the poor girl, and now she was left alone to fend for herself. Green eyes snapped as Caroline felt a need to lash out, but she held it down. Anger would only scare the girl away.

"Welcome, Miss Surlock. I don't have much in the way of refreshments or seating, but if you don't mind a hard-backed chair and a bit of water, I'd be happy if you would join me."

"Oh, no," she replied quickly, glancing at the door. "I can't stay. I just came by . . . because . . . well . . ."

"What is it?" Caroline questioned kindly.

Missy's eyes grew distraught and her lips pursed until in a rush she said, "I'm delivering soon and I'm afraid!"

Caroline stood very still.

Missy continued. "I've heard all around town how you're good with doctoring kinds of things, and I was wondering . . . well . . . if you could help me deliver?"

The words were out, and Caroline could see the relief spread across Missy's face. Help her, she had asked. Someone had actually come to her, without being browbeaten or cornered, to ask for her help. Caroline stood speechless, her heart filled with joy. After all these years someone had come to her. Oh, the feeling, she rejoiced to herself, not having realized until then how very much she had missed being sought out for her cures and skills.

"I can't pay you coin, but I can clean and such," Missy rushed to say.

Caroline focused her gaze on the girl and smiled. "That won't be necessary, Miss Surlock. I'll be happy to help you when your time comes."

"Are you sure?" Missy asked, as if unable to believe she had heard correctly.

"Of course I'm sure." And she was. She was as certain as she had ever been, and she wasn't going to let a little thing like not knowing the first thing about delivering a baby dampen her mood.

CHAPTER

✳

10

PERHAPS NOT KNOWING the first thing about childbirth couldn't dampen her mood, but hours of unsuccessfully perusing her medical book in hopes of learning such information managed to do it quite nicely.

Caroline slammed the old leather book down on the tiny table next to her bed.

"Childbirth!" she muttered aloud as she flicked yet again through the yellowed pages. "Good Lord, Caroline Bromley, what were you thinking?"

She had taken a meager meal to her room, telling Emma she had a good deal of work to do before tomorrow. Caroline wondered how long she could come up with plausible excuses for missing the evening meal. One week, two, maybe three? She could not bear the thought of sitting through a two-minute cup of coffee with Shane Rivers, much less an entire meal.

Emma placed a great deal of emphasis on the family, however extended it might be, sitting down to supper together. Caroline would be lucky to get away with a week! But in the back of her mind, she was constantly aware that at any time Shane could reveal her past, making it unnecessary to come up with excuses at all.

She would be eating elsewhere anyway!

But she didn't wonder about excuses for long when she remembered that Shane Rivers was the least of her worries just then. Childbirth and, specifically, how it was done need be her only concern. Page after page, throughout the three-inch-thick tome, references to childbirth were few and far between. If a person had to rely on those scant mentions, then the book, she came to the maddening conclusion, was useless. Dr. Murphy of *Murphy's Medical Book* was either an idiot or felt that only an idiot needed to be told how the miracle of birth was accomplished.

Caroline groaned and fell back onto the bed, her arms flung out on her sides, deciding that both explanations were true. She certainly felt like an idiot for getting herself into such a mess.

By the time the moon had traveled well into the heavens, Caroline still had not come up with a solution to her dilemma. She debated going to the kitchen to seek out a bit more food. The small bowl of stew and the single tortilla she devoured hours ago had done little more than take the edge off her growling hunger. But she didn't dare for fear that someone might be there— a certain someone to be specific.

Instead, she took the stairs that led to the promenade, where guards patrolled the land.

"*Buenas noches, señorita,*" a guard called.

"*Buenas noches, Pedro.*"

She slipped along, her arms wrapped around her against the crisp cool nighttime air, until she reached the farthest corner, which would afford her some privacy. Leaning up against the low wall, Caroline looked out over the land, her elbows resting on the ledge. To the south she could see a sprinkling of lights from the fires of other settlements in El Paso on the north bank of the Rio Grande. The black ribbon of darkness that was the river divided those lights from the larger glow of Paso del Norte on the south bank. When the breeze shifted ever so slightly, she could hear a few bars of mariachi music or the hoots and hollers of boisterous men playing cards or drinking whiskey at Ben Dowell's notorious saloon.

To both the east and west she could make out the jagged peaks of the mountains that formed the valley. She had come to love the stark beauty of this rugged desert land and knew she did not want to leave it.

"It's beautiful out there. Even in the dark."

Caroline twirled around at the sound of the voice. His voice.

"Shane," she whispered.

Her heart pounded. He stood no more than a few feet from her, so handsome that he took her breath away. He wore a loose-fitting white shirt and thigh-hugging black pants. His hair was long and loose, trailing down his massive back. The shirt sleeves were rolled up on his forearms, and she could make out the corded muscles that bespoke years of hard work.

Tears stung her eyes. God, how I love him, her mind cried, eyes nearly fluttering closed as the feelings washed over her. But then she cursed. Loved him, she corrected herself forcefully, before she turned back to the landscape.

Though his footsteps were silent, she could feel him approach. She knew she should tell him to leave, but the words stuck in her throat. He took the remaining steps until she knew he stood scant inches behind her. She could feel his heat. And she could feel, as well, her unbearable longing.

"I missed you at supper." His deep voice rumbled in the night.

Her eyes pressed closed. She could hardly breathe.

"I hope someone brought you something," he continued. "After a hard day in this heat, especially for someone unused to it, you need to maintain your strength."

His caring words were almost her undoing. But she held on.

He chuckled. "If I remember correctly, however, I suspect my worries are misplaced. You were always making sure everyone was well tended. I can't imagine you would let yourself waste away from hunger."

"Go away," she finally managed, her voice strangled, taut. "Leave me alone."

Cicadas called to their mates, filling the sky with their cries. Mariachi music strummed rhythmically in the distance, caught on a shimmering strand of breeze that wrapped around Caroline in her quandary.

Slowly, gently, Shane reached out and touched her shoulder. "I can't seem to do that."

"No," she cried hoarsely, refusing to turn around to face him.

"Caroline," he whispered before he leaned down and kissed her neck.

She sucked in her breath. Her mind whirled. With the simple kiss, her uncertainty, along with the past, fled from her thoughts. And when he pulled her into his arms, pressing her back against his chest, tears streaming down her cheeks, she didn't resist. She turned her cheek until it pressed against his. She reveled in the feel.

They stood that way, time suspended, until Shane wrapped his arms more tightly around her, their hands intertwining, fingers curling together at her waist, each clinging to the other.

"I've never forgotten you," he whispered into her ear. "Though I should have."

Caroline tensed, and when she would have questioned him, he pressed one finger to her lips then turned her in his arms like a doll with no will of its own, and kissed the tears from her cheeks, his eyes never leaving hers. And then, like all those years ago, her breath caught in her throat and she turned her head ever so slightly until her lips met his.

He groaned at the touch, savoring the contact, running his hands up her arms to the slim column of her neck. Their kiss became heated. He nibbled at her lips, his tongue flicking, feeling. She hesitantly opened her mouth at his insistence, her body melting into his when their tongues intertwined. She pressed closer, innocently seeking the fire his fingers ignited as they danced over her skin.

"Shane," she murmured once again, her eyes closed.

He pulled back to look into her eyes. He held still until her eyes fluttered open, vivid green washed with desire. His grip tightened on her arms.

"Why is it, Caroline Bromley, that you have an uncanny ability to ensnare me?"

Her eyes began to clear, to question. But when she opened her mouth to speak, he forced her back to him with a groan, his lips capturing hers in a savage embrace.

His mouth slanted over hers, almost brutally, seeming to punish. "Oh God," he groaned against her lips, his hand trailing down her back, pressing their bodies together.

She felt his heart pounding against his ribs, though when pressed together so tightly, Caroline was uncertain where his heartbeat ended and hers began. Reason was abandoned as her fingers found their way into the thick strands of his long dark hair. Her senses reeled when his tongue demanded entry to the hidden recesses of her mouth once again to explore and taste, leaving her shaken with longing.

"Caroline," he murmured. "Sweet, sweet Caroline."

Her body was flushed with wanting, awash with waves of a new and overwhelming need. With trembling limbs she clung to him, lost in the swirl of mounting desire, no longer willing to question.

His hands trailed up over her hips and along her sides until he clasped her under her arms and lifted her off the ground. Setting her on the ledge, he moved between her legs. Sensation coursed through her body when she felt the heat of him between her thighs. A fierce longing pulsed within her. He kissed a fiery trail along her cheek and down her neck before he pressed his lips to the curve of her breast. Her arms wrapped around his shoulders and she clung to him, wanting to feel his bare skin on her own.

As if he understood, his strong dark hands worked the fastenings at the front of her dress. When finally the last button gave way under his touch, Shane found his efforts frustrated by her thick muslin chemise. "Curse these layers of clothes," he said impatiently as his fingers pushed the offending garments away.

Her body glistened in the moonlight. Skin so soft and creamy that his breath stuck in his throat. He was visibly awed by the rose-tipped peaks already grown taut with passion. "Beautiful . . ." The low, reverent groan was extinguished when he took one nipple in his mouth.

Caroline cried out, and her head fell back as his lips followed where his eyes had already gone, leaving her in agony and astonishment. His hand cupped her hips, pressing himself closer to the heat that burned between her thighs, only to let up then press again, and again, harder, until she thought she'd go mad.

In some clouded depths of her mind, Caroline realized as his hands and mouth awakened her body, that she was finally on the threshold of learning where his kisses would lead. Her body yearned to know. But the murky depths began to clear and her mind began to reassert itself, insinuating fine tendrils of memory into the unhealed cracks in her heart.

Lonely nights. Hurt and anger. Pain. The fallen woman. All because her body had sought this man's touch, had sought to know. Just as she did now.

The pounding in her heart and licks of fire across her skin almost swept the memories from her thoughts. But her mind held firm. She had been a fool once. She could never forgive herself if she were a fool again.

With that, sanity filled her mind in a blinding rush. She frantically pushed Shane's head aside, causing him to step back, pulling her to the ground as he did so. With a snarl she wrenched her body away from him.

"No!" Her immense eyes flashed sudden, overwhelming contempt for him.

Shane flinched as if he had been struck. "Caroline,

what's wrong?" His eyes narrowed in question, clearly not understanding what had altered their course.

"If you have to ask, you don't deserve to know," she hissed as she yanked her dress back together, hastily fastening the long row of frustratingly small buttons.

He stood watching her, confusion etched on his high brow. "You've changed," he whispered.

Her hands stilled in their task and her eyes grew incredulous. She threw back her head and laughed, a strange strangled sound filled with both mirth and despair. "I would hope so," she said with a sneer, bringing her eyes to meet his. "I would hope I'm no longer such a fool. I loved you once. More the fool, I. But no longer and never again." She laughed once more, though now all semblance of mirth was gone. "I'm no longer some silly young girl who trembles with desire and loses control at your mere touch. I am a woman full-grown, Shane Rivers, in charge of my person and in charge of my life. You'll get nothing more from me."

She quickly finished off the buttons then forced herself to move away, despite the urge that bade her rush back into his arms, despite the cold, empty ache that filled her at the loss.

"I am leaving on the next stagecoach. Until that time, do not touch or talk to me again."

Nearly blinded by rage and loss, she gathered her long skirts, more to stop the trembling of her hands than to keep the hem from dragging. Then she hurried along the rooftop, unmindful of the guards who stopped and stared at her reckless flight.

Shane looked on, his large frame quiet and still, as he watched her disappear. A breeze caught his raven-black hair and blew it into a cloud around his face. Reaching up, his hands shook as he brushed the strands away. He stood rooted to the spot, straight and immobile.

At length he jerked away and turned to the wall, his eyes narrowed—and strangely burning. Confusion played on his chiseled countenance, bringing a feral, almost savage frown to his face. Questions swirled in his mind as he looked out over the land—questions he knew he should have asked her. Why was she here? Where was her father? And what had caused her to change? Where was the laughter and the smiles that had enchanted him all those years ago?

He had been sitting on the north side of the rooftop smoking a cheroot when he had seen her climb the stairs. Even in the moonlight he had been able to discern her exhaustion and worry. He had wondered if there was more to it than just her days teaching in a strange land. He had approached her, telling himself he was simply going to ask her all the questions he knew he should ask. But something had stopped him. The smell of lemons in her hair? The sudden nearness of the woman who had graced his dreams for years? He didn't know the answer. Instead, he had leaned down and kissed her, refusing to ask questions he suddenly found he was not sure he wanted answered. And with one whisper of her voice, with one touch of her skin, the questions were forgotten. Though now they rushed back with renewed intensity.

Leaning up against the wall, Shane pulled in a deep calming breath, staring up into the heavens. But whatever calm he managed to find was shattered when Emma stepped out of the dark with Henry at her side.

"I can't believe what I have just had the misfortune to overhear," she declared, her anger barely controlled. "How could you?"

She clutched a woolen shawl around her shoulders, her faded blue eyes snapping with rage. Henry took her arm. "Emma," he said simply.

Emma shook off his hand and stepped closer to Shane. "Tell me, damn you. How could you?"

Shane turned to his grandmother, his face hard. "How could I what?" he asked quietly.

A strangled cry sounded in Emma's throat, and she nearly flung herself at him, but was stopped by Henry's restraining hand. "She has become like a daughter to me. And now this!"

"How much did you . . . hear?"

"Enough! And frankly I don't want to know any more. I don't want to know the details. But I have suspected something was wrong since the day you walked through the door and found Caroline." She pummeled the air with her fist like a frustrated child. "Somewhere and somehow you obviously ruined the girl. That is all that is pertinent." Emma jerked her head away, a ray of the bright moon catching on the tears in her eyes. "Have you no sense of honor?"

Shane tensed. He was uncertain if his grandmother's tears were shed for Caroline or for his lack of honor. Surely by now she had learned not to waste them on him. "Emma—" he began, but was cut short.

"If you want to remain my grandson," she said stiffly, "you will marry Caroline . . . and right as best you can your grievous wrong." She took a deep breath and her eyes momentarily met Henry's. "She may not get the love and caring she deserves, but clearly you have

put her in a position where she feels she can marry no other. As a result, I demand you give her the
respectability of your name." Emma hesitated, her body
seeming to give in to defeat. "If not"—she sighed—"I
expect you to leave the hacienda at first light."

And with that, understanding washed over Shane
like a raging tidal wave, catching him up in the churning mass. He closed his eyes against comprehension.
But it would not be shut out. He realized that perhaps
the understanding had been there since the moment he
saw Caroline in the *sala*, and he had simply not been
able to face the possibilities. But now he could avoid
the truth no longer.

Suddenly it all made sense. He realized what the difference was about her—her eyes, those beautiful eyes,
once so filled with innocence and trust, were now filled
with misery and pain. The hatred he had told himself
was only a figment of his imagination was real.

Rupert had been wrong. He had not been able to
keep the sheriff and mayor quiet. And Caroline had
been ruined by their nearly chaste kiss.

Doubt surfaced. Even if Rupert hadn't been able to
keep it quiet, was society truly so narrow-minded and
unforgiving of such an innocent kiss? But the picture of
Caroline's hair tumbling down her back and her skirts
hiked up around her legs came to mind, and he realized
it hadn't looked so innocent. After that, the lies must
have spread through the small town. Why else would
she have come to such an outpost? He was a fool to
have thought anything else.

Guilt assailed him. Why hadn't he returned to San
Antonio to make sure she was all right? he wondered.
Why had he listened to Rupert in the first place when

his heart had told him to stay? He shook his head.

She obviously hated him because he hadn't tried to convince the mayor and sheriff that she had been attacked. He had said nothing because he knew they wouldn't have believed him, not when they had the chance to snag a half-breed for their noose. But she obviously hadn't realized that. And in the end, Caroline had suffered because those very same men had wanted him dead. No wonder she hated him.

Guilt was soon replaced by anger and a fierce protectiveness. He wanted to lash out, to make everyone who had hurt Caroline pay. But more important, he found he wanted to marry her. She might not get her life with God or even a husband she deserved, but he had seen to that five years before. The only thing left to do was try to clean up the mess he had created.

The idea leaped full-blown into his head as though it had been there all along and was finally free to take flight. His mind swam.

Marriage to Caroline. Yes, marriage. Husband and Wife. Children. Growing old together.

To have and to hold.

And he would. He would never let her go again.

You're a savage. The words loomed in his mind, pushing away all else. Shane flinched at the image of his mother standing back and watching, his back bared to the hot burning sun, and the whip. He could see his small hands clutching the wooden post, his knuckles white with red lines running across them, until the image changed and his hands clutched another man's neck.

His hands fisted at his side and his eyes narrowed.

He would not give in. He would not give in to the savage. He promised himself then, standing on the rooftop, the moon and the stars as witness, that Caroline would never see that side of him—he would prove to himself that he was worthy of her.

The faded memory of hope and purpose, long absent from his life, filled his mind. And with the renewed convictions came excitement and joy, the kind Shane Rivers had not known since he was a very small boy.

Emma and Henry stood silently by until Emma decided Shane had no response to give. With a despairing sigh, she took Henry's arm and they departed without a word. Henry helped her with the stairs, one hand secure on her arm, the other holding a lantern high to light the way. But when they reached the bottom, she stopped.

"What is it?" Henry asked when she started to retrace her steps.

"I want to tell Shane about the wedding gift I've decided to give him when he marries Caroline," she said, a trace of excitement lacing her words, the anger surprisingly gone.

Henry sighed, catching her hand. "*When* they marry? I think you should be thinking *if* they marry. I saw no indication that he will wed her. And if he didn't marry her before, what makes you think he will now?"

"Whether Shane realizes it or not, he is a man of honor, and always has been. I spoke out of anger earlier. Overhearing such a tale infuriated me because I have grown so terribly fond of Caroline. But in my heart I know Shane will do right by her. Everything will work out." She shivered against the slight breeze. "And I will give him the vineyards and winery he loves so much as a wedding gift."

Henry stared at Emma. "Whether he has honor or not remains to be seen," he said, ignoring Emma's glare. "And why now, after all he has apparently done, will you reward him for doing what he should have done in the first place?" He tenderly pushed a strand of gray hair behind her ear. "I think you're trying to bribe him with gifts to make him stay."

Her chin came up, her eyes narrowed with conviction. "Yes, I want him to stay, even if I have to bribe him. Is that so terribly wrong?" she cried. "And beyond that, I owe Shane."

With force, Henry pulled Emma close, his hand tightly gripping her arm, the light flickering wildly at the quick movement. "How long are you going to try to make up the past to Shane?" he demanded. "What happened was not your fault!"

Someone crooned a melody in the distance. The faint bleat of a goat sounded somewhere in the darkness beyond the small circle of amber light. "I may not have struck the blows or uttered the words, but I stood back and did nothing to stop it. As a result, I am as guilty as the rest." She pulled her arm from his grip. "But you're right about one thing. I cannot bribe him. First, I will wait and let him do the right thing, then I will make my gift, and my peace—if not with him, then with myself."

CHAPTER

✳

11

CAROLINE MADE HER way across the deserted court-yard to the kitchen very early the following morning. Her mind raced with frantic thoughts of Shane Rivers and her stomach grumbled with hunger. Hunger, how-ever, was the only issue she was willing to deal with just then. Hunger she understood.

It was still early enough that the roosters hadn't crowed and the sun hadn't eked its way up the horizon, early enough that she felt certain she was safe from all save loaves of bread and kitchen cutlery. She had plenty of time to get a bite to eat before anyone else raised an eyelid.

Pushing open the kitchen door, Caroline breathed a sigh of relief when indeed she found the room empty. She fumbled to light the lantern before turning her attention to the shiny copper pots and pans that hung from the *vigas* that lined the ceiling. Her countenance became rueful when she realized she had no idea how to retrieve one of the cooking implements, much less how to use it.

But she was not to be deterred in her mission.

Long benches nestled beneath either side of the kitchen table. With little effort she dragged one to the center of the room. She gathered the heavy brown twill of her skirt and carefully climbed on top of the shiny wood. Her first leap nearly toppled her to the floor. Undaunted, however, she tried a couple more wobbly jumps until she finally managed to snag a pan.

"Ha!" she cried in triumph.

Next she searched for food. She found eggs, ham, bread, butter, milk, and coffee. Confidence built, pushing her on in her desire to cook in a kitchen that was so very different from her own back in San Antonio. Not that she was all that proficient in the one she was familiar with, she conceded, but she had managed.

Tying a muslin apron around her waist, she rolled up the long sleeves of her high-necked cotton blouse and stood before the large, newfangled stove Henry had shipped in from back east as a surprise for Emma. Whether it was a marvel of modernity or not, Caroline would just as soon have an old cast-iron kettle over an old-fashioned fire, since she had no idea how to make this monstrosity perform. But what, she wondered, was she to do? Eat a cold meal of bread, butter, and milk. Nonsense. She would deal with the stove after she had everything else ready. Perhaps by then a servant would be awake. She could let them get the stove fired up.

For now, all she needed were utensils. A hunt through the pantry provided a bowl, a long knife, and a fork. Now to begin, she thought with a self-congratulatory smile.

But the smile soon gave way to a scowl of frustration when first one eggshell then another cracked into a million pieces, filling the bowl with more shell than egg. "Durn blast it!"

"Durn blast it?"

Caroline twirled around at the sound, egg yolk and shell flying through her fingers as she did.

"Is that any way for a schoolteacher to talk?" Shane asked as he watched the streams of egg splatter against the wall.

Panic filled her green eyes, but was quickly replaced by anger. "Do you never announce yourself in a civilized manner?"

Shane leaned against the doorjamb, his hair just about dry from his bath, his face cleanly shaven. He eyed the long streams of egg that now stretched through her fingers before they dropped with a plop to the floor. "Ugh," he said with a grimace, ignoring her demand. "I can only hope your teaching efforts are more successful than your cooking efforts."

"Get out!"

He pushed away from the door. She watched as he approached, his hard muscles playing crazily beneath his soft shirt, doing the exact opposite of her command by walking into the room. Heat surrounded her, and if the oven had been going just then, she would have thankfully blamed the heat on that. But it wasn't.

"I told you last night to stay away from me," she hissed, taking refuge in anger.

"Perhaps I should take over here," he stated, ignoring her angry words.

Her eyes narrowed. "What are you talking about? I am perfectly capable of cooking!" She shook egg and bits of shell off her fingers into the bowl then wiped the remainder on her apron. "For myself!"

"Hmmm. I seem to remember differently. I distinctly recall your father saying to me on several occasions that while you were an exemplary teacher and healer, your cooking had nearly killed him more than once."

Caroline's mouth fell open. "That's a lie!"

"Is it?" he asked, with a slight nod of his head toward the yolk-splattered wall before he walked over to the table and took up an egg. "I happen to recall a roast that was burned to a crisp on the outside and raw on the inside." He cracked the egg on the side of a clean bowl with a simple flick of his wrist and smiled.

Despite herself, Caroline eyed his efforts and grumbled under her breath. "It may have been raw on the inside, but only because you and Father came waltzing in like nobody's business, demanding to be fed," she bit out while snatching up another egg, not to be outdone, and cracking it much as Shane had.

A grimace stretched across his face as he watched Caroline's egg ooze out onto the table. "I don't recall you seeming to mind," he stated with infuriating arrogance.

Heat scorched her face as she recalled the specific incident. She certainly had not minded. In fact, she remembered she had positively gushed over the man. "I was my father's hostess. What was I to do? Kick you out?"

Shane eyed Caroline, one brow arched in disbelief. He tossed her a towel. "Wipe your hands and sit down while I finish this up. Emma will yell the house down if she comes in and finds her precious domain a wreck."

Caroline wiped the mess from her fingers as best she could, anger simmering, ready to explode. "Did you wake up and plan to ruin my day or did it just happen?"

Shane looked nonplussed at Caroline's caustic barb,

but then he flung back his head and roared.

"Obviously you planned it," she bit out unreasonably, embarrassed by his laughter. "I told you to leave me alone, Shane Rivers, and I meant it." Then she tossed the towel on the table, spun on her heel with a flourish, her skirts billowing, and headed for the door. "This horrible cook has to get to school."

A smile still slashing across his face, Shane glanced out into the darkness before he quickly grabbed her hand and gently forced her down onto the bench. "School won't start for . . ." He glanced back outside at the early-morning darkness. "Let's just say you have a while before your students converge on the schoolhouse. Time enough to eat."

"I'm not hungry," she stated, though just then her traitorous stomach choose to announce otherwise.

"Really?" he asked with a wry glance at her midsection.

Caroline started to stand, but Shane gently pushed her back down. "Truce, little one. I'll not have you starve on my account. Just sit there and pretend I'm not here. You don't have to talk to me or look at me, just eat when it's ready."

Caroline crossed her arms like a disgruntled child and decided to stay, but only just long enough to eat.

"Good," was all he said when she remained on the bench, then returned to the matter of making the meal.

Caroline sat back and tried to pretend he wasn't there, but found it nearly impossible to do. Not only did his presence command attention, but his showmanlike culinary skills brought a reluctant grin to her lips.

"What's this? A smile?" he asked with a rakish slant of dark brow. "Could it be that Miss Caroline Bromley, the hacienda's very own schoolmistress, finds some humor in this situation?"

Caroline's reluctant grin turned into a scowl as she ignored his question. With a chuckle he turned back to his task. Even with her continued best efforts to do otherwise, she found herself watching him work while he told her stories and laughed at his own jokes just as he had done all those years before. He didn't touch her or kiss her, and in spite of herself, she felt the knot of anger start to ease.

He sliced ham and buttered bread, grated cheese and scrambled eggs. She watched with growing astonishment at the meal that came to life before her.

"Where did you learn to cook like that?" she finally had to ask.

With a flip of the dangerous-looking knife and a devilish smile, Shane said, "Five years in a war teaches a man many things."

"You went to war?" she asked, clearly surprised.

"Yes." Nothing more.

"Which side did you fight on?"

"The losing side."

"After all those years in Washington, you fought for the Confederates?"

"I'm a born and raised Texan, my dear. And losing cause or not, my loyalties remain to the South." He poured the eggs into the hot pan. "And what about you? What have you been doing these last years?"

Her stomach clenched. He asked the question with an outward calm, and Caroline wondered if he truly didn't know or if he was toying with her. "A little bit of this and a little bit of that," she offered with a nonchalant tilt of her head.

Shane glanced back at her but didn't press the issue. Instead he had the audacity to ask, "Why haven't you married?"

Caroline nearly choked. *Why hadn't she married?* He was either dim-witted or truly oblivious to what had happened to her after he had so callously fled. She swallowed with difficulty. Either way, as far as she was concerned, that was how it would stay. She was not about to reveal the pain of her life in San Antonio. Especially to Shane Rivers.

"I haven't married because I'm ornery and opinionated and I scared them all away."

Something dark flashed through his eyes. But then it settled. "Opinionated, I know; ornery, I'm learning; but I doubt you could scare any of them away. You're much too lovely."

Their eyes locked and held. Her heart beat wildly. And that made her mad. A mean streak she didn't know she possessed surfaced. She studied her fingernails, only glancing up after she said, "There you are wrong. Women like Henrietta Whitley are much too lovely to scare people off. Have you seen your *ex*-fiancée recently?"

If she had expected some great show of emotion, she was to be disappointed. He simply turned back to the stove and stirred the eggs, turning them over to keep them from burning. "No, I haven't," was his answer, moving the skillet to the side of the heat so he could focus on another pan.

Caroline ran her tongue over her teeth. "Then you probably didn't know that she is very near to marrying Dean Fowler."

This time she got a response. Even with his back to

her, she could see that his hand stilled and his body tensed. And that hurt her all the more. He obviously still loved Henrietta and was jealous. She looked away.

Slices of ham suddenly sizzled in a skillet. The smell of warm bread gently wafted through the room.

"How is your father?" he asked, breaking the quiet.

"He's dead."

Her pronouncement caused Shane to jerk around so abruptly, a knife still clutched in his hand, that Caroline jumped in her seat. She watched, fascinated, as a multitude of dark sentiments drifted across his face, before the chiseled planes went hard, making her suspect she had only imagined the emotions. But she knew better. She had hurt him as she had intended. And since she had meant to wound him, she should have been pleased. But she wasn't. She simply felt callous.

"I'm sorry," she offered, studying her hands.

Shane stared at her until she was forced to look into his eyes. "No, I'm sorry. Sorry that he passed away. And sorry that I didn't know."

And suddenly between them came a wary truce. They talked, though mostly Shane carefully asked questions while Caroline adeptly avoided answering, over a feast of eggs mixed with melted cheese, tomatoes, onions and green chilies, fresh bread dripping with butter, and thick slices of ham grilled to perfection.

Caroline was so hungry and intent on the meal that she did not notice the tension that began to build in Shane with each answer she failed to provide. She did not realize that he inferred a great deal from what she did not say.

"We've determined that you didn't marry. But what

about the church?" he asked suddenly.

"Church?" She appeared confused. "What about it?"

"Apparently you didn't get your life with God either."

"What are you talking about? What do you mean my life with God?"

He stared at her as he recalled Rupert's declaration that his daughter wanted a life with God. Shane saw that his question clearly confused Caroline. What could this mean? he wondered. He hated the answers that skipped through his mind. But still he couldn't bring himself to believe that his friend would have made up such a tale.

Eventually, he forced a chuckle. "You spent so much time at the church," he found himself saying, "I was convinced you'd become a nun."

Caroline glanced at him as if he were crazy. "How could I have become a nun? I'm Methodist." She shook her head and grinned. "Besides, more than once Reverend Hayes chastised me for my ungodly way. I'm afraid that had I ever wanted such a life—which God forgive me, I can't imagine—I never would have succeeded."

Shane's body stilled as her statement sank in, the meaning undeniable. Rupert had lied.

Incredulity filled him.

Stiffly, he pushed himself up from the table, not knowing what he could say or what he should do. "I see you've finished your coffee. Let me get you some more."

She considered. "Perhaps just a bit. Then I really must get to school."

He took her cup to the stove while Caroline quickly

cleared the table. She turned back from the counter as he held out her coffee. But when she grasped the handle, Shane didn't let go.

They stood facing each other, the cup held between them. Her eyes opened wide, startled. The ease evaporated, and the same desperation he had seen in her eyes the night before returned. Shane wished suddenly that he could return the innocence to her gaze. He wished he could turn back the clock. And while he would not erase their passionate embrace, he would have selfishly made her his wife.

"I heard you were in town yesterday inquiring about the stagecoach." He looked into her haunted green eyes. He wanted desperately to caress her porcelain cheeks and smooth her fiery hair. His face grew fierce. "I don't want you to leave, Caroline."

Panic fled as anger descended upon her. He didn't want her to leave, her mind mimicked.

"Why?" she asked heatedly, wanting to hear what this man's excuse could possibly be.

"Why?" he repeated when he found he had no idea how to answer her. What could he tell her? That he knew she had been ruined? He thought of her pride. No, he couldn't tell her he knew. She would despise what he was certain she would see as pity. He had to court her sweetly, gently, to convince her that he wanted her simply for herself. She deserved that.

"Why?" he asked again.

"See, you have no answer," she accused as she stepped back and let go of the cup just as Shane finally let go as well.

The colorful earthenware fell from their grasps to shatter on the tile floor in multicolored pieces. They stared down at the mess, neither able to move.

After an eternity, Shane spoke. "Is that what happened to you?" he asked softly, pained. "Do you feel the pieces can no longer be put back together?"

Caroline sucked in her breath and abruptly turned her head, tears glistening in her eyes. "I said I'm leaving. And I am."

Shane reached out and cupped her chin in the palm of his hand, forcing her to meet his eyes. "Where will you go, Caroline?"

She recoiled against his touch, but his hand held firm.

"I can get another teaching position somewhere else," she stated, heated conviction lacing her words.

He chuckled. "I'd forgotten what a little fighter you are, regardless that the odds are against you." He traced the line of her jaw. "But fighter or not, you delude yourself, Caroline. It will be difficult to find employment elsewhere." His hand dropped away. "Don't put yourself through any more. Stay here. I'm going to put the pieces back together. I promise."

Her heart galloped in her chest. Her skin was alive with feeling where his simple touch had passed. She longed to believe him. She took a deep breath, relishing the thought. But too many years of hurt stood in the way for the wish to take hold—too many years of her father's admonitions and warnings. She thought about Shane's promise and how he genuinely seemed to care. But that was a lie, her mind told her. If he had cared for her, he never would have left her. And she realized then with a heart-crushing certainty, that just as he had made promises to her five years ago to escape the sheriff's noose, Shane Rivers made promises now because he wanted something from her once again.

Grief seared her. She was already painfully aware that he didn't love her. And now with her new realization that he wanted something from her once again, she could only conclude that like so many other men over the last five years, he found her easy prey. Plain and simple, he wanted to seduce her. Is that not exactly what he had been trying to do since he got here? Every time she turned around, it seemed he was trying to press her with kisses.

She backed away, but he grasped her arm.

"Caroline?"

One simple word, uttered by his deep voice, caressed her senses, filling her with unbearable need. And that was impossible. Tears resurfaced, stinging her eyes. Humiliated, she jerked free of his hold. She had to get away. She had to find the means to leave El Paso. She couldn't take another six weeks of meeting him like this. Because deep down inside she knew, shame washing over her, that soon she would give in to his demand. She would succumb to his kisses even though he had no love to give. Once again she would be willing to act without decency, regardless of the fact that this time she knew God was watching. And then she would never be able to forgive herself.

With careful movements, as if she might shatter, she turned toward the door. His curse made her resolution waver, and the sound of his fist crashing against the hardwood table made her pause. She took a deep breath. Leave! her mind screamed. And she would have, but his words stopped her cold.

"I never should have listened to Rupert," he ground out, more to himself than to her. "Maybe I wasn't good enough, but I was better than what you got."

His words struck her with a force that nearly doubled her over. She turned slowly. "What are you talking about?" she demanded.

His dark brows came together in a uncertain frown. "Didn't Rupert tell you?"

"Tell me what?"

He studied her closely, then turned away. "It's nothing. Forget it."

Caroline reached out and grabbed his arm, her nails biting into his flesh. "When did you speak to my father?"

A sharp weariness passed through his eyes. He should have known. Not only had Rupert been wrong when he said Caroline wouldn't be ruined, and not only had he lied about Caroline wanting a life with God, he had never told her about his nighttime plea in the jailhouse.

Shane nearly laughed when he realized the extent of Rupert's betrayal. Caroline didn't hate him because he had failed to convince the others that she had been attacked by an intruder, but because she thought he had willingly abandoned her to a miserable fate.

"Caroline, I told you, it's not important. Forget it."

"No, I won't forget it. Tell me," she demanded, her voice rising. "When did you speak to my father?"

With a sigh, not knowing what else he could do, Shane gently took hold of both Caroline's arms and told her of his encounter with Rupert in the jailhouse. "I thought he was right at the time. I thought you were better off without me," he finished.

Caroline felt as though she had been physically struck. It couldn't be true. Her father knew how much she wanted to marry Shane. Her father wouldn't have done that to her. No! her mind screamed. Her father loved her!

"Caroline." Shane's voice rumbled through the room as his face creased with worry.

Her haunted green eyes filled with hatred. She felt deeply and brutally betrayed as never before. She thought Shane could not hurt her any more than he already had. But now he added to his crimes with his venomous words.

"You're lying!" she hissed. "You used me to get out of being shot or hanged, then you tossed me aside like who knows how many others you have encountered along the way. You lied to me back then, damn you, just as you are lying to me now!" Tears mixed with her rage. "You're lying!" she choked out once again, as if to convince them both.

She jerked from his grasp, intent on getting away. But her flight was halted when she ran straight into Diego, who chose that unfortunate moment to enter the kitchen.

"Good morning," he said, catching her in her head-long flight. He steadied her, looking at her closely. "What's this?" he asked. "Tears from our school-teacher?" His gaze dropped to the floor and he noticed the broken shards of pottery. He glanced from the cup to Shane. "What have you done to her, cousin?" he asked with a faint lift of curious brow.

Reina stepped in behind Diego. She took in the tense scene that was playing itself out in the early-morning hours. Her smoldering gaze ran the length of Caroline, disdain written in her eyes. "I have wondered all along what such a prim and proper little schoolteacher was doing all the way out here in El Paso," she said with a sneer. "But maybe you're not so prim and proper, eh?"

Caroline blanched at the words that struck so close to the truth. Her worst nightmare was becoming reality before her. All her fears about the truth being revealed were coming true. She wondered again how she would survive the humiliation until the next stagecoach arrived.

Shane's jaw tightened and he glared at Diego.

If Diego was aware of Shane's anger, he chose to ignore it. "Do *you* know why our schoolteacher has traveled so far from her home, cousin?"

An insidious smile stretched Diego's lips into a taut line. Shane took a step toward his cousin, their eyes locked and filled with loathing.

Caroline watched, her breath lodged painfully in her throat, as unexpected anger between these two men pressed every other emotion out of the room. Shane took another step closer, seemingly no longer aware of Caroline, aware only of Diego. She didn't understand all that lay beneath the surface of the confrontation, but knew instinctively that much more than the simple words they spoke was at issue. At that moment, however, none of it was her business. Her only concern was to get away. She had to escape.

Caroline pried her arm from Diego's grip. "Shane did nothing. The days of heat have made me clumsy," she mumbled before she turned on her heel and fled from the room, never looking back.

Shane broke the furious standoff between him and his cousin. Fighting, he knew, would do no good. Instead, he watched Caroline as she hurried through the courtyard. He hesitated, his angry gaze finding Diego again before he too quit the room.

Reina and Diego watched Shane's receding figure.

"When I think back on it," Diego said thoughtfully, "both Shane's and Caroline's reaction to the other when Shane first arrived was . . . strange." His eyes narrowed in contemplation. "What indeed brought someone as obviously refined and knowledgeable as Caroline Bromley to such an outpost?"

"*Miss* Caroline Bromley," Reina added. "I suspect that somehow, somewhere, our *unmarried* schoolteacher knew Shane, perhaps more intimately than her appearance would lead one to believe. But soon," she continued, "Emma will turn the hacienda over to you, and then you can send Miss Caroline packing. After all, Cielo el Dorado is yours."

Diego cursed. "No, it's not! It's my grandmother's . . . and then there's Shane—always Shane."

Reina reached over and smoothed Diego's brow. "Soon he will leave," she said. "He always does."

Diego snorted. "I'm not so sure. Shane seems different somehow. I watched him walk over the land. I saw the way he looked around. He wants it, I can tell. I know that look. Damn him!" His voice rose, became agitated. "The hacienda is mine!" he raged. "Not some heathen's son who's rarely here. I'm the oldest, but since Shane's mother is my grandparent's oldest child, the hacienda will go to Shane."

"You don't know that for certain, Diego," Reina said, her voice soothing, though her brow creased with worry.

"No, but I can guess. My grandmother always loved Shane more. Though if my grandfather were still alive, things would be different, just like they used to be. And then the hacienda would be mine!"

Diego turned to leave.

"What are you doing?" she asked.

"Leaving. What does it look like?"

"Where are you going?"

"To Ben Dowell's."

Anger filled her. "You spend more time in that damned saloon than with me!"

He eyed her speculatively. "The company is more entertaining."

CHAPTER

✳

12

SHE HATED HIM.

If she had had a knife she would have plunged it to the hilt, impaling his heart. In that instant Caroline longed to feel Shane Rivers's lifeblood spurt from his body. Yes, she hated him, and she knew she would hate him forever.

Caroline made her way to the schoolhouse without so much as a wave or hello to a single soul she passed. Her mind spiraled with thoughts of escape. And not just from the kitchen.

She had to get to town after school and check again on the stagecoach. Though she knew it was much too early for the eastbound coach for San Antonio, perhaps there was another—any stagecoach, going anyplace, at this point, would do. Or by chance, there might be an individual who was preparing to travel. Whichever, something had to be going somewhere, and she planned to be going with it.

Caroline refused to sit back, waiting for the next blow to fall. She painfully and a bit shamefully admitted to herself that for all her promises that she was going to take charge of her life and be adventuresome, ever since Shane's arrival she had let herself fall into old habits. And that was unacceptable. Once again she found she was afraid of life and living. She must do something. Especially when faced with a man who was prepared to tell such hideous lies about her father to achieve his goal. And lies they were, she emphasized to herself, nothing more.

She was halfway to school when someone cried out in pain, pushing everything else from her mind. Caroline found the cook's assistant from the working side of the hacienda had sliced her hand with a large knife. She ran to her room and gathered her medical supplies, then hurried back to the injured woman.

A small group convened in the working kitchen to watch as Caroline carefully washed the wound. They stood in awe as she deftly stitched up the deep cut then covered it with a mixture of sweet lard, beeswax, and some resin.

"You must be careful with that hand now, Leticia," Caroline said as she wrapped the woman's hand.

"Will I cook again, señorita?" Leticia asked.

"Certainly. No tendons or muscles were cut. You were lucky. If you let it heal properly, you should be back in the kitchen within a couple of weeks." Caroline began gathering her supplies. "I'll want to check the wound every day for the next couple of days. Infection is our biggest worry."

"*Gracias, señorita.*"

The crowd meandered out of the kitchen once the excitement was over, and it was a moment before Caroline remembered school. With a start, she jumped up, dispatched her bag back to her room via a young woman, and dashed to the schoolhouse.

She came around the corner in a flurry of skirts and was brought up short at the sight that met her. There, lined up outside the schoolhouse, were her students, with Esteban at the lead. Wounds, stagecoaches, Shane Rivers, and Diego Cervantes were forgotten as a simple joy filled her. Her efforts were paying off.

Caroline took the last few steps slowly. "Esteban," she asked, "could you please ring the bell to begin class?"

Esteban glanced over the line of children. Then he smiled. "*Sí, señorita.* I would be happy to."

Taking measured steps, Esteban approached the old cast iron bell that hung from a sturdy cottonwood post. He hesitated a half second then grabbed the long rope and pulled with all his strength. The bell clanged wildly.

Caroline pressed her eyes closed, reassuring herself that mountains could be climbed.

After crossing the yard, she took the boy's arm in a firm grip. "Thank you, Esteban. That will do."

The children snickered and giggled while Caroline herded them through the door and into their seats. The room grew hushed as she approached her desk. Looking around at the faces who surreptitiously glanced from her to Esteban, she lowered herself to the chair. "Ahhh!" she screeched, before she clamped her mouth shut and stood.

Perhaps mountains could indeed be climbed, she mused to herself, but slowly, very slowly.

Leaning over, Caroline retrieved a harmless garden snake. With what she hoped could pass for a grin, she calmly handed Esteban the snake. "You seem to have misplaced something."

Esteban's eyes widened briefly before he regained his composure and accepted the snake. He pulled a burlap bag from his shirt, a sigh of relief sounding from his lips once the coarse fabric was removed, then shoved the reptile in the bag before he sat back down at his desk.

Shaking her head, Caroline wondered what she would find crawling in a drawer or falling from above a door next. But, she reminded herself, the boy was there, in his desk, and wasn't that exactly what she wanted? Well, yes, she conceded. And maybe she could wear him down with patience.

Looking over her students one by one to see who was there and who was not, official roll call having long since been abandoned, her eyes came to an abrupt halt. Hortense the hog had returned, a new bow tied around her neck. Caroline sighed then stifled a grunt of laughter. Hortense, she acknowledged, was the best-behaved pupil she had. With that, she turned her attention to other things, deciding it was not worth the effort to expel the sow. At least not today.

"This morning I thought we'd put on a play," she announced, as though having snakes and hogs in class were nothing out of the ordinary.

"A play!" the students squealed in unison.

"Yes, a play."

And so they did. A small production but, by the end of the day, a huge success. The greatest breakthrough came in the form of Esteban. It became obvious as the day progressed that the boy loved to act.

"You're very good at this, Esteban. Have you ever acted before?" Caroline asked.

"No," he replied, his brown fingers still stuck between

the buttons of his shirt, his stance regal. "I have never acted. But I like. In fact, Señorita Caroline, I think we should act for the Fall Fiesta."

"The Fall Fiesta?" Caroline inquired. "What is the Fall Fiesta?"

Beth rolled her soft brown eyes. "It's a fiesta in the fall. Everyone knows that."

Well, that explained everything, Caroline thought to herself sarcastically. To the class, however, she said, "I still don't know what it is. What is a fiesta?"

"A party!" they shouted, and immediately pretended they were at one, and a raucous one, at that!

It took several minutes to calm the masses down. Once this was accomplished, Caroline tried to turn the class to reading. She had no interest in continuing a discussion about a fall fiesta, regardless of what it was. If it occurred in the fall, which apparently it did, she wouldn't be there to participate. And she wasn't about to get herself mixed up in something that would ultimately end in disappointment for her students when she left. As a result, she opened her reading book with finality. But the children wouldn't have it.

"How about acting out *The Silver Cradle*," Billy suggested.

Caroline groaned and wondered, not for the first time, if she was ever going to get control over her students. Would it ever get easier?

Opal clasped her hands to her breast and said, "I think that is a wonderful idea! And Hortense could play the part of the mule."

The class hooted their appreciation at the picture their young minds conjured up of the class hog as a mule.

Good God, Caroline moaned to herself, things were getting out of hand. But the children wouldn't let up, and before she knew it, she was agreeing to the play since she had not been able to come up with a reasonable explanation as to why they shouldn't put on the production for friends and family at what was apparently a special time of the year. She certainly couldn't tell them she wouldn't be there. Instead, she sighed her resignation and began questioning the students about the importance and meaning of the Fall Fiesta.

Of course, not a single child knew what was being celebrated at the annual affair. They only knew the important things.

"There is lots of food."

"And games."

"And dancing."

"Dancing?" Caroline asked.

"Yes, dancing."

The following day, the schoolroom was dismally hot, worse than usual. Caroline could not keep her mind on simple addition and subtraction or *Newgate's Reading Primer*. Neither could the children, though they had little trouble finding other items of interest—teasing, making faces, all behind their teacher's back—until a yelp of pain brought Caroline to full attention. Someone had tied Opal's braids to her chair back. Caroline knew very well who the someone was, but of course, as usual, she had no proof. Billy, with a smile so angelic it made him look all the guiltier, sat behind and one over from Opal.

"What am I going to do with the lot of you this day?" she asked, with a shake of her head.

"Let us go home," Billy offered with enthusiasm.

"Hardly," she responded, her tone dry.

Billy turned to his hero, Esteban, for answers. The older boy merely shrugged his shoulders as he slumped in his chair. Caroline turned when she heard a heavy sigh to find Beth, dreamy-eyed, staring at Esteban, her chin resting in her palm.

"I have it," she announced, thinking of the Fall Fiesta. "We're going to have . . ." She screwed up her face in consideration. What could she call it and have it still sound reasonably schoolish. "Hmmm," she said before her eyes opened wide with inspiration. "Practical lessons! That's it!"

The class responded to her excitement even though they had no idea what she had in mind. Billy jumped up from his seat, followed by several others. The children practically bounced off the walls with energy— everyone, that is, except Esteban, who eyed Caroline with a mixture of amusement and interest.

"We are going to learn to dance!" Caroline exclaimed, her hands pressed against her chest, the delicate white skin outlined against the dark fabric.

The room grew suddenly silent. Fifteen pairs of eyes stared at her as if she had gone mad. Esteban snorted into the silence.

"Dance?" Billy said with a sneer. "Only girls dance."

"What do you mean?" Caroline asked in exasperation. "Just yesterday the lot of you told me everyone danced at the Fall Fiesta. Don't you want to learn how?"

Billy glanced at Esteban for the answer to this question. Esteban looked at Beth. After a moment he stood. "I dance," he announced.

His eyes returned to Beth, who blushed to the roots of her hair. But her blush of pleasure increased to mortification when Esteban turned away and looked at Caroline.

"But first you teach," he commanded.

Caroline started to balk, but when Esteban gallantly held his hand out to her, and the students, with the exception of Beth, chanted and cheered her on, she curtsied and took the young gallant's hand. She alternately hummed the music and explained the intricate steps of the quadrille until most every child could mimic some approximation of the European dance.

When Caroline had finished her lesson, Esteban bowed perfectly then turned once again to Beth. "Now I dance again."

Beth still glanced painfully at her shoes.

"With Beth," he said as he approached the young girl.

He came to stand before her chair until Caroline knew for certain that the only vision before Beth's eyes were Esteban's black-booted feet. Still, the girl did not look up. And then Esteban did something so sweet and tender that Caroline inhaled sharply. He knelt down on one knee before Beth, looking more a young prince before his princess than a young troublemaker before his lovesick classmate, and held out his hand. "Dance with me."

Beth looked up at him then, her longing and mortification having magically disappeared, replaced with a strangely arched brow, clearly questioning his command.

Esteban laughed and stood, his hand still proffered. "Please, Beth."

"I'd be delighted."

They walked to the center of the room, tables and chairs pushed haphazardly out of the way to make an impromptu dance floor, he in a much-mended shirt and faded trousers, she in a cream-colored cotton blouse and striped skirt. Beth curtsied and Esteban bowed as Caroline began to hum the tune. The entire class joined in, humming the tune and clapping the rhythm, as at first slowly, then more rapidly, Esteban and Beth moved through the intricate steps.

It wasn't long, however, before the rest of the class lost interest in simply providing the music and began to dance themselves. Billy, trying to copy Esteban, held out his hand to Opal, who shyly accepted and was pulled into a never-before-seen version of the dance. With that, everyone else simply started dancing, whether with a partner or alone, whether the quadrille or some invention of their own, it did not seem to matter.

Caroline looked on until she knew her instructions and music were no longer needed. She turned away, glancing out the window, her eyes full of longing. As the children continued to laugh and dance she sat down in a chair. Why, she wondered in despair, did her heart have to ache so at the simple sight of such gallantry as that which Esteban had performed? She studied her hands as she narrowed her eyes, trying to block the pain and lies from her mind. But then, as Beth had earlier, she found two black leather boots, much too large to belong to one of her students, standing before her.

Her heart seemed to stop. And she held her breath.

The laughter and gaiety quieted, the children growing hushed.

"May I?" His voice rumbled through the room.

Caroline thought she would swoon, then chided herself for such a weak-willed notion. Her eyes traveled up the length of him, from high-polished boots to long hair swept back from his forehead, to prove to herself that her ears had not deceived her. Shane. More handsome than any man had a right to be. Asking her to dance.

Hatred and shameful desire warred within her. But in the end, her newfound hatred for this man won out.

Shane extended his hand much as Esteban had earlier. "May I, Miss Caroline?" he repeated.

"I couldn't possibly," she stated coldly.

Opal jumped up and down and cried, "Yes, you can! Yes, you can!"

And then the whole class began to chant, stomping their feet on the wooden floor until the entire room vibrated. "Dance, dance, dance."

"I don't think you're going to be given much choice," Shane said with an infuriating smile, "unless you'd like to cause a riot."

Glancing around the room, Caroline took in the hopeful faces. Each child eyed her curiously. The hard line of her scowl reluctantly pulled into something that would pass for a smile and she nodded her head. "All right," she finally agreed, though the simple words came out small and low as she glanced up and met Shane's eyes.

Shane clasped her hand, but despite her acceptance, she tried to pull free. They stared at each other. Years of pain passed between them. After long, quiet moments ticked by, she straightened her spine and stood. He nodded and smiled, looking satisfied. Caroline nearly laughed when the thought crossed her mind that aside from their ages, there was not a great deal of difference between Shane Rivers and Esteban Gonzalez.

The children let out a whoop of delight when Shane bowed and Caroline curtsied as they came to the center of the makeshift dance floor. The room quickly filled with sound as the class broke into raucous humming and Shane swept Caroline not into the circumspect quadrille but an intimate waltz.

The instant their bodies came together, Caroline felt a surge of feeling, intense, almost overwhelming in its need. She glanced up into Shane's eyes and the laughter was gone, replaced by stormy depths, and she thought he must have felt it, too. They glided across the rough-hewn planks of hardwood. He held her closer than he should have, especially considering the fact that he should not have been holding her at all. He smelled of the wind and the sky, of wild grasses from the riverbank. Their eyes held, though neither spoke, as if unwilling to break the magical moment.

Around the room, floating on a tidal wave of sensation, they danced as if they had danced together all their lives. Caroline followed his lead with an ease she had not thought possible. Their bodies fit together like two pieces of a whole as they moved around the room, unaware of anyone else.

Perhaps it would never end.

But then the children's music ceased, the magic vanishing into the afternoon light, and the spell was broken.

It was a moment before Caroline's mind awoke from its floating, dreamlike state to collide with the harsh edge of reality. She caught sight of the children's curious stares. She glanced back and seemed surprised to find herself in the arms of Shane Rivers. Her lips pursed and her green eyes darkened.

She yanked away, her cheeks burning with shame. "I think we've all had enough for the day," she said to the children. "Class dismissed."

She didn't wait for the stream of students to file out the door. She hurriedly gathered her bonnet and books and walked quickly, though calmly, past the scattered furniture and out of the schoolhouse, the feel of Shane's arms around her seared into her mind.

Silence hung in the air. The only sound came from shuffling feet and a bee buzzing as it tried to find its way outside. The children glanced from the now empty door to Shane, uncertain of what would happen next on this day that had been filled with so many surprises. Not a single child was all that interested in scooting out the door in pursuit of their freedom as they normally were. The stranger, who they all had heard was Mrs. Emma's grandson, was proving to be much too intriguing.

"What was that all about?" Esteban asked Shane, accusation etched on his swarthy face.

Shane stared at the empty doorway. He thought of the feel of Caroline in his arms. How right it felt. And somehow he had to make her see it, too. He glanced back at Esteban and shrugged. "Perhaps she doesn't like to dance."

Esteban tilted his chin. "Me thinks, señor, she does not like you."

A smile slowly settled on Shane's lips. He looked toward the door through which Caroline had vanished. "Maybe. But she'll change her mind. I'll see to it."

CHAPTER

✴

13

CAROLINE WAS MUCH too busy over the next few days to make it into town as she had planned. Much to her delight, after she had so deftly stitched up Leticia's wounded hand, people began to wait before and after school to have her tend their various ailments.

Today, however, she promised herself as she made her way to the schoolroom that she was going to go. The minute her students were dismissed, she was going to be on her way.

But then, she nearly stopped in her tracks when she considered the possibility of running into Shane in town. She had heard more than one woman around the hacienda whisper that if they wanted to gain Señor Rivers's attention, he could sometimes be found after work at Ben Dowell's Saloon. The rumor had triggered a fierce response, but she simply chalked it up to disgust. Obviously, he was a drinking man—it had nothing to do with other women wanting his notice.

She consoled herself with the fact that she would not run into him at this hour. The man worked until well past dark most evenings. She had kept track of his schedule to better ensure avoiding him. Though he hadn't made it easy, she had managed to elude him—for days. More than once he had started making his way toward her, and she managed to slip away, though not before catching sight of a pounded wall or a kicked tree root when Shane was thwarted. She smiled at the memories.

Class that morning proceeded surprisingly well. Not that there was not a mishap or two. But as the sun progressed through the sky Caroline was pleased. Mathematics and reading had taken place, and maybe, just maybe, she thought, her students might have learned a thing or two.

As had been their habit since their first "practical skills lesson," Caroline began a new practical lesson when there was no more than an hour left of school.

"Today we are going to learn how to build and bank a fire," she explained once she had the children outside. "First we must find an area where we are certain we won't catch anything on fire," she said, studying the landscape.

Despite her preparations, Caroline was rather nervous about the endeavor. Every evening before going to bed, she used the books from Emma's extensive library to teach herself the skills she would teach the following day. Her own lesson on building and banking a fire the night before had gone only marginally well. But there was no help for it. She had no other lesson planned. Besides, she reasoned to herself, how hard could it be to build and bank a fire? She simply must have been tired when she had practiced last night. With that, Caroline began.

She chose a spot, then instructed the children to clear away every twig, leaf, and small rock within a five-foot radius so they could build their fire.

"Esteban, please bring the wood," she directed as the last pieces of debris were removed.

Esteban did as he was told with a look that was not altogether optimistic. "Where do want it?"

"Right here," she said, pointing to the very center of the clearing.

Caroline smiled gaily as she began to offer her instructions. Talking ceased as the children, who had lived their whole lives practicing "practical skills" but who had never bothered to enlighten the señorita of this fact, looked on skeptically as Caroline gathered her long skirt then knelt in the dirt to construct her fire.

"Señorita," Esteban began hesitantly, "I have never seen a fire built in such a way."

"You've just not seen it done *this* way."

Esteban glanced over at the other children and shrugged his shoulders as if to say, "I tried."

Caroline struggled with the flint and was on the verge of resorting to the easy way, using matches or even a tinderbox, when a much-worked-for spark fell onto the kindling and ignited. Pushing up from the ground, she failed to notice that Shane stood to the side, watching this display with something close to shock on his face.

"There," Caroline pronounced as she dusted her hands. "What do you think of that?" she asked as she twirled around to her students, triumph sparkling in her eyes.

The question was barely out of her mouth, however, when fifteen sets of brown eyes opened wide and Señorita Caroline was rolled to the ground. By none other than Shane Rivers.

Caroline sputtered and choked on dust and indignation. "What are you doing?" she demanded, pummeling Shane's massive body as she lay beneath him on the hard-packed desert floor.

"Putting you out," he retorted dryly as he slapped the last flames from her skirt.

"What are you talking about?" She squirmed around and caught sight of the hem of her skirt—the blackened hem of her skirt. "How did that happen?"

In one easy motion Shane leaped up from the ground. "How did that happen?" he echoed incredulously, cursing without regard for the youngsters.

She pulled herself up, ignoring Shane's attempts to assist her, and dusted the dirt and dried grass from her clothes with quick, efficient strokes. Caroline stepped back and stumbled when her heel caught the hem of her charred attire. Her eyes grew wide as she tried to regain her balance.

Shane's arm shot out and steadied her. He eyed her warily. "One of these days you're going to do some permanent damage to yourself," he stated impatiently, tearing his eyes away from hers.

"Permanent damage!" she cried, outraged.

"Yes, permanent damage." He jerked his head back, his heated gaze locking with hers. "You, Caroline Bromley, are an accident waiting to happen. Always have been."

Caroline burned with mortification, but through the haze of emotion she took notice of the children's fascinated stares. In front of the very people whom she was trying to impress with her authority, she was making a spectacle of herself. And all thanks to Shane Rivers!

"Mr. Rivers," she said stiffly, scalding the odious man with angry eyes. "I believe I've had enough of this discussion."

"Go ahead," young Billy said with a smile. "Fight all you like. We don't mind. Do we?" he asked the others.

"No," they responded with enthusiasm.

"Well, I mind," Shane cut in. "We can *finish* this discussion on our way to town."

"Finish! On *our* way to town!" Her eyes narrowed and she wondered if there was no end to this man's impertinent presumptions. "I'm not going anywhere with you!"

"I'll accept no refusals, and that's final."

"Who . . . do . . . you . . . think—" she sputtered, red-hot anger surging in her cheeks. But she was cut short when Emma joined them, a smile on her face.

"I heard you were going to town," the older woman said, placing her hand on Caroline's forearm. "I wondered if you could bother yourself to pick up a few things for me?"

Shane stood back and watched, a boyish grin suddenly teasing at his lips.

Caroline sent Shane a soul-searing glare before she regained her composure and smiled at Emma. "I'd be happy to."

"Good. I'll run in and make up a list while you get ready."

Caroline stared at Emma's retreating back and conceded that at least now she wouldn't have to think up an excuse to get herself to the depot to check on the next stagecoach. But even that didn't lessen her ire at Shane Rivers.

"Come on," Shane interrupted her thoughts. "We'd best hurry." He turned to Esteban. "See to it that the fire is put out." Then he took Caroline's wrist in a firm but gentle grip and pulled her along after him.

"Class dismissed," she called over her shoulder as she tried to keep up with her tormentor.

Once around the side wall, Caroline jerked her hand away, the suddenness of her act gaining her release. "I am perfectly capable of walking by myself!"

"I'm not so sure about that."

He made the statement with such calm arrogance that Caroline wanted to strangle him.

"Besides," he continued, "I'm afraid if I lose sight of you, you'll manage to avoid me as you've been doing all week."

Triumph surged. She really had gotten to him. Small consolation for the way he had humiliated her—but it would do—for now. It was all she could do to keep the smile from her face. "Avoiding you? That's absurd," she lied quickly, quashing whatever guilt she felt with the quick thought that he deserved no better. "And if you believe I have, then you think too highly of yourself, sir."

Shane looked down at her with a mixture of grim humor and reproach. "You, Miss Bromley, aren't telling the truth. And I'm tired of chasing you around and coming up empty-handed."

"Then don't chase me around," she stated with a sharp nod of her head.

"Don't hold your breath."

Caroline grumbled as she fell in step alongside Shane. Once inside the stables, Shane grabbed a brown-paper-wrapped parcel that lay on a worktable. Tossing her the package, which thankfully she caught, he said, "Open it."

Shane, however, was caught by surprise when she tossed it right back.

"Thank you, but no," she said, her polite words and angelic smile in sharp contrast to her caustic tone.

The surprise faded and Shane chuckled. "It's from Emma. She'll be returning soon with her list and what will I tell her? That you turned your nose up at her gift?" One dark brow raised quizzically.

Caroline muttered. She had to bite her tongue to keep from cursing. He stood before her, a lazy lick of black hair falling forward on his forehead, making him look more devastatingly handsome than ever. That only added to her ire, and she longed to smack him upside the head to wipe the arrogant smile right off his face. But in spite of her wayward thoughts, she caught the package when he tossed it back. She grumbled while untying the string that secured the brown wrapper. She could not imagine what it could be. And as she unwrapped the package her grumbles gave way to a small shiver of excitement like a child feels at Christmas. For the moment she forgot all else. She had so rarely received gifts in her life.

Her excitement, however, died a quick, unmerciful death when she pulled a tan linen blouse and a brown broadcloth skirt from the wrapping. Upon closer inspection, she almost squeaked her protest when she found that the skirt was split up the middle, looking for all the world more like extremely baggy trousers than anything any self-respecting woman would wear. "What's this?"

"Riding clothes," he responded simply.

"From Emma?" Disbelief stretched across her features and her nose wrinkled in indecision.

"Yes, from Emma."

"She expects me to wear such a . . . wear this?" she finished lamely.

"Yes."

Well, Caroline mused, she could not for the life of her imagine where Emma thought she could wear such an outfit, but she would deal with that later. She didn't ride horses, and she sure wouldn't ride in a wagon in this, though Shane and Emma didn't have to know that, she reasoned. She would simply smile, offer her thanks, then bury the clothes in a deep hole by the river.

"I'll be sure to thank Emma," she finally responded with a strained smile. "She is so terribly thoughtful." She turned back to rewrap the clothes.

"I can tell from your face how terribly thoughtful you think she is, but I'm not interested in your sincerity. I'm interested in you having some practical riding clothes. Now get inside and put those on."

Her hands stilled in their task. She gritted her teeth. He was not making this easy. She took a deep breath then released it slowly. "What I am wearing is perfectly fine to ride into town."

Shane eyed her, his impatience growing. "Not for riding astride."

A heartbeat passed before what little bit of calm Caroline had managed to find vanished into the straw-filled stable. "Astride? A horse!" she cried, snapping her head in his direction as she tried to comprehend his ludicrous statement. "We'll take the wagon, of course. I can't ride astride, especially in this," she added, holding up the package, all attempts to be polite and gracious forgotten. "I can't wear this . . . skirt around town. I'd cause a scandal."

Shane went still. An aching world-weariness passed through his eyes. At length, he pulled a deep breath, then exhaled slowly as he ran a hand across his face. "You won't cause a scandal here, Caroline. Never. This is your home."

They stared at each other for long-drawn-out moments before he abruptly turned away. Her mind rushed with staggering thoughts. The awful split skirt. The pain in his eyes. And Shane calling this her home. If only . . .

"Go change, Caroline."

"But—"

"Go change. Now," he demanded, his voice like tempered steel, "before I strip that god-awful thing you're wearing right off your back and dress you myself."

Her galloping mind reined in. She remembered, thank God, before it was too late, that she hated him. "I'm going, Mr. Rivers, but not without lodging my protest." Her voice was level, though she quivered inside, feeling awkward and uncertain, and having no idea what else to say.

"Protest acknowledged. Now go change."

Caroline reluctantly appeared in the doorway with Emma's list in her hand and her new apparel on her back. Gone was the practical attire that hid her curves from view, replaced by the sturdy blouse that pulled tight against full breasts, then tucked into the waist of the split skirt that flowed around gently curving hips. Long waves of red hair were pulled up and back with soft tendrils falling loose to curl about her face. Full red lips were pulled into a tight grimace. Green eyes still snapped their protest. And she was beautiful.

Shane stared at her for a good long while. He had to remind himself he had been the one who forced her to change, and now that she had, all he wanted to do was send her back to change again . . . or bury himself deep in her body until he was lost. But she couldn't change if they were going to ride into town, and he was determined that they go. He needed time with her. Time alone.

She had ignored him and avoided him, and gotten herself into more trouble and near scrapes in the short period he had been there, that every time she stepped out of his sight, he had come to question if he would ever see her again. Truly he wasn't lying when he said she was an accident waiting to happen. Burning her skirt up was minor compared with some of the things she had gotten herself into.

His frustration mounted daily. As a result, every time he turned around, his promise to court her sweetly nearly fell by the wayside. The more he got used to the idea of Caroline as his wife, the more determined he became to make it happen. And God, he promised, he was going to see the deed done, Miss Caroline Bromley willing or not. It was for her own good.

He muttered a curse under his breath. "Let's go."

She stood up straight in her scandalous attire and pulled on her bonnet, eyeing the two horses suspiciously. A mixture of emotions filled her. Riding. A horse. Caroline was torn. Her new sense of adventure demanded that she ride the darned animal, though years of being careful, not to mention her firmly ingrained sense of propriety, demanded she ride in a wagon.

But then Shane raised an infuriating eyebrow and said, "Don't tell me you're still afraid to ride."

Well, that did it. Caroline pulled back her shoulders, stiffened her spine, and said, "Don't be ridiculous. Of course I'm not afraid to ride."

"Glad to hear it."

They rode out of town at a brisk walk, Shane strangely silent, Caroline nervously chatting to her horse.

"We are going to get along just fine as long as you obey the rules," Caroline informed her mount.

Just a short time later, after Shane pressed their mounts into a slow trot, he determined that *no trotting* appeared to be one of Caroline's rules.

"Whoooa," Caroline called, bobbing up and down on the horse, her feet, along with stirrups, flapping like pigeon wings against the horse's sides.

Shane grumbled under his breath and slowed their pace. He sent her a disgruntled scowl and grabbed her reins. "What are you doing?" he asked impatiently.

Caroline swayed in the saddle when her horse stopped, her hair and bonnet hanging askew on her head. She probably would have fallen into a heap on the dusty trail had Shane not swiftly reached out and steadied her.

"I am riding, sir," she stated regally, though the effect was somewhat diminished by a face gone pale and green eyes that were having difficulty focusing.

"Riding like kernels of corn over a hot fire maybe, but not like a rider who has any intention of staying on the horse for any distance. Hell, Caroline, don't you know how to ride?"

"Of course not," she snapped. "What do I look like? A hoyden who rides astride in a split skirt?" She glanced down at herself and grimaced. "Next I'll be chewing tobacco and spitting on the ground. Good God," she moaned, "what has become of me?" Her shoulders slumped, wilting like silken petals on a hot humid day. Scorching-hot dry air wrapped around her, bringing beads of sweat out on her forehead. Then she sighed. "I've gotten myself into this mess. I might as well see it through."

She clucked to her horse, sounding more like a chicken than a rider coaxing her mount forward. Shane nearly laughed out loud, but hung his head in despair instead, holding tight to their reins.

"If you continue to ride like you were, after a few less than enjoyable miles, you'll never ride again. Let me show you how it's done."

Caroline eyed her nemesis with dubious eyes, but eventually conceded the truth of his words. Besides, she was going to be adventurous, wasn't she? Here was a perfect opportunity. Take advantage of it, girl, she chided herself. And so she did.

After Shane gave her a quick lesson on riding, pointing out the fundamental elements of travel, they proceeded along the well-marked trail, alternating between a fast walk, a brisk trot, and eventually a slow, smooth canter that brought a glorious smile to Caroline's lips. Her bonnet had long since fallen back to her shoulders, her hair loosening from its pins to fly behind her.

She rode like the desert wind, free and alive. Caroline Bromley, the ruined woman, ceased to exist. With the new clothes and the amazing ability to ride, the old, restrained Caroline dropped away onto the rock-strewn landscape.

"Oh, Shane!" she shouted across the short distance that separated them, forgetting for the time being that she hated him. "What a feeling! The wind in your hair, the sun on your face. It's indescribable!" For the moment she felt whole and new, and she wished she could ride forever.

Shane glanced over at her. He could not remember the last time he had felt such joy for such a simple pleasure. But it wouldn't last. He knew that soon her anger would resurface, because now he understood the cause. She thought he had willingly left her. If only somehow he could make her understand the reason why he had left. But to make her see the truth would also force her to see that while *he* hadn't lied, her father had. Could he do that to her? He didn't see how.

His mind tried to drift. An image of mahogany skin and flowing black braids from his childhood pushed at his mind. His eyes narrowed and he pushed the images away. Regardless of the fact that she was likely to hate him forever, and regardless of his past, he was doing the right thing to marry Caroline. If only to provide her with the security of his name. He had to believe that.

They rode side by side, neither willing to break the silent camaraderie that had unexpectedly sprung up between them. They slowed to a walk, making their way through craggy cottonwoods and shimmering poplars. Birds chirped overhead and cicadas beckoned to their mates.

They reached El Paso in good time, but didn't stop there. When Shane continued through the town toward the river, Caroline asked where they were going.

"Paso del Norte, across the river."

"We're going to Mexico?" Caroline asked, excitement and trepidation lacing her words.

Shane eyed her with amusement. "Yes, Caroline, we're going to Mexico."

"Oh, what an adventure!"

After crossing the Rio Grande, they came to the town that did not look much different from its counterpart directly across the river. Paso del Norte was simply larger and older than El Paso.

A young boy stood outside the mercantile.

"*Hola*, Señor Rivers. I take care of your horses, *sí*?"

"*Sí*, Pepe." Shane tossed the boy a silver coin. "I expect you to take good care of them."

"Of course, señor. Do I not always take care of Midnight perfectly?"

When Shane helped Caroline dismount, she glanced over at his horse. "You still have Midnight?"

"Yes, we're still together."

"He's still beautiful, you know."

Shane looked at Caroline. The sun caught in her hair and danced in her eyes. "So are you."

Red inched up into Caroline's cheeks. But before he could say another word, she turned and hastily strode up the wooden steps to the mercantile, hating the rapidly growing confusion she felt.

After business was taken care of, Shane showed Caroline around the old Spanish town. The mission loomed tall to the west, silhouetted against the gnarled masses of the reddish Sierra Madre mountain range. Walking through the dirt streets of the town, they passed every sort of vendor, hawking their wares. There were chickens and vegetables, tin lamps and cookware, anything one could possibly need.

Shane bought Caroline sweet Mexican candy, which she reluctantly accepted but enthusiastically ate. Strolling among the vendors, they came to an old man whose carved art was displayed on a long table.

"They're lovely," Caroline said reverently. "But what are they?"

Shane picked up one of the wooden pieces of art. "*Retablos* of the patron saints. Most *retablos* have the saint simply painted on the wood. These are special, as the saints are carved into the wood. It's an age-old art that is passed down from generation to generation."

The *retablo* carver nodded his agreement.

"*Son muy bonita*," she complimented the man.

With an arch of dark brow, Shane chuckled. "*Muy bien, señorita*," he complimented her on her Spanish. "I didn't realize you spoke the language."

"*Un poquito*," she responded, grinning like a child, holding her index finger and thumb up and slightly apart to indicate the amount of Spanish she actually knew. "And only with great diligence on my part. And out of self-defense."

"You're doing better each day, I've noticed," Shane said.

His words were unexpected and threw her off balance. She blushed painfully as if the surge of color burned her cheeks. Her sense of newness and rebirth vanished as harsh, inescapable reality surged forth.

"Has it been that bad?" he inquired, his voice gentle and caring.

Tearing her eyes away from his, she did not answer. She looked back at the *retablos*. With one long, graceful finger she traced the outline of a figure that caught her attention.

"Our Lady of Remedies," Shane said, "the patroness of the River Kingdom. You have chosen the Virgin Mother who protects women in the river valley from the evils of the world." The words were spoken slowly, as if they pained him. He reached out to her as he had wanted to do so often during the last several days.

Caroline gasped when the back of his hand gently grazed her cheek and she spun out of his range. Her foot caught in the hem of the split skirt and her body lurched forward, into the path of a racing carriage.

Time hung suspended. Breathlessly, painfully, all those who stood around watched in horror.

Shane's mind worked as if it swam in churning river mud. Dread, fear and despair consumed him. "No!" he roared, forcing his limbs from inaction. With lightning speed he reached out and grabbed the soft flesh of Caroline's arm and yanked her to the safe haven of his embrace, her skirt billowing in the wake of the rushing carriage.

They stood clasped together, each shaken to their core, neither aware of the relieved stares that surrounded them. Shane held her tightly, every muscle tense.

After a moment she pushed away from him, her breath shaky, her smile curiously embarrassed as she turned back to the table of *retablos*, uncertain at that second where else to turn. Shane came to stand next to her. He reached down and traced the outline of Our Lady much as Caroline had done earlier. "Perhaps you need this, sweet Caroline," he said, his voice oddly strained.

At first she didn't respond. They stood side by side, Caroline painfully aware of Shane's strong hand stroking the *retablo*.

"Why?" she finally whispered. "Do I need protection from getting run down in the street . . . or from you?"

Shane's eyes darkened, his forehead creasing as he grasped her arms and forced her to meet his gaze. "Maybe both. But rest assured that as my wife I will protect you from the dangers of the street . . . we will see how successful the Blessed Mother is in other areas."

Eyes opening wide as the meaning of his words slowly sank in, Caroline staggered on comprehension—comprehension that he stood in the road *proclaiming* that she would be his wife! God, when would he cease to say things that stole her breath away and threatened to steal her sanity?

"As your wife?" she demanded. "I am not your wife and never will be. You saw to that years ago."

"I said I was going to put the pieces of your life back together. Two of the pieces are a proposal and an acceptance that I remember quite well."

"Five years ago, maybe!"

"No maybe about it. I've tried to court you long enough without getting anywhere. The courtship is over, Caroline Bromley. You and I are betrothed."

Caroline stammered and sputtered in disbelief and outrage at such brazenness. "I don't know who you think you are! And I cannot imagine what has brought on this sudden change of heart. But if you think for one second I'm going to stand by and grin while you waltz back into my life and think you can pick up where you left off—forget it."

His steely grip loosened until it was nearly a caress. "We are going to be married, Caroline. Don't you forget that."

CHAPTER

✳

14

MARRIAGE!

Caroline's lips pursed and her smooth brow furrowed. Shane unnerved her now more than ever with his talk of marriage.

Marriage indeed! Like he meant it!

Through her sleepless night, some unfamiliar voice in her head told her that he did mean his words, though she still had no idea why.

Her heart suddenly pounded against her ribs. Years of her father's words filtered through her mind. *Don't ride, Caroline dear. You'll only get hurt.* She thought of all the men she had come to know, only to have them disappear from her life unexpectedly, without explanation. Her mind reeled. *Caroline, I don't know what I'd do without you.*

She sucked in her breath. She felt sick. It was not possible, she told herself emphatically. Her father had not been the type of twisted man who could have done the things of which Shane accused him. Her father had been kind and gentle. He had always been there for her. He had loved her.

Her breath came out in a sharp burst. The sick feeling

turned quickly to renewed and intensified hatred. Shane Rivers had planted a poisonous seed in her mind against her father, and now it had started to grow. She felt like a traitor, and she felt ashamed after all her father had done for her. It was Shane Rivers who was the liar and deceiver, not her father, her mind raged. She knew from experience that only a fool would believe Shane Rivers's words and declarations.

And who did he think he was that he could so arrogantly and autocratically boss her around? she demanded to know. She was a freethinking, independent woman who was no longer amenable to being told by some man what she could or could not do. Especially by some conceited, arrogant . . . libertine.

Marriage indeed! she cried again.

If only her wits did not flee in the face of his breathtaking, stormy-eyed gaze. And to think she had told him that she was a woman who was in control of herself. She had nearly gotten herself run down in the street for all her control. Well, she promised, she would show him control yet!

She gathered her skirt with a vengeance then ventured out of her room into the courtyard. No sooner had her foot touched the smooth-stoned path than a voice came out of the growing darkness. Caroline's step faltered for a heartbeat before she hastily gathered her skirt all the tighter and quickened her pace in pursuit of the relative safety of the *sala*.

Shane chuckled then stubbed out his cheroot. "Always in a hurry. Slow down, I have a thing or two I'd like to discuss."

"Discuss them with someone who cares," she shot back over her shoulder. "I certainly don't."

"Well, you should. They concern you."

He caught her after a few bold strides and brought her around to face him. With frigid disdain she pulled her shoulder away from his grasp.

"Always so prickly." His voice was soft as he reached out to caress a lock of red hair that had fallen free of her chignon. "I believe we have some planning to do," he said as he wrapped the strand of hair around his finger.

Caroline's eyes flashed. Trying to free herself, she yanked her head away. "Ouch!" she yelped when she only succeeded in pulling her own hair. "Let me go! This instant!"

Instead, he tangled his hand further in the fiery locks, pulling her closer. "But perhaps we should seal our betrothal first, then make plans."

Anger flashed like silver-white lightning in her eyes; her lips pursed in protest.

In answer, Shane pulled her closer still. "Just a simple kiss will do, sweet Caroline," he whispered with an infuriating smile.

"You can get your plans and your kisses elsewhere, Mr. Rivers—as I'm sure you've been doing all along." There was a second of shocked silence as the implication of her statement sank in, before Caroline fervently wished she could bite back her careless words. But the deed was done and she cringed at the knowing look that quickly came to Shane's eyes.

"Jealous, little one?"

"In your dreams, you hard-hearted blackguard!"

Shane threw back his head and roared.

"Let me go!"

"Not until we've sealed our betrothal . . . my little jealous one."

Outrage suffused her. She sputtered and spit and searched for some cutting rejoinder. But before something suitable surfaced in her fury-riddled brain, a sound in the distance caught her attention.

"What's that?" Shane asked, mischief in his eyes. "Sounds like someone's coming."

Caroline stilled before she hissed, "Let me go!"

"First my kiss."

The sounds of voices grew louder and nearer. "Ahhgh!" she groaned, but finally reached up on tiptoe and pressed a fleeting kiss to his lips.

His arm came around her like a band of iron. She pressed her fists against his chest, trying to free herself. But no matter how hard she pushed, he held her secure. His lips whispered across her cheek to her neck, and she felt a velvet shiver tingle down her spine. A tiny gasp escaped her lips and her traitorous body melted against his. Her head fell back and he ran his tongue along the slender white column. Shivers of longing coursed through her body, making her burn.

"Caroline," he groaned softly into her ear, pressing her hips against the hard length of his need. "You make me crazy. I want to feel you beneath me." He ran his hand down her neck until he cupped her breast through her gown. He circled her already taut nipple, making her shake with feeling. "And you want me, too."

The simple words doused the flames. And in a flash of furious temper, she yanked herself free.

It was a moment before he gained control of his raging passion. He had only meant to press a chaste kiss on her lips. But at the feel of her sweetness pressed against him, his better intentions fled. He would have cursed himself for his lack of control had he not been caught up in watching her as she wound herself up, words he was sure would not have been misplaced in a saloon threatening at her lips. But somehow, through an amazing show of self-discipline, Shane thought with regret, Caroline bit the words back.

Choking on her anger, red mottling her cheeks, Caroline glared at him for one more second before, with a strangled cry, she turned on her heel and marched off.

"You'd best decide on a date for our wedding," he called after her. When she failed to stop or respond, he added, "If you don't decide soon, I'll do it for you." Then, ignoring the snarl he would have sworn he heard waft back to him, Shane followed Caroline into the *sala* for the evening meal.

Supper that evening was filled with preparations for the annual Fall Fiesta. The inhabitants of Cielo el Dorado talked about the date and the invitations, and about who would do what. Everyone seemed to put forth their best effort at pleasant conversation. All, that is, except Caroline, who sat in her chair, staring at her plate morosely. She was falling apart. One touch from that man and she turned into a moon-eyed, weak-kneed mass of swooning desire. Good Lord, she admonished herself, didn't she have more resolve than that?

Not until the conversation eventually turned to weapons, and Shane reacted vehemently against the idea of women using them, did Caroline perk up.

"Guns, you say," Caroline stated, surprising all those around the table who had nearly forgotten she was there. All, that is, except Shane, whose slate-gray eyes glittered suspiciously.

Diego glanced from Caroline to Shane. A slight smile parted his lips. "Yes. Everyone living on the frontier should know how to use firearms." Diego turned to Emma. "Grandmother can take out a jackrabbit at a hundred paces. Isn't that true, Grandmother?"

"I don't know if I still can, but there was a day. . . ." she responded with a dreamy smile of memory.

"See, even Grandmother knows how to shoot. You should also, Miss Caroline," Diego announced. "And I will be happy to teach you."

Shane's dark countenance darkened even further. "Diego," he warned.

Diego chuckled. "What, cousin?" he asked with feigned innocence. "With Caroline being so fond of 'practical skills,' I would think this was perfect for her."

"Surely," Shane began tightly, "her *success* with practical skills has not gone unnoticed by you?"

Choking off his laughter with a cough, Diego hesitated a second before he set his napkin aside. "A mishap or two, perhaps," he offered with a negligent grin. "But I would be the one in charge of instruction for a shooting lesson, not the other way around."

"Diego," Shane bit out, leaning forward, his elbows planted aggressively on the table.

But before another word could be spoken, Caroline clasped her hands. "I think it's a grand idea. When can we begin?"

"Caroline," Shane warned.

Diego chuckled. "We will start tomorrow."

"Perfect," Caroline chimed. "As soon as school is out."

Shane started to speak, but stopped. He knew she

took great pains to thwart him. If he said something now, it would only make things worse. He would simply have to say something to Diego later. Without Caroline around.

Angrily, he pushed himself up from his seat and walked over to retrieve a snifter of brandy. Talk of shooting exploits filled the table. Everyone seemed to have a story to tell that bespoke their great prowess with firearms. Shane watched Caroline smile and laugh as she listened avidly to the tales.

Emma set her napkin aside and joined Shane at the sideboard. "She seems happier, I think," she ventured as Shane offered her some brandy.

He glanced over at Caroline. "Does she? It's hard for me to tell."

Emma smiled. "I was thinking that a wedding during the fiesta would be lovely."

Shane's lips spread with grim humor. "Before we can start making plans for a wedding, I have to prevent our schoolteacher from getting herself killed, and then I must convince her to marry me."

Astonishment skipped across Emma's face. "But I would have thought she would be thrilled . . . or at least she would want to marry."

"Caroline Bromley has a mind of her own, and she is determined to prove that to me over and over again."

Taking a slow sip of the amber liquid, Emma took in the room filled with her family. "You love her, don't you?"

Pewter eyes grew cold. A cutting edge sharpened his tone. "What I feel doesn't matter."

Emma sighed. "You feel as though I've forced you into this marriage, then."

With effort, he forced himself to relax. "No, Emma. You only provided me with the means of obtaining something I wanted and felt I had no right to have."

She turned questioning eyes on him. "What do you mean?"

"Nothing," he said slowly. "But rest assured, you have not forced me into anything."

"Then you want to marry her?"

Shane stared across the room at Caroline, whose eyes were graced with a smile that he rarely had the pleasure of seeing turned toward him. His heart beat heavily and his eyes darkened.

"God help her, but yes, I want to marry her."

CHAPTER

✳

15

SHOOTING, CAROLINE DETERMINED, was not as difficult as it appeared. Certainly, it was enough of a challenge that she felt a sense of accomplishment when she finally managed to hit something she intended to hit. And she knew with a certainty that her shoulder would be black and blue by the following morning. But, all in all, it was well worth the effort, even considering the fact that in the end, Emma had taken Shane's side and pleaded with her not to go. The older woman had come into Caroline's room saying Shane had been unexpectedly called out to the northeast quadrant early that morning. As if that was going to make her stay. Caroline shook her head. Shane Rivers had no say in her life. And by all that was holy, she was going to prove that to the man one way or another.

"Why don't we go over the next rise," Diego said, taking her arm and leading her still farther from the hacienda. "There's another area that's perfect for more difficult target practice."

For some reason Caroline could not put her finger on, a shiver of unease ran down her spine. But she shook it off. "How long have you lived at the hacienda?" she asked, trying to retain her calm as they walked side by side.

Diego glanced down at her curiously. "Ten years. Since Emma came to the area and purchased Cielo el Dorado."

"Then you must have come with her."

"Yes, I did."

"What about Henry Driver?"

Diego stiffened. "He came with us as well."

"And Reina?"

"Aren't you full of questions." But then he shrugged and said, "We met her once we had arrived. Reina's parents helped my grandmother learn the area when we first came to this land."

"Where are Reina's parents now?"

"Dead," he stated simply.

"The fever?"

"No. An Indian raid."

"Oh," she said uncomfortably. "What about your parents?" she asked in hopes of changing the subject.

"Dead as well."

Caroline flinched. So much for changing the subject. "I'm so sorry."

"They died when I was only a boy. I hardly remember them," he stated dispassionately. "Like Reina's parents, they were killed during an Indian raid."

"Here at the hacienda?"

"No. Years earlier in East Texas, by the same tribe that captured my aunt."

"Your aunt!"

"Shane's mother."

Caroline staggered at the unexpected information. "Shane's mother was a captive?"

"Yes, for eleven years."

"What happened to her?"

"Eventually, my grandfather recaptured her." His grip tightened on Caroline's arm. "And when she returned to us, much to everyone's ... surprise, she had a son."

"Shane," she breathed.

"Yes, Shane," he confirmed with a curt nod.

"I didn't know."

Diego slowed his pace and then smiled. "Would it have changed anything if you had?"

Birds glided on the wind up above—herons, eagles— big, powerful birds of this desert land.

"No," she finally responded. "No, I guess nothing would have changed."

They walked on, picking their way across the rugged desert.

"Where is Shane's mother now?" Caroline asked as they came to a small flat clearing.

"She married a trader named Davis Withers and moved to St. Louis the year before we traveled to El Paso. They only come to the hacienda for the Fall Fiesta. You will meet her then." He forced a smile to his face. "You will love the fiesta. It is a time of great fun."

Caroline laughed. "So my students have told me."

His ambling gait slowed. He stopped and took her hand. Menace crackled in his eyes. "Will you save a dance for me, Miss Caroline ... or will they all be saved for my cousin?"

Words failed her. She could only stare. Diego dropped her hand and chuckled harshly. Unease pressed in on her. "Why don't you like Shane?" she asked, trying to understand the hatred that crackled between the cousins. She didn't know why, but she sensed that it was important—that at some point she would need to know. "Is it because he was born of the Comanches who murdered your parents?"

Diego stared at her. "Relationships are never as simple as they seem. Now, enough of such talk."

She shook off the strange premonition. The heat must finally be getting to her, she mused. What else could explain her sudden wild and overactive imagination? Premonitions, indeed. But despite her admonitions, she couldn't quite shake her disquiet. And through the haze of unease, she began to realize that her view of Shane had altered, though how exactly she couldn't say.

She looked out over the land. The sun sank steadily in the western sky. Suddenly shooting lost its appeal. "I think I've had enough for the day. Let's head back."

"Nonsense," he said with a cold smile. "Just a little longer." Diego took her hand firmly in his.

Her mind raced. Fear commandeered her senses and this time she couldn't shake it off. She cursed herself for coming with Diego in the first place. "Really, Mr. Cervantes." Caroline tensed. "I need to get back."

"Diego!"

Relief flooded over her at the sound. Her legs felt weak. She turned quickly to the voice. Reina Valdez was no more than twenty feet away and striding purposefully toward them. Caroline had never been so thankful to see the woman in all her life.

"Emma is looking for you, Diego," Reina stated heatedly, watching as Caroline pulled her hand away from Diego.

Diego's eyes narrowed on Reina.

"And," Reina continued, "afternoon coffee is ready in the *sala*."

After several seconds the lines on his brow visibly eased. "Then we must not keep grandmother waiting."

Gathering the few items he had brought along, Diego headed back to the hacienda without so much as a nod to Caroline. Only Reina seemed aware of the school-teacher's presence. She stood and stared long and hard at Caroline before she, too, turned and followed Diego. Caroline stood in the clearing, unnerved by the strange episode, though with no exact idea why.

Afternoon coffee was a treat that Caroline normally looked forward to. Guests from El Paso usually joined them and provided news from town. But, more important, she enjoyed the afternoon respite because Shane rarely attended.

The smell of coffee filled the *sala*. The table was covered with cakes and *posteres*, thick cream and precious sugar. All was perfect this day, Caroline thought with a scowl, except one thing.

"Shane, I'm so glad you came in from the fields," Emma gushed as she handed her youngest grandson a cup of coffee.

Caroline sipped hers and tried not to notice anyone else. But try as she might, it was difficult not to note how tiny and delicate the earthenware cup looked in the large sun-golden hands of Shane Rivers. Fingers, long and strong, looked as if they should fumble with the small cup, but did not. And she had the sudden thought of those fingers holding her and caressing her. Her body tingled. But then she cursed under her breath, a scowl marring her brow. She'd not have it, she scolded herself.

"What brings you in so early, cousin?" Diego asked with an obvious sneer. "No more fields to tend or weeds to pull?"

"The shooting," Shane responded simply, as if that should explain.

And of course it did. Caroline knew he was furious that she had gone out to shoot with Diego. She had sensed it from the minute he walked through the door. Caroline nearly smiled. Served him right, the boorish man.

"You should have seen her," Beth offered.

Diego jerked in his seat. "What do you know of her shooting?"

"Me and Esteban watched from up on the cliff."

"Esteban and I," Caroline corrected automatically, seemingly unconcerned about Diego's sudden outburst.

Shane, however, eyed Diego over his cup.

"Esteban and I," Beth conceded.

"You should not have been there," Diego interjected heatedly, before catching Shane's eye. "You might have been hit," he added, his face mulish.

Esteban laughed. "This is true. At first nothing was safe. She was shooting like a crazy person!"

"But then you should have seen her, Mrs. Emma," Beth added with a sharp glare at Esteban. "She was great. Isn't that right, Esteban?"

"I guess so," he offered reluctantly. "She did get better."

"Miss Caroline should try her hand at shooting game," Beth proposed.

"Oh, heavens. I don't think that's such a good idea," Caroline responded dubiously, carefully testing her aching shoulder.

"Sure it is. You were great," Beth persisted. "And there is a whole flock of ducks down by the river. Just on the other side of the long grass."

Shane scowled. "Caroline has no business shooting anything, much less anything that moves."

Emma groaned. Diego leaned his chair back and smiled. And Caroline shimmered with hot waves of indignation.

"I can shoot or hunt anything I want, Mr. Rivers," she stated caustically.

"Perhaps I should give you another lesson," Diego offered.

Caroline smiled across the table at Diego and started to speak.

"Don't you dare," Shane cut in with a meaningful glare at Caroline, before he pushed out of his chair and strode from the room.

Don't you dare. Ha! Caroline thought to herself only minutes later as she stalked through the working-side courtyard, looking for a gun. "How dare *he* tell me what to do," she muttered, her mind rolling with resentment. She'd show him.

In the end Caroline found the same gun she had used earlier. A sign, in her mind, that it was meant to be. When a voice in her head tried to question her obviously obstinate and childish behavior, she, with great effort, pushed the thoughts from her mind. She was unwilling to study the fact that at the drop of a hat, her traitorous heart seemed all too willing to forget that she had begged Shane Rivers to marry her once and he had wanted nothing to do with her. Well, she wanted nothing to do with him now! Besides, she added to herself reasonably, she wanted to lengthen her list of adventures, and what better way than by hunting. Goodness knows, she never would have done such a thing before!

"Where are you going, señorita?" Esteban called out to her.

"Hunting," she replied, and she meant it. Though when suddenly faced with the cumbersome carbine and an aching shoulder, she realized it was one thing to talk about hunting and something else again to actually go.

"I don't think this is such a good idea, Señorita Caroline," Esteban cajoled, following in her wake. "Señor Shane said not to."

"I don't care what *Señor* Shane said or didn't say. I am going to get a duck for supper. Now hurry on home, Esteban."

Caroline stopped in her tracks when a sudden thought occurred to her, Esteban nearly running into her back. "You're not going to turn traitor on me and tell, are you?"

Esteban groaned. "No, I will not tell the señor. But I will go with you on your hunt to make sure you are safe."

"Now, Esteban, that's sweet, but totally unnecessary."

"No, Señorita Caroline," he stated stubbornly. "I go."

Caroline sighed. "Suit yourself."

She slipped out the back gate, around the side and back to the front, Esteban close on her heels, without a single guard catching sight of them. Stealthfully they made their way through the brush until they came to the edge of the long grasses. They crawled through the strawlike vegetation, their bodies invisible to any who surveyed the land, including the ducks. From the rooftop, when Caroline had studied the distance she would have to travel, she thought it no great trek. From the ground, however, she began to wonder if she would ever reach her destination.

Her arms began to ache unbearably. Her elbows and knees, she was certain, would never be the same. Sweat trickled down her back, and her skirt tangled in her legs. When she parted the grass to see how close they were getting to her prey, she saw nothing but more grass. She sighed and hesitated.

"Either the river is farther away than I thought, or the ducks have disappeared," Caroline whispered over her shoulder.

"We could turn back," Esteban pleaded.

Caroline wavered. But then she thought of Shane and his dictatorial commands, and she became more determined than ever to persevere.

"You go right ahead," she hissed back at the boy. "I have a job to do."

Esteban hung his head between his scraped elbows before he inhaled deeply and crawled along behind his teacher.

They came to the water after what seemed an eternity, but when Caroline peered through the brush, there wasn't a single duck in sight.

"Where have they all gone?" she murmured in despair.

"Perhaps Beth was not correct about the location," Esteban offered.

Frustration and disappointment filled her, and she nearly dropped her head onto her arms in defeat. But the image of Shane loomed in her head, sufficient motivation to keep her going.

"They're here, I saw them. And after all this, by God, I'm going to get a duck!"

And then suddenly, out of the tall grass that sprouted from the river, the ducks rose majestically into the sky.

Shane made his way through the hacienda. Without acknowledging what he was doing, he glanced about in hopes of catching sight of Caroline. Strange, he thought, she was nowhere to be seen. Walking from courtyard to courtyard, he still found no trace of her. And no one had seen her in quite some time. Nor had they seen Diego.

His blood began to boil. Undoubtedly, she had gone out with Diego again. Fear raced through him, and jealousy did as well. He had seen the way his cousin looked at her. And Caroline had been all too eager to accept his offer of instruction. Damn her stubborn hide!

His search continued with no success, his fear and jealousy converging into anger that turned rapidly to fury. Then suddenly a shot rang out uncomfortably close to the hacienda walls.

Everyone within Cielo el Dorado stopped their chores. Thoughts of Indians and outlaws passed through their heads. Shane raced to the front gate with Emma close behind him. They froze in their tracks when Caroline leaped up from the field of long grass, a smile slicing across her face, her hair disheveled, weeds and twigs clinging to her dress, and a dead duck hanging from her hand. Esteban surfaced reluctantly beside her, looking alternately proud and fearful.

Pure, unadulterated relief washed over Shane. The relief, however, was short-lived and quickly replaced by anger when Diego strolled up, wiping tallow grease from his hands, making it clear he had been in the tack room the whole time. "Perhaps she did not understand your command, cousin," he offered with a smile.

Shane glared at Diego, a growl rumbling in his chest, then he set out at an angry pace across the land. Dangerous emotions pushed him on. He made short work of the hundred feet or so that separated him from Caroline. He watched as the look on his quarry's face turned rapidly from excitement to concern as he grew closer. He came to a bone-jarring halt directly in front of her, too relieved and too angry to speak.

Caroline looked up at him, a shaky smile quivering on her lips. "Would you have preferred rabbit?"

With a strangled curse, Shane grabbed the gun, then Caroline's arm and without a word pulled her back to the hacienda, the duck swinging wildly back and forth in her hand. Caroline had to run every few steps to keep up, and no matter how she twisted and turned, she could not gain her release.

"Let me go you . . . you tyrant," she ground out.

Abruptly, Shane stopped and turned to face her. "Tyrant? Tyrant! I'm a tyrant because I try to keep you from getting yourself killed?" His voice crackled with fury. "Your actions continually betray a regrettable lack of thought. Obviously your father failed to instill in you the proper respect for authority. Fortunately, it is an oversight that I have every intention of rectifying—now!"

Caroline's eyes opened wide with worry and insult. She slapped at his hand. "You will rectify nothing! Do you hear me?"

Shane's eyes glittered dangerously. He clasped her arm and pulled her so close that her head was forced to tilt back to meet his eyes. "Damn you, Caroline Bromley. When will you use your head? All it takes in this harsh, unforgiving land is one false move, or one unfortunate meeting with the wrong stranger, and no one will be able to save you. Not me, not any of the guards." His grip turned harsh and violent, his eyes intense. "Do you hate me so much that you will continually put yourself in danger just to thwart me?"

His words made her wince and she looked away.

"Do not blame her," Esteban stated, stepping forward. "It is my fault, señor, not Señorita Caroline's. I insisted we go."

Slowly, Shane turned an arctic-cold glare on the young boy. "You apparently want to be taught a lesson as well, Esteban—for lying."

Esteban wavered for a moment but held true. "It is the truth."

"Esteban," Caroline commanded, though her voice held little of the strength and pride it had earlier. "This is not your battle."

Shane's heart clenched in his chest. Her words were like water to fire. His eyes dimmed like burned-out ashes. He took in the look on her gentle face. The brazen courage and pride that had etched her features were now replaced by despair, as so often happened when he was around her.

Suddenly he wondered if he was right to pursue Caroline, if truly she would be better off married to him, or if he was simply giving in to his own desires. He stared down at her, longing for some clue, wishing for some hint of the truth. She only stared back, hatred lacing her gaze, providing him with an answer, he realized, that he was unwilling to accept.

He sighed and released her. "Go take your kill to the kitchen. It looks as though there will be duck for supper."

They feasted on a succulent meal of roasted duck and roots and greens gathered from the gardens and pantry. Shane sipped his wine, his mind racing with plaguing thoughts. Caroline sat silently across from him. He watched as she dejectedly eyed the meal set before her. The roots, he noted, gave her little pleasure, and the duck . . . well . . . Caroline, it would seem, had no interest in eating the perfectly prepared fowl.

"Is something wrong?" Shane's deep baritone cut through the chattering group.

Only Caroline noticed, however, and her eyes glanced up from her meal. "No, nothing's wrong."

"How's your supper?" he persisted.

"It's fine. I'm just not all that hungry."

"You, not hungry? Why do I find that hard to believe?"

Caroline made a face. "Such compliments you shower on me. You'd best be careful, they might go to my head," she retorted dryly before she glanced back at her plate and suppressed a groan. She picked at the vegtables and poked suspiciously at a soft unrecognizable lump of less than firm green mush. With her nose wrinkled in concern, she finally took a bite. Her eyes opened wide in pained surprise.

Shane had to stifle his laughter when for a moment he thought she would spit the food out. Obviously thinking better of such an idea, she chewed as quickly as possible then gulped an entire glass of the hacienda's finest wine to wash the whole mess down. She lowered the crystal to the table and glanced around as if looking for more. Shane chuckled and their eyes met.

"You didn't like the sotol, I take it," he said quietly without disturbing those who were near, filling her glass with more wine.

"Sotol?" she asked.

"A variety of cactus."

"Ugh. I should have known."

Shane leaned forward, his elbows resting on the table. "I suspect they wanted to give you a taste of some local fare."

She glanced around the table, then lowered her voice. "It's awful!"

Shane considered her over his glass. "Now I understand why you're not eating the sotol, but what's wrong with your hard-won duck?"

Caroline glanced at her plate and, upon finding the bird still there, seemed surprised. Blood crept into her cheeks and she shrugged. "I don't know," she began quietly. "When I used to buy chickens from the mercantile or from the farmer down the way, they were already . . . dead. Somehow after seeing my duck alive . . . flying through the air for one last helpless, fateful flight . . ."

Tears gathered in her eyes and Shane was touched by such feeling as much as he was amused. Certainly Caroline would never make it on a farm. "The first time is hard for everyone. You'll get used to it."

"Never!" she exclaimed, suddenly vehement. "I will never hunt again."

"That certainly suits me," he responded dryly.

Caroline glanced at him. "I forgot. You're not still angry, are you?"

Shane nearly sucked in his breath at the sight. She looked up at him with those big green eyes, a flash of the innocence he had thought but a memory shimmering in their depths. "Would you care if I was?"

Minutes ticked by, neither one of them aware of the laughter and bantering that went on all around.

"I guess not," she finally answered with a sigh, the flash of innocence evaporating into the amber light.

His heart clenched in his chest. How could he span the chasm that yawned between them? And he wondered if it was too late. Five years too late.

He started to reach out to her, but let his hand drop when he saw the sudden panic that flared in her eyes. The look impaled him, and his heart bled quietly. Gripped by his inadequacies, he turned away.

CHAPTER

✴

16

CAROLINE STOOD BEFORE the mirror. Her red hair was still the same, and her eyes were no more or less green than before. Certainly her pale white skin had taken on some color; it was inevitable in such a sun-washed land. She could even detect a smattering of freckles across the delicate bridge of her nose. Despite that, her features, she conceded, were still the same.

But somehow, she thought as she ran her fingers gently over her face, she seemed different. And she had no idea why.

Shane Rivers came to mind and her heart beat faster. She turned her head away from the mirror, trying to turn away from her thoughts. As she glanced out the window the colorful early-morning sunrise beckoned. She wanted to feel the cool air on her face as if that could clear her head.

Caroline took the steps to the rooftop so she could walk along the promenade, seeking a moment of quiet solace. She chose a distant corner so she would remain undisturbed. The smell of roses and hyacinth wafted on the delicate breeze that came toward her. The sky was black quickly fading to purple and blue—clear

with echoes of stars. The guards had told her a storm
would be upon them before night's end. An El Paso
storm, another guard had added, chuckling. The type
that came down upon the land with all the pent-up
rage of the gods, and then was gone as quickly as it
had come. For now, however, as she looked up at the
sky she could hardly imagine a storm.

She took a deep, calming breath before she allowed
her mind to turn to the caldron of thoughts about Shane
Rivers. She no longer knew what she felt, though certainly confusion could adequately describe her emotions. Her body, mind as well as limbs, felt as though
it had passed through the wringer. And not solely due
to the scrapes and bruises from her hunting misad-
venture. A gamut of feelings played in her head. She
grappled with anger at Shane's domineering attitude,
hate over his lies, and most maddening of all, desire
for the infuriating man.

And as had happened so many times over the last
weeks, she wanted to give in to him, in spite of his outrageous behavior and his hideous lies. But she didn't
know how.

A tiny whimper escaped her lips. She didn't know
how to stop her father's admonitions from playing over
and over again in her mind like a waterwheel in rushing water. She didn't know how to dry up the words
that seemed to make it impossible to give in to her
yearnings. Was she so immature that she could not
forgive and forget? she wondered painfully. Couldn't
she take Shane at his word that he truly wanted to marry her? Shouldn't Shane's offer of marriage negate her
belief that he simply wanted to seduce her? Shouldn't
his proposal drown out the truths about traitorous men

she had learned from her father? And did the reason for Shane's wish to marry her really matter?

White-hot shame engulfed her. Of course it mattered. She still wanted deep and abiding love—not a marriage she entered through some strange twist of fate. Pride swelled. And therein lay the problem. Not only did she fight her parent's words, but she could not understand why Shane wanted to marry her now. And, more important, why would he tell her such monstrous lies about her father? For all that she had thought she knew Shane Rivers years ago, she realized now that she had not known him at all.

Caroline thought about Shane's past. It was as if she had thought of him as springing to life on the day they met. She had been vaguely aware that he had lived in Washington, but beyond that, until she had come here, she had known nothing else of his life. She wondered what it had cost him to be the fruit of a captive coupling. Did coming to this world under such circumstances excuse the man's behavior? Did it allow him to leave her at the altar, then show up years later demanding that he take control of her life and that they marry? Did it excuse his lies? She thought not.

But then she wondered if it was possible that she was the biggest liar of all. Was she clinging to her hatred of Shane and denying her desire for him in hopes of proving to God, or simply to herself, that she was not without decency?

A faint noise brought her out of her reverie. She turned her head, and when she did she saw him. He stood in the distance, alone, looking out over the river, seemingly mesmerized by the swirls and eddies of the flowing water. Her nostrils flared, her eyes burned, and she nearly cried out for the sheer power and beauty he emanated.

Her hand reached out, and she wished with all her heart, regardless of all her earlier musings, that he would turn around and find her. She knew that if it were he who stood watching her, she would feel it, she would know it in her heart and seek out his eyes.

But Shane didn't turn.

They stood quietly, separated by so much more than mere distance, he staring at the water, she staring at him, as the sounds of the morning drifted over the land. She waited longer than she told herself she would, willing him to turn, knowing at that moment that if he did, she would go to him regardless of the past. But still he failed to sense her presence.

Her face grew somber. Suddenly the simple movement became enormously important. Leaning forward, she clasped her arms around her body.

"Turn, damn you," she whispered into the cool morning air, unconsciously reaching out to him.

But he didn't.

Slowly her hand fell. She fought off despair as a tight, burning ache filled her soul. Suddenly she felt so alone, so very alone. With a sigh, she looked away and retreated to the safe haven of her father's beliefs, chastising herself for a romantic fool as she slipped away through the growing light.

The river moved as quickly as if it cascaded from a waterfall. Shane watched the flow without seeing, his eyes intense. He stood quietly, his hands pushed deep in his pockets, no movement except for an occasional strand of hair caught by the breeze. And then suddenly he turned.

He looked back at the hacienda, uncertain why he turned, or what it was he sought. His eyes were drawn to the promenade. Searching the rooftop, he found guards looking out over the land. Nothing more. With eyes narrowed and lips pursed in thought, he looked back to the west, taking in the purples and blues that were fast turning to oranges and yellows as the sun forced its way into the sky. He frowned at the deep, inexplicable sense of loss that surged through him.

He returned to the hacienda to gather his horse and his men, along with the tools they would need for their work. The small group set out for the day.

The northeast quadrant was the rockiest and least fertile land of the hacienda. But livestock was known to stray this far, and Shane meant to see that all cattle and goats were found and fences were secured.

The day passed, and as it did Shane grew concerned. His body stiffened with alarm as he found signs of passage across the land that could only mean one thing. But perhaps he was wrong.

As the afternoon sun traveled westward Shane felt the growing need to return to the hacienda. The laborers were more than happy to head back early. Shane left the men before they reached the gate, then made his way to a secluded part of the river. And there his worst fears were confirmed.

The man stood on the sandy bank, his long black braided hair shining blue in the late-afternoon sunlight. Wide black eyes stared off into the distance, though Shane was certain the man had heard his approach.

"You have not forgotten all you learned, my brother," the Indian said.

He was not nearly as tall as Shane, but every bit as well defined—a formidable figure. He wore a dark blue breechclout and soft leather moccasins. His skin was the color of saddle leather, polished smooth.

"Life's lessons are not easily forgotten, I'm afraid," Shane responded, his tone unwelcoming.

"Always the philosopher. And now I suspect too much of the white man's schools is in you, making you hard." The man's broad, flat face wrinkled with a smile.

"One works with what one is given, Little Bear," Shane stated.

A strange softness crept into the Indian's eyes, but then it was gone. "I am no longer Little Bear, Fast As the Rivers. I had my vision quest many years back now."

A flicker of yearning flashed across Shane's face. The thought-to-be-forgotten smell of smoke and bear grease teased his mind. "I offer my congratulations."

"Black Bear, I am called now. The fearsome beast came to me in my dreams, and upon waking, my dream became a reality." Black Bear held up a string of huge teeth that hung around his neck.

"Then Black Bear has become a great warrior," Shane offered.

"Like you would have been had you stayed."

The yearning slipped away. "I was given no choice, now, was I?"

Black Bear nodded. "The gods had other plans for you."

"What do you want, Black Bear?" Shane asked tightly, not wanting to prolong this confrontation any longer than necessary.

Black Bear sighed. "Yes, too much of the white man is in you. In too much of a hurry. Do you forget the way of the People? I have brought the peace pipe to share, that we might be brothers once again." He pulled a pipe from a beautifully hand-carved leather pouch.

"I have no time for offers of peace. Why are you here?" Shane demanded again.

Black Bear returned the pipe to his pouch. "It is time for you to find the People, Fast As the Rivers. Your grandfather has sent me for you. He is desirous of your return."

Shane's hand clenched at his side. "What are you talking about?"

"The headman, your grandfather, has sent me. I have come to show you the way to the People. Though as quickly as you found me this day, I think you could have found us on your own, had you only tried. Strong One says it is time for you to return to your true family."

Shane looked toward the mountains, then pressed his eyes closed. He said nothing for a great while, then he looked back and his eyes locked with Black Bear's. "I have no Indian family. That is my message to Strong One."

Black Bear stared at Shane as if making some decision. "He will not be pleased, my brother."

"That is of little concern to me."

Black Bear's eyes flashed, but he said nothing. He merely leaped on his Indian pony and rode from sight.

Shane watched him go. Anger grew until it threatened to defeat him, because he knew, as he knew the sun would rise, that he would see Black Bear again. The tribe wouldn't leave him alone this easily. And now he was forced to face the fact that no matter how hard he tried, he couldn't escape his past.

With stiff movements he returned to the hacienda to put his horse away. Once in the stable, he deftly lifted the saddle from Midnight's back. He brushed the horse's coat and mane. Checking each hoof, he cleared away any rocks and debris to ensure the well-being of the soft triangular frog. With water and food secured, Shane led Midnight to his stall and put him up for the night.

The simple task of putting his horse away did little to diminish his anger and frustration. His jaw was taut when he came around the corner from the working side into the main courtyard. He was taken aback when he caught sight of Reina running out of the schoolhouse, anger and tears distorting her face. Concern filled him. But his concern quickly turned back to anger, so easily reignited after his meeting with Black Bear, when next he saw Diego exit the same building.

Diego stopped at the sight of Shane. A hard smile curved on his face. "Don't think she only wants you, cousin," he stated, nodding toward the schoolhouse, before he threw back his head and laughed.

Another time Shane would not have given his cousin's remark a second thought, but this time, filled with anger that was fast turning irrational boiling inside of him, he let go of his hard-won control and lashed out.

Diego's laughter was cut short when Shane's fist connected with his chin. Diego's hand flew to his jaw as his startled black-brown eyes tried to comprehend. But surprise turned quickly to fury. He flew at Shane, cursing and screaming like a madman. Shane didn't care. In fact, he relished the blows, he wanted the pain.

They fought and tumbled along the hard-packed earth, drawing a crowd. They fought each other, both fighting for years of real and imagined hurts.

"I will kill you," Diego spat out, rolling on top of Shane, blood dripping from his nose.

Shane merely blocked the blows until Diego pulled his fisted hand up in the air, readying it to strike with the greatest possible force. Just as contact was nearly made Shane jerked and flipped his cousin on his back. In seconds, he had Diego under control and pinned to the ground. Shane waited until their eyes met. "This time I stop because you are family, Diego. But if you ever go near Caroline again, cousin or not, I will teach you a lesson you will not soon forget."

He then released Diego with disdain and leaped up from the ground. Wiping the blood from his face with the back of his arm, he pushed his way through the crowd toward the schoolhouse. He took the steps in one wrathful leap and threw open the door.

Caroline was alone, writing lessons on the blackboard for the next day. She twirled around, chalk still held firmly between her fingers. When her eyes focused on Shane, her hand fell to her side in relief. She stepped away from the blackboard. "You scared me to death," she began with a rush of breath. But her relief was short-lived when in the next second Shane moved toward her, his step menacing, his face frozen in a feral mask.

"What's wrong?" she stammered.

When he failed to answer, she tried to sidestep his approach. He reached out with deadly speed and grabbed her arm, forcing her up against the wall.

"Have you turned your charms on my cousin?" he demanded, his voice seething.

"What are you talking about?" The expression in her eyes grew incensed. "What are you implying, sir?"

"Don't play the little innocent with me!"

"I've never *played* anything with you. Never! And you insult me when you imply otherwise." She gritted her teeth. "*I* have always been honest with you. Now let me go," she demanded, her anger mixing with growing fear.

He seemed unaware, or certainly unconcerned, about her fright. He only clasped her arm tighter.

"Let me go! You're hurting me!" She tried to pull free, but his grip held her immobile. "What's wrong with you? Have you gone mad?"

Shane pulled her close until her lips were only inches from his. "Perhaps," he replied. "But mad or not, right or wrong, you are mine." He dipped his head until he claimed a brutal kiss. "Only mine," he breathed harshly.

Struggling against his iron grip, Caroline turned her head away from his lips. "Don't do this, Shane," she whispered, her voice tight.

But Shane was given no opportunity to stop or answer when a sharp knife hurtled through the air and stuck into the wall with a resounding *twang*.

Young Esteban had arrived.

"Me thinks, señor, you had best leave Señorita Caroline alone."

Shane turned slowly. He impaled the boy with furious eyes. "*I* think you had best leave before I teach you a lesson long in coming."

The sharp brown features of Esteban's face creased

with worry, but his shoulders remained rigid. "I will not leave the señorita," he declared. "I have come to protect her."

The world went silent. *Protect her*. The words assailed Shane. Protect her from the savage. His head swayed back, his breath hissed through his teeth. A young boy was trying to protect Caroline from him. He looked down at her and for the first time noticed the fear in her eyes. What had he almost done? he demanded of himself. What would have happened had someone not intervened? The answer that came to him pierced his mind. He had wanted her to hurt, as he was hurting. He had wanted her to feel, as he was feeling. The realization sickened him, leaving him cold and empty.

His grip loosened, allowing Caroline to slip free. He didn't try to stop her. He let her go and simply watched as she hurried down the neatly lined aisle, herding her young savior swiftly out the door.

Silver spurs dug into the horse's sides as Diego whipped his mount into action and galloped toward town. His thoughts spiraled. Shane couldn't get away with this! His cousin would pay, Diego promised himself.

Racing through the crowded streets, Diego took little notice of the people that were forced to run to get out of his path. Reining in, he threw his leg over, jumped to the ground, and tossed the reins to the young boy in front of Ben Dowell's Saloon.

Diego barged through the door, causing heads to pop up from muffled conversations. Several muttered then went back to their drinks. Diego paid them no mind; he merely strode across the floor, spurs jangling on the hardwood.

"Bottle of tequila," he called.

Ben Dowell stood behind the bar wiping a glass with a cotton towel. "Afternoon," he said, turning away to stack the tumbler in a pyramid of glass, impatience flickering in his eyes as he glanced at Diego in the smoky mirror that ran the length of the back counter.

"Tequila, Dowell. I'm not interested in pleasantries."

"You in a hurry to find oblivion, or do you just want to dull the pain?" the saloon owner asked with a nod at Diego's rapidly swelling eye.

"Cute, Dowell. Am I going to get my drink or do I need to go across the river?"

"Keep your shirttail on," Ben said as he pulled a liquor bottle from beneath the bar and set it on the wooden counter along with a glass. "You really should have someone look at that eye."

Diego poured a glass and virtually threw its contents down his throat. His eyes watered and he sucked in his breath before he poured himself another.

Ben watched the proceedings. "From what I've heard, that pretty little schoolteacher you all got over there at the hacienda is a damn fine healer. Maybe she should have a look at that cut over your eye."

Liquor spewed from Diego's mouth.

"Hey!" Ben shouted. "What the hell you doing, Cervantes?"

"She knows nothing, you understand. Nothing! And soon she will be gone. Back to San Antonio where she belongs."

Ben wiped the counter down and turned away from Diego with a grumble.

Diego continued to drink. Once the pain had dulled a bit, he noticed a short man with clothes clearly not of the area, standing at the end of the bar eyeing him. "What you lookin' at?" Diego demanded, his tone belligerent.

The man smiled and moved closer. "I couldn't help but overhear you mention San Antonio."

"What about it?"

"I've recently left that very town on my way to California."

Diego sneered. "The gold rush is over, fella."

The man chuckled and nodded. "But opportunity still abounds."

"A fortune hunter. We've seen them through here by the thousands over the years. Always filled with crazy dreams," Diego said with great disdain as he poured himself another drink.

The man eyed the bottle hopefully but said nothing. Carefully, almost cautiously, he climbed up onto the stool next to Diego. "Dean Fowler's the name," he offered, extending his hand. When Diego failed to respond, Dean dropped his hand to his side. "Just the talk of San Antonio brought me over here. Friendly faces. A kindred soul . . . who just might have a bit of help for a man down on his luck. Fellow San Antonians like to stick together."

Diego turned to face the man and glanced over his fancily clad form. "I'm not sure who you're talking about being down on their luck, but Caroline Bromley hasn't a penny to her name, much less one to spare for you."

"Caroline Bromley, did you say?" the man questioned, suddenly intent.

Diego eyed the other man. "You know her?"

"Not well, really. I knew more of her than anything." He tittered like an old, crabby woman. "I guess everyone knew *of* her."

Diego's hand froze on the glass. "What do you mean?"

"Well, I'd not like to be the one to spread rumors," Dean began, eyeing the bottle of tequila.

This time Diego noticed the glance. "Dowell, another glass."

Dean sighed when a full glass of liquor was set before him. He sipped the harsh beverage.

"You were saying?" Diego prompted.

Smacking his lips delicately, Dean turned to Diego. "It was said that Caroline Bromley was a heathen half-breed's woman before he ran off and left her to her fate." He snorted and took another sip, then tossed the remainder down his throat much as Diego had earlier. His face contorted before he sighed again, then nodded his thanks when Diego poured him another.

"I don't doubt the story a bit, however. I knew the heathen myself." His eyes grew distant and his hand came self-consciously to his neck as he remembered, then he began to tell the story of Caroline Bromley.

Time passed. At length, Dean's tale rambled to a stop. From a table nearby, someone called for another round, breaking Dean's reverie. He looked back at Diego and cleared his throat uncomfortably. "But who's to say? In hindsight, I'd say Miss Bromley was a fine woman. One who I'm sure is always willing to help a person in need," he added meaningfully, taking a long, slow sip.

Diego grabbed the glass away, his patience at an end.

"Hey," Dean sputtered, nearly falling from the stool.

"The half-breed. What was his name?" Diego ground out the words.

Dean hurriedly wiped the spattered drops of tequila from his coat.

"What was his name?" Diego pressed.

"Rivers. Shane Rivers," Dean responded with one last brush at his attire.

Diego's mind reeled. His speculation was confirmed. Caroline Bromley was Shane's woman. Miss Caroline Bromley was a whore. His scowl lifted as elation filled him. His grandmother would never abide a whore in her house.

"Diego!"

Both Diego and Dean turned to the startling sound of a female voice in a purely male domain. Diego's eyes turned cold. Dean's eyes glowed with appreciation.

Reina sauntered up to the bar.

"Miss Reina," Ben Dowell said from the end of the bar. "What can I do for you?"

Her brown-eyed gaze swept over the bartender. "Nothing, señor. I will be on my way soon."

She ignored the muttered comments from the mix of Mexican and American men that filled the tables of the town saloon.

"I've been looking for you, Diego," Reina said, her lower lip full and pouting as she reached out to touch the cut on his brow.

Diego slapped her hand away and turned back to his drink.

Dean stood from his stool and made a slight bow. "I am Dean Fowler, pleased to make your acquaintance."

Reina glanced back and forth between Diego and the new man. She extended her hand. "I am Reina Valdez."

Taking her hand, he leaned over and brushed her knuckles with a fleeting kiss. "I am your servant," he said, straightening.

Reina started to pull her hand away, but stopped when she furiously conceded that Diego had little interest in her this evening. She eyed Dean more intently. When she would have showed the man her charms, intent on making Diego jealous, Diego stood up from his stool.

"This fine tequila shouldn't go to waste," he stated. "Perhaps the two of you would care to share the remainder."

"Oh, what a fine idea," Dean responded effusively.

Reina's eyes narrowed with anger. "Diego!"

But Diego did not heed her; he simply started for the door.

"Cervantes," Ben Dowell called. "You gonna pay, or what?"

Diego searched his pockets and came up empty-handed. "Put it on my bill," he called back.

Reina watched as the wooden door slammed shut. Gradually, she became aware of the men who stared at her. Then she laughed to cover her despair. "Pour me a drink, Señor Fowler. Suddenly I find myself with a great thirst."

CHAPTER

✳

17

CAROLINE SAT ON a small wooden stool in front of the mirror, brushing her long fiery tresses. She was startled from her thoughts when a knock sounded at the door.

"Who is it?" she called.

The door pushed open and Emma entered. "I thought you might like some company," she said as she casually strode about the room, running her finger along the edge of furniture until she came to the *retablo* depicting Our Lady of Remedies. She smiled but said nothing.

Caroline eyed the older woman. Though she was delighted to see her, she suspected this visit was more than casual.

"Shane seems taken with you," Emma finally said, casting a quick glance at Caroline.

Caroline's mouth went dry. Please God, she prayed, don't let Emma have learned of my past. Forcing herself to remain calm, she took up her brush once again and busied herself with her hair. "I don't know what you mean."

Emma smiled and turned to the window, which had become a shadowed mirror against the blackened night. "I believe you do but are afraid to admit it, maybe even to yourself. And I think it's because you don't understand my grandson." She lowered herself onto the edge of the bed. "Shane's life has been . . . different than most of ours."

Caroline's heart slowed, barely, but it slowed.

"Emma," Caroline said, setting the brush aside. "I really don't see how—"

"Hear me out, please." Emma's smile faded, replaced by a hard line that aged her face considerably. "He has had a more difficult time than most. As a result, he has different thoughts running through his head . . . causing him to do things that perhaps most of us don't comprehend."

Caroline studied Emma in the small vanity mirror, having no idea where this conversation was going or, for that matter, what it meant, and why Emma felt compelled to tell her these things. It didn't appear that Emma had finally learned of her past. Certainly, if she had, she gave no sign of it. But even as relief filled her, she felt an odd, uncomfortable sense of emptiness creep over her as Emma simply continued to speak of Shane, staring off into the distance, seeing things that only she could see.

"Yes, Shane is different. He fights so many demons. I can only hope that one day he will win."

The words startled Caroline. Win what? she wondered. Didn't everyone have battles to fight?

Emma turned away from the window and focused on Caroline. "Yes," Emma stated heatedly as if Caroline had spoken her thoughts aloud. "Shane *is* different. Surely by now you have learned he is half Indian. I've never learned what his life was like while he lived among the Comanches, but his life was hell once my husband captured him and brought him to our home in East Texas." Emma's face became ravaged. "Oliver Shelton, Shane's grandfather, resented Shane's birth, resented all it represented."

Caroline did not understand. "What did Shane represent?"

"His grandfather's inability to take care of his own. Many people died in the raid that made my daughter, Miriam, a hostage—many who followed Oliver from Georgia to what was then the frontier with promises of a better life, only to meet their death. When Miriam was taken, Oliver vowed to get her back, no matter the cost." Emma looked at the *retablo*. "He should have left her there, left both Miriam and Shane there, because East Texas was never home to Miriam again. It was never home to Shane at all. Home was with their Indian family. A family that Miriam, against all odds, apparently was welcomed into."

"And your husband resented that?" Caroline ventured, still trying to understand, finding suddenly that she desperately wanted to know.

Emma considered. "No, not that specifically, though certainly it was part of it. If she had come home by herself, nothing would have changed. Her father would have been able to ignore the fact that she had been a hostage. But she didn't return alone. She came with a child—an Indian child—a constant reminder that he had failed to keep his friends and family safe. Oliver never forgave his daughter that—nor her son. And for that transgression, he made them pay."

Caroline stared at her hands, trying to comprehend.

Emma took a deep breath. "Oliver killed Shane's father."

Caroline's head snapped up. "No!"

"I'm afraid so. As I said, Oliver intended to make his daughter and grandson pay. My husband had always been a hard man, but when Miriam returned and Shane came with her, Oliver turned . . . The only word I can think of is crazed. He killed Great White Wolf to punish Miriam for . . . loving a heathen, and to punish Shane"— Emma shrugged—"for his very existence."

"They must have been devastated to learn of his death."

"They didn't know."

Caroline looked confused.

"None of us did for years," Emma explained. "Oliver didn't tell anyone. Instead, he told Miriam she was a whore whose so-called husband didn't want her back because she had borne him a white-eyes child. And when Miriam protested that Oliver's words were untrue, that Wolf would come for her and her child, Oliver only laughed, never telling her the man was dead." Emma's lips tilted in a mockery of a smile. "As months turned to years and Wolf failed to come, Miriam came to believe her father. Gradually, she began to take out her anger and pain and feelings of betrayal on her son. In her mind, her Indian family didn't want her because she had a half-white son. Her father didn't want her because she had a half-Indian son. So she took it out on Shane, because she saw him as the downfall of her life. You see, she was detested by her father and ostracized from polite society. She had lain with a heathen."

Emma wrung her hands. "I understand the reasons now, but I didn't at the time. If only I had . . ." Her voice trailed off.

Caroline searched for something to say but found nothing. What was there to say about such a terrible tale except I'm sorry. And that, she knew, was wholly inadequate.

"Yes," Emma continued. "Miriam took it out on her son. And amazingly, he took it. He took everything his mother and grandfather dealt out."

Emma's breath caught in her throat. "Even after his mother had given in and come to believe that her husband didn't want her, Shane remained adamant that his father would find him. It was terrible to watch the boy, day after day, waiting for his father. Year after year, he made Indian clothes to accommodate his rapidly growing size. He even made presents to give his 'family' upon his return. And then one day it stopped. No explanations given, the watch simply ceased and the clothes were once and for all packed away."

Caroline sat perfectly still, tears stinging her eyes at the picture of Shane as a boy. Every bit of the healer in her wanted to take that little boy in her arms and heal what surely was a wounded heart. Her mind reeled, however, at the thought that Shane the boy had turned into Shane the man—a man who had hurt her so deeply.

"And that was the day," Emma added quietly, "when I realized he had come to hate his mother."

Caroline jerked out of her reverie, unwilling to believe what she heard. "Hate his mother? How can a child hate his parent?"

"Believe me. Shane hated his mother. Though who could blame him?" Emma took a deep breath. "And then I learned of Oliver's treachery. Eight years after he had brought Miriam and Shane to East Texas, he boasted, in a drunken fit, of what he saw as his greatest success. He told me how Great White Wolf had perished at the end of his rifle. For the first time in my life, I defied my husband and told Shane and Miriam. But by then it was too late. Too many years filled with hate and pain had left both my daughter and grandson scarred. When I told them, Miriam didn't believe me. I suspect after all those years of hate, she couldn't afford to. Shane had looked on, devoid of emotion. But I have always felt certain that somehow he already knew.

"Not knowing what else to do, but knowing he deserved more than what he would ever get from my husband and daughter, I gave him money that I had hid away over the years and told him to go make a new life for himself.

"Soon after Shane left, my husband died, leaving me a wealthy widow. God forgive me, but I went down on my knees in thanks. That's when Miriam married her trader and moved away. I decided to move to El Paso and buy the hacienda, to start over, even at my age. But Shane was already gone, and I had no idea how to find him. At seventeen, Shane Rivers was out in the world with no foundation of love or support."

Emma grew quiet.

"I'm sure he had your love in his heart," Caroline offered hesitantly, her head spinning with the sadness and tragedy of the story.

"My love! Ha! I was as bad as the rest. I should have done something for the boy sooner, much sooner, but I didn't. I sat back and watched for eight years and did nothing. At the time my husband seemed so all-powerful that I couldn't think of defying him. Now, so many years later, I find it hard to forgive myself." Her hand fisted against her skirt, her face marked by deep lines of regret, until suddenly she sighed, defeated.

Emma rubbed her arm as if it pained her. "Of course, this is Shane's story to tell, not mine. But I felt you should know, and I didn't think Shane would tell you—I don't think he knows how." She reached out and touched Caroline's hand. "The light died in Shane's eye the day he realized his father wasn't coming for him. I haven't seen the light since. At least not until he arrived here at Cielo el Dorado and found you."

With a tired smile, Emma moved toward the door. "Whether or not you know it, Shane needs you. Give him a sec—give him a chance."

Caroline closed her eyes, her heart pounding against her ribs. Could she? Could they start again? Could she forgive and forget? Could she move beyond the past? Then suddenly she wondered, could he?

"Good night, Caroline," Emma said as she slipped from the room.

Caroline stared at the closed door for what seemed like ages. In searing detail the images of her shared past with Shane began to dance before her eyes, every nuance vivid until they wavered and changed and she saw Shane as a boy, unloved and unwanted. Hurting. Perhaps his past still didn't excuse his more recent actions, but certainly it made them more understandable.

A moment passed before Caroline felt the rush of cool air that suddenly filled the room. When she did, she found Beth standing in the doorway, her words tumbling out in a rush.

"Missy Surlock. Baby," she gasped, out of breath.

"Calm down, Beth," Caroline said gently, though

sternly, her mind flickering between the present and the past.

"It's time," Beth breathed. "Missy Surlock is having her baby and she's calling for you."

Caroline's mind snapped firmly into the present. "Oh, dear Lord, Missy has gone into labor!" she exclaimed, flying about her room, gathering the things she thought she would need.

"I told Pedro to saddle your horse," Beth stated.

"Thank you. Let Emma know where I've gone. I'll return as soon as I can."

No sooner were the words out than Shane burst through the door. "What's this I hear about you going out?" he demanded.

Caroline's hand stilled in its frantic chore as she took in Shane Rivers. Missy Surlock was momentarily forgotten as all she had just learned about this man came back to her. Caroline's heart ached for him. The healer in her surged again, and she nearly reached out to gather him in her arms and hold him to her heart.

"Caroline!" Shane stepped closer. "Where do you think you're going?"

Caroline blinked then blinked again as she snatched her hand back down to her side. "I'm going to help Missy Surlock," she said by way of explanation, turning back to her supplies. "She's in labor."

"Let the doctor from town help her. A storm is moving this way and you're not going out in it."

"He's right," Beth conceded, in her all-knowing twelve-year-old voice. "They come on all of a sudden, washing out roads, with huge hail and gusting winds. Not a pretty sight."

"I promised," was Caroline's answer as she pulled

on a heavy cloak to protect her from the possible rain, her eyes determined, her gaze locked with Shane's. "I'll not go back on my word."

They stood facing each other, unaware of anyone else. The chasm yawned between them, seemingly unbridgeable, until Shane reached across and took Caroline's arm. "Then I'll take you."

They rode toward El Paso, Shane thankful for the full moon, Caroline unaware of the dangers of riding at night. Outlaws and bandits, or even Black Bear, were the least of his worries when faced with the possibility that with one false move either one of their horses could go down. As a result, Shane kept their mounts to a slow but steady pace, and they made the trek in a quarter hour.

The moans of pain could be heard from fifty yards away. At the sound, reality set in. Pain and suffering didn't bother Caroline, she had seen them countless times before. But pain and suffering from childbirth were altogether a different matter. She froze.

"What's the matter?" Shane asked when Caroline stopped dead in her tracks just outside the door.

"Oh God, what have I done?" she whispered, torn between duty and fear.

"What are you talking about?" He turned her to him, forcing her to look up into his eyes. "What has happened between here and the hacienda?"

A shrill cry of pain pierced the quiet. Caroline's eyes grew wild with panic. "Oh, Shane, I can't. I was a fool for ever having told Missy I would help."

"What do you mean?"

"I can't deliver this baby." She started to step away from the door and another sharp cry from within made her flinch.

His grip tightened on her arms. He forced her to meet his eyes. "You can do this, Caroline."

"I can't," she cried, trying to pull away. "I'll go find the doctor. A midwife. Somebody. Surely someone around here knows how to deliver a baby."

"There's no time for that. From the sounds in there, her time is near. She needs you. You *can* do it, and you will, because you're a healer. A fine healer."

"I'm a healer of cuts and bruises!" she cried, her voice rising. "As a single female, I have never had the opportunity to deliver a baby, nor was I ever in a position to learn how it was done!"

Pewter eyes implored her. "Reach inside yourself. Reach inside yourself to that place where you have the strength to overcome adversity. Just as you have done all these years." His hard-chiseled countenance softened. "You can do it, Red."

Red. The name wrapped around her. The name he used to call her when she had felt certain they shared some bond, that they were destined to be together— as if there still remained some glimmer of truth to the thought.

Thunder rumbled in the distance. Caroline glanced over her shoulder toward the sound. *God was watching.* The thought insinuated itself in her mind. Her heart clenched. God was angry once again, she felt certain. But then a silver-white, breathtaking bolt of lightning streaked across the sky, shedding light on the world for one brief space of time. And in that moment Caroline had the sudden thought that she was not being punished, after all, that she was being given a second chance at destinies intertwined. Why else would she have ended up in this desolate outpost?

Why else would she have been forced together with Shane over and over again during the last weeks? Why else would she be continually learning more and more about Shane's life?

And then it came to her with startling clarity that in this world so filled with ambiguity, she had never been so certain of anything as she was certain that she and Shane were somehow meant to be together. It was as if their worlds had come together then forced apart unnaturally, and it had taken years to find their way back to each other. But she realized now that it was bound to happen. Inevitable. And truly it was time to put the past behind her.

She looked back at Shane, wanting to tell him all that she felt, all that she had realized. But whatever she might have said was curtailed when a gut-wrenching cry sounded from the small house. Her shoulders straightened and she took a deep breath.

"That's my girl," he whispered before he turned her back to the door.

When they entered the tiny tumbledown shack, it took a moment before their eyes adjusted to the semidarkness. Eventually, Caroline made out the rounded form of Missy huddled beneath the covers of the bed. The one-room adobe building held traces of an earlier prosperity—a beautiful cast-iron headboard, a large feather mattress set against a crumbling mud-and-straw wall. Caroline knew on sight that Missy Surlock was a victim of circumstance.

Caroline's sense of joy and second chances evaporated. The unfairness of the world suddenly threatened to overwhelm her. The strides she had made to put her past behind her vanished when she realized that the girl lying on the bed could easily have been her.

A tired moan brought Caroline from her thoughts as Missy's contractions began to come again. While Caroline was unprepared for such a procedure, instinct took over, guiding her, helping her.

Shane stayed at her side, offering his help whenever it was needed. He built up the fire to boil water, after which, upon Caroline's instructions, he tied lengths of rope to the headboard to be used as makeshift hand-holds. Rummaging through an old trunk, Caroline found beautiful white baby blankets and downy clothes. She nearly wept at the obvious change some unknown force had wrought in Missy's life.

"Thank you for coming, Miss Caroline," Missy said quietly once the contraction had ended.

"Don't you think twice about it," Caroline said as she straightened bed linen and mopped Missy's brow. "I'm happy to help."

The next contraction came on quickly and violently, turning sweet Missy Surlock into a raving wildwoman. Caroline forced her charge to take the handholds before she hurried Shane out the door.

"I'll be right outside. Call if you need me," Shane said as he held tight to Caroline's hand.

For a second Caroline could not bring herself to let go as a trickle of renewed fear swept through her.

"You'll do fine, Red."

With that, Caroline took a deep strengthening breath of nighttime air, squeezed his hand, then pulled back and shut the door.

"Mama!" the girl shrieked.

Caroline whirled around and rushed to the bed.

"Mama!" Missy screamed again, her face twisted in pain. "Why did you leave me?"

The anguished sound filled the room. "It's all right, Missy," Caroline cooed.

But Missy was not so easily calmed. She screamed and cursed like a sailor, and through this Caroline gleaned that Missy's parents had most probably died of the fever, leaving Missy alone in a strange land. As she soothed the young woman's brow and whispered words of encouragement, Caroline knew she had to find a way to help Missy Surlock, even beyond this delivery.

For two long and arduous hours both Caroline and Missy battled the pain of labor. Missy's gasps were punctuated every other minute by shrieks of agony. Caroline tried to keep both of them calm. But the task was difficult when niggling doubts began to surface. What if something went wrong? she wondered. What if she couldn't save mother or child? But the worries had barely formed when, in a crescendo of pain, Caroline caught sight of the baby's head.

"It's coming! The baby's coming! Just hold on, Missy. Just a few minutes more."

Indeed, it was just a few minutes later when Caroline announced, "It's a boy."

The girl's eyes fluttered opened and she smiled before she drifted off into the sleep of the dead.

Caroline washed the baby and bundled him in a blanket. With great care, she placed him on the bed so she could tend to his mother. No more than a few hours from when Caroline and Shane had arrived, both mother and son were clean, and as comfortable as either was going to get.

Voices sounded from outside. Presently, Shane entered with an old Mexican woman. The kindly woman was from down the way and had come over during the birth and offered to stay with Missy and the baby through the night. Once Caroline was convinced she could do no more for Missy and that the girl simply needed sleep more than anything, she consented when Shane said they should go.

They walked out into a night filled with streaks of lightning followed quickly by resounding thunder.

"I'm proud of you, Red. You did a wonderful job."

Caroline looked up at him. Every inch of her ached with exhaustion. Even her mind ached from the conflicting emotions of the last several hours. At that moment she had no idea what to feel. But then she took in Shane's clearly proud countenance and she felt her spirits soar.

He took her hand and pulled her close. She could feel the steady beat of his heart against his ribs. She felt safe and right and she never wanted to let go. And she realized then that she didn't have to—she didn't have to let go because they *would* be together—forever.

Laughter gurgled up inside her. She felt alive and excited. "I did do a great job, didn't I?"

With a low chuckle Shane tightened his hold. "Yes, you did. Once this gets around, your line of patients will only get longer." He shook his head. "And I'll have an even more difficult time getting you alone."

Caroline smiled. "Well, Mr. Rivers, I think I might be able to fit you in. . . ." She pretended to consider. "Perhaps the second week in December might work."

"That's well over a month from now, you little baggage," he said, his dark gray eyes filled with mirth.

"And you're dreaming if you think I'm going to wait that long."

Caroline's smile grew to laughter. "Impatient, are we?"

For a second it looked as though he could hardly believe the unexpected change in her, as though he might question her. But then he seemed to think better of such an idea, and deep, rumbling laughter filled his chest as he pulled her closer still. "I've got no time for saucy wenches, at least not just now." He leaned down and pressed a hungry kiss to her lips. "For now, we'd best hurry back to the hacienda. With any luck we might make it back before the storm breaks."

CHAPTER

✳

18

As LUCK WOULD have it, no sooner had Shane and Caroline turned toward home than the first drops of rain began to pelt the earth. Within seconds, the storm was down upon them in a gushing deluge. Shane guided their horses to a deserted cottage just beyond the road. Caroline waited in the open doorway while he put the horses in a small lean-to off the side, saw to their needs as best he could, then ran to the house. Stepping from the biting rain into the musty warmth of the one-room shanty, he shut the door behind him.

The tiny room washed black by darkness.

Caroline tensed. Her heart suddenly pounded in her chest. She couldn't seem to catch her breath as the darkness enveloped her. The day had left her exhausted and spent, with few reserves of strength from which to draw. She was tired, susceptible. And when panic threatened she was unable to hold it back, unable to hold back the painful, distant memories that she had locked away long ago.

She reached up, her hands fisting against some imaginary foe. "No!" she cried, her voice edged with fear. But regardless of her protestations, her mind was forced back to that time seemingly so long ago, in her kitchen just when her candle had flickered out.

"Caroline!"

It was a moment before her mind grasped that her name was being called. "Shane?"

"I'm here," he said, moving closer.

Hysteria laced her mind as the memory of muffled footsteps closing in on her grappled with the present. "Open the door, light a lantern. Something. Do something!"

Muted light and rain spilled into the room when Shane flung open the door. He turned back to find Caroline standing deathly still, cast in the silver glow of the stormy light. She choked back a sob.

"What is it, Red?" he demanded, taking the few steps that separated them.

When she didn't move, he removed her wet cloak then pulled her into his arms. She fell into his embrace, pressing her head against his shirt, unwilling to speak. She took a deep breath, breathing in the smell of horse and leather and wet wool—breathing in sanity. And just as she had been doing for the last five years, once again finding herself in the light, she cast unwanted memories aside.

His hand came to her face. His fingers were cool, soothing her brow. "What happened?"

"Nothing."

"That was not 'nothing,'" he countered quietly.

"Just afraid of the dark," she murmured into his solid chest. "Silly little schoolgirl fears."

He tightened his hold. "I've known you to be many things, but silly has never been one of them."

Finally, she pulled away, refusing to meet his eyes.

The floor was fast becoming soaked from the driving rain.

"I'll build a fire," she offered, stubbornly refusing to answer his questions. She moved toward the hearth. "Then we can close the door."

Shane eyed her closely, seeming to decide not to press her, then forced a chuckle. "Not on your life. I've seen what you can do with wood and flames. I'll build it while you rummage around for a blanket."

Dried logs lay forgotten in the fireplace. Within minutes Shane had a small fire burning. Caroline found a blanket. Shaking dust from its folds, she set the woolen fabric on the rough-planked floor in front of the heat. She stepped back to take in the room.

"Oh, Shane, look," she exclaimed.

Shane followed her gaze. "What is it?"

"A mirror!" She hurried to the darkened corner.

She took hold of the side and tried to pull it from its dusty resting place.

"Step back, Caroline. You're going to hurt yourself." He picked up the mirror with ease and brought it near the fire.

Caroline found an old rag and wiped the dust from the wooden frame and silvered face. "It's beautiful."

And it was. Full-length, oval, and finely etched around the edges. "Who could have left such a thing?"

"Emma will know who was here last. Many times folks have to move on, and with each stop, they have to leave more and more behind. They start out back east with a wagon load of finery and come to find all they need is practicality."

"But wouldn't they have sold it?"

Shane considered for a moment. "Perhaps they went where they didn't need money. Much as Missy Surlock's parents have obviously done."

"What do you mean?" She hesitated. "Oh. They died." Her face tightened. Her throat burned. She had tried so hard to keep her emotions at bay, throughout the delivery ordeal and then throughout her panicked recollection. But now, at the thought of someone else's misfortune, all that she had suspended threatened to come crashing back.

With tight control, she lowered herself to the floor, her long skirt pooling around her, to sit before the heat of the fire, trying to hold on to her wavering calm. Shane stretched out on the blanket behind her, his weight resting on his elbow. He watched as she sat with legs crossed, her elbows on her knees, staring into the flickering flames.

"Do you want to tell me about it?" he finally asked.

After some time she said, "No."

"Sometimes it helps to talk about your fears."

"No," she repeated, her voice strained. "It only makes them worse."

"Red." He reached up and touched her shoulder.

Her breath caught in her throat and she began to shake. She felt vulnerable and unequipped to deal with this world. For every stride she had made with her students, and for all her growing sense of strength, Emma's story, Missy's situation, and memories of the past combined and seemed to negate all her progress.

Shane leaned forward and saw the glimmer of tears in her eyes. He pulled her around until they faced each other, though her eyes remained fixed on her hands.

She sat before him, steeped in golden light, the glint of tears staining her cheeks. Her face shone like a flame, shimmering, burning. Her hair tumbled wildly, and her porcelain-white skin burned with color. He took her in, all at once, though each separate detail stood out clearly in his mind. He willed her to meet his gaze, and after a moment she did. She looked suddenly like a fairy-tale flower, too fragile for the real world. He felt the need to touch her, to soothe her fears away.

"Hold me," she whispered. The words were spoken in a soft imploring voice that wrapped around him, making him groan. "Please, hold me," she whispered again.

After so many days of her taunting and avoiding him, his heart rocked in his chest, unable to believe her request. But her statement hung in the air, unretracted. And when she looked at him with those haunted green eyes, so captivating, so alluring, he took her in his arms as gently as if she were a porcelain doll.

Cradling her against his chest, he thought only to comfort her. He held her close, murmuring gentle words into her ear. She reached up and traced his face with her finger, and when it came to his lips, he took the tip in his mouth. With the touch, the world and all its problems disappeared. He kissed her then, his lips meeting hers in a fleeting embrace, brushing delicately together. Carefully, he kissed her again, along the gracefully arched line of her milk-white neck. He pulled back to look at her, to take in the promise of her eyes, the warmth of her body.

The golden glow of the fire illuminated her flushed face. As always, her beauty stirred him. It was not an ordinary beauty, rather a beauty of the wild prairies and majestic heights of the Rocky Mountains, beauty that a man could not capture or hold, only delight in, savor. Her beauty was not just that of face and body, but of mind and soul as well, astonishing him that she wanted his touch.

She reached up and lightly touched his cheek. "Love me, Shane."

He knew he shouldn't. Not like this. Not until they were married. He knew he should simply stand and go out into the night and check the horses. And yet, like all those years ago, he pulled her to him, slowly. This time his kiss was unyielding, until tentatively she began to respond. "Caroline," he groaned deep in his chest.

Forgetting his misgivings, he gently lowered her to the blanket and stretched out beside her. His body began to burn, slowly, intensely. He nipped at the corner of her mouth, trying to pull back, telling himself he should get up and leave. But like a man out in the cold, he sought her warmth, and in the end he was unable to pull away, unable to turn back from this treacherous journey.

His tongue sought entrance to her mouth. At the touch of tongue on tongue, Shane forgot everything, his only thought being of Caroline, her feel, her warmth. *Caroline*, his mind repeated, over and over, matching the thrust of his tongue.

"I want to see you, sweet Caroline." His finger worked the tiny fastenings of her dress, and when the cool air touched her skin, she turned her head away. "Don't hide from me, Red." With a barely felt touch of his knuckle, he turned her head back. "Look at me. Look at us."

Drawing a deep breath, she closed her eyes, but when she exhaled, they opened again and her fingers found the fastenings of his shirt. "Then I'd see you as well," she said, her voice barely audible over the rain.

But when she started to push his shirt from his shoulders, he stayed her hand. He kissed each knuckle, then wrapped her arm around his neck, pressing her to his hard length, tracing the curve of her ear with his tongue.

A gentle moan escaped her lips when his fingers lightly circled her breast, sending burning shivers to the very center of her being. He dipped his head to flick his tongue across the rosy peak. His arm forced its way beneath her back, bringing her closer to his seeking mouth.

But then, without warning, his body tensed.

When moments passed and he didn't move, Caroline started to pull away. "What—"

Her words were cut off when his hand came to cover her mouth. "Don't move," he whispered in her ear.

Silence. And then it happened. A faint hiss and rattle sounded through the tiny room.

Gossamer images fluttered before Shane's eyes as his mind flashed to another time. A young Shane. Long black braids, running, smiling, laughing; Little Bear at his side, racing, competing. And throwing a knife, over and over again, until Shane was the best.

Unaware of thought, with quick, stealthful movements, Shane rolled away and reached down to his boot. Not a heartbeat had passed before he grabbed a neatly concealed knife and hurled it through the air. The dull thud of metal piercing wood and the sudden mad rustle of snake on the floor echoed against the walls.

The smell of rain and dust mingled in the growing

heat from the fire. The mad rustle ceased as the snake succumbed in the last throes of death and the room grew quiet. Caroline glanced over at the reptile, pulling her dress together. "Ehhh," she offered, her lip curling with disgust.

Shane grinned like a schoolboy.

Caroline shook her head. "You know this isn't the first time I've noted that there isn't much difference between you and Esteban Gonzalez."

Shane's grin grew devilish. "I'm a better throw."

Despite herself, Caroline laughed. "Are you, now? I can think of a few times Esteban has displayed amazing accuracy. Once, not so long ago," she remarked.

One black brow arched. "Luck, I tell you. For all we know, he was aiming for my head."

He rolled to his feet and approached the rattler.

"Perhaps you would kindly dispose of our unwanted guest," Caroline remarked in her schoolmistress tone.

"I'll set it outside, but I'll take it back to the hacienda with us when the rain stops."

"Take it with us? Good Lord, why?"

"Haven't you heard of rattlesnake stew?"

Caroline pulled a face. "Thankfully not."

"Ah, little lady, then you are in for a treat. You thought I scrambled an egg to your liking—just wait until you taste this culinary delight."

Her nose wrinkled. "If it's anything like roasted duck, I'll pass."

"Your unfortunate fowl can hardly compare with the feast I am prepared to make for you."

Caroline snorted as Shane deftly wrapped the dead snake in an old piece of burlap then placed it outside beneath the front step.

He returned, dusting his hands. "Looks like it's clearing up. We should be on our way within the next half hour or so."

He sat down on the blanket beside her, looking pleased.

"Where did you learn to use a knife like that?" she asked while he wiped the blade on the rag she had used to dust.

He turned until he faced the fire, a slight smile flitting across his face. "When we were kids, Little Bear and I used to practice for hours."

"Who is Little Bear?"

"An Indian," he said simply, his tone suddenly void of emotion.

"Little Bear," she said, considering. "What were you called?"

His eyes grew distant, and Caroline could make out the orange flames of fire reflected in the slate-gray depths.

"Fast As the Rivers," he said finally, saying the name in the Indian tongue. "Had I ever had my vision quest to become a warrior, my name would have changed, just as Little Bear is now called Black Bear. But he was Little Bear to me, and he was my friend . . . my cohort in crime, some might say." He smiled. "We were always into some kind of trouble. My father was continually forced to punish me for some escapade . . . but I always knew he was proud." He chuckled. "Once, I galloped through the compound on a packhorse and snatched a freshly cooked slab of venison. My father scolded me severely. But we both knew I hadn't knocked over a single pot or pan. A week later he gave me my own pony."

Silence filled the room.

"Was the pony Midnight?"

"No," he finally said. "I bought Midnight many years later back east. No resemblance between the two. Sky was an Indian war pony. Short, stocky. Midnight is the descendant of an award-winning Thoroughbred. Long and sleek. Altogether a different horse. But Sky was a good horse," he continued. "My mother was scared to death that I was going to get myself killed riding around like I did."

He started to replace the knife in his boot, but Caroline stopped him. "Can I see it?"

Shane hesitated before he offered her the blade. With great care, she took the clearly very old weapon in her hands. He reached over and pointed to the faded colors worked into the handle. "A yellow rising sun over three blue lines. The land, the sea, and the sky. These are the markings of my father's people." A smile tilted his lips. "Years ago I saved my mother from a rattlesnake with this very knife."

Reaching up, Caroline touched his cheek. Without thinking, she said, "Your mother must have been so proud of you."

Shane visibly flinched. His eyes lost their focus. His mind drifted in the garden of memories.

"Look mother!" Shane called proudly, his young thin chest puffed up with pride as he pointed to his knife stuck exactly in the center of a ring on the ground. His mother smiled, her hair in thick blond braids, her blue eyes glowing. Then Shane's mind snagged on old and half-forgotten memories that he had hoped to keep long buried. Suddenly he saw his mother and another childhood. Tight uncomfortable clothes, backbreaking work, hate-filled words, and the whip. He saw

*his knife stuck in a bull's-eye on a wooden wall. His mother
looked at him, her blond hair tangled, and her blue eyes seared
him with her hatred. "Don't show me your heathen tricks,"
she said.*

Shane jerked Caroline's hand away from his face.
"No, my mother wasn't proud of me."

"Shane," Caroline said, reaching out once again.

"No, Caroline," he warned, his eyes cold and hard
as it all came rushing back. Black Bear's unexpected
visit, fighting with Diego, taking his anger and frustration out on Caroline in the classroom—a relentless
onslaught of reminders that he was a savage. Now,
when more than ever he had reason to forget, he was
forced to confront the very thing he had spent an eternity trying not to remember. And he knew then that no
matter what promises he had made to himself under
the heavens, he could not escape his past, he could not
escape who he was. He was a fool to have tried.

Anger and despair permeated his being, filling his
soul. He felt like a wick in a candle with the wax
nearly gone. And strangely he was afraid. Through
years of living with his grandfather in East Texas and
even through years of war, he had never been afraid.
But at the thought of how he would certainly end
up hurting Caroline worse than he already had, fear
wrapped around him and held him like a vise.

He took a deep breath. "Stay away from me."

Caroline watched helplessly, the look in his eyes forbidding, and she knew in that moment that she should
heed his words. But she couldn't. Her father's words
tried to resurface. But she had told herself it was time
to put the past behind her. And it was. It was time
to forgive Shane his lies, because no matter how mis-

guided they were, she had come to realize that Shane Rivers truly believed his accusations. And she knew suddenly that she could forgive him, because despite all logic, she knew she still loved him. Yes, she loved him, she conceded, though she shouldn't. Dear God, help her, for truly she shouldn't. But in spite of what her mind told her, her heart wanted to give in. She wanted to give in to his domineering ways. Give in to his demands of marriage, give in to the demands of her love. She wanted to be there, and be there she would.

Regardless of repercussions.

"Don't push me away, Shane," she whispered. "Let me love you."

She saw his hand fist at his side. The restraint she placed on herself made her head suddenly feel light. She wanted to touch him. And so she did. She reached out and stroked his arm.

"Leave me alone, Caroline," he said through clenched teeth.

She drew a deep breath. "No," she said simply. "I can't seem to do that." She repeated the words he had spoken that first night they had met again by the river.

Surprise flickered across Shane's face, but only for a moment. His slate-gray eyes narrowed. Reaching down, he tilted her chin until their eyes met. His look was so hard and cold Caroline had to force herself not to step back.

"I'll not say it again. You don't know me, Red. You don't know what I am capable of doing to you. You play at games that aren't really games. And you'd do well not to forget it."

Caroline persisted in her touch, to show him that she did know him, despite what he thought. "That's not true, Shane."

"It is true!"

"No," she whispered, and boldly moved closer despite the look that was so full of anger and loathing. Before her courage deserted her, she pressed her head to his chest and her hand to his heart.

He flinched as if burned. With measured movements, he pulled away from her and stood up from the blanket. "The rain has stopped. We'd best be going. Emma will be worried." His words were short and curt.

Caroline came to her knees. "Hold me."

The logs crackled and popped as the fire burned in the hearth. Shane stood immobile. Emotion played havoc with his granite features until something happened, and he snapped. "Hold you," he ground out. "What? Like this?" he demanded, grabbing her arm, yanking her to her feet, forcing her around until her back was pressed up against his naked chest, the edges of his shirt fluttering on either side of her.

She faced the full-length mirror. She saw her fear in the reflection, but held it at bay. Her dress was only partially fastened. Shane reached up and ripped the buttons free. He ignored her gasp and brought his hand up to her breast.

"Like this?" he demanded again. "Do you want me to hold you like this?"

"No," she whispered.

"What? You want this?" He grabbed a handful of material in a deadly grip and pulled, revealing both breasts.

"Shane, don't do this."

"Have you changed your mind?" he hissed.

She could see him in the mirror. His face was ravaged, strained. Hard lines creased his brow, thick veins stood out on his neck.

"Just seconds ago you were begging me to hold you," he added, pulling her bodice away.

Caroline tried to break free from his grip, but he held her captive. She saw anger mix with pain on his face, and she realized that, like a wounded animal, he was lashing out at the very person who was trying to save him from the trap. He was a product of two opposing worlds, but belonged to neither. A man who had no home, no refuge, a man who was filled with anguish. She had to make him see that he had sanctuary with her.

She bit her lip against crying out when he ripped her dress still further, telling herself she would be his home, she would be his refuge. And with that thought she vanquished her fear. Strength surged. The measure of a person is taken when times are hard, she told herself.

"You'll not hurt me, Shane Rivers," she stated firmly as his hands roamed crudely over her nearly naked body.

Then as if to prove her wrong, he pulled her dress free, the coarse material dropping to form a pool of muslin at her feet. He made short work of her undergarments. Then he held her body in a painful grip, her back to his chest, and forced her eyes to the mirror. "You must watch, sweet Caroline, as I prove you wrong. For rest assured, I *will* hurt you. Irreparably."

He forced her legs apart with his boot. Her chin came up a notch as she watched his finely sculpted hand begin to violate her body, sliding from her breasts to the triangle of hair between her thighs. Her body flinched against the impending intrusion, her breath caught in her throat, but she refused to look away.

"You won't hurt me, Shane." A statement of fact. Her words held no doubt.

His hand stilled and their eyes locked in the hazy mirror. Anguished, she watched myriad emotions play havoc with the chiseled planes of his face as his anger melted to despair. Drawing a deep, ragged breath, his jaw cemented. But when he started to let her go, defeated, she quickly slipped around until she faced him. This time she didn't ask him to hold her or kiss her. She had learned. Instead, she reached up and locked her arms around his neck and pulled him down to her lips.

She did not ask, she took, and when he would have pulled away, she said, "No!"

They stared at each other for a lifetime, a battle of wills waging war in the deserted house, until she pulled him closer, and with a strangled cry he lost himself in her embrace.

Their love was frantic. Each surrendering, each forgetting all else.

He ran his hands over her body, testing, feeling, as if he couldn't believe she was really there. The heel of his hand grazed the side to her breast, before he cupped the soft underswell. "You're so beautiful," he said, his voice taut.

He turned her in his arms until she faced the mirror once again. He held her tight when she resisted, his forearm secure beneath her breasts, the throbbing evidence of his desire hard against the small of her back. His hand lowered to the triangle of hair between her thighs, this time with exquisite care. Instinctively, she tried to cover herself.

"No, Caroline. Open your legs for me. Let me show you how it should be done." His words were a demand.

He gently forced her to widen her stance. With maddening attention, his fingers teased the lips of her sex. Against better judgment, she surrendered to sensation. Her head fell back against his chest as she began to tremble and sigh under his touch. A whirlwind of feeling coursed through her body, tingling, pounding, centered in the core of her being.

His fingers penetrated, slowly, carefully, again and again, until unconsciously she spread her legs further.

"Yes, Caroline. Let go."

His fingers went deeper, his thumb brushing against a terribly sensitive spot that she was certain would make her go mad. Her body started to move of its own volition. Her hips shamefully sought his touch. But when she caught sight of the wanton display in the mirror, red singed her cheeks and her body stilled. She turned her head away and futilely tried to cover herself.

"No, Caroline. Look at me." When she didn't, he forced her head back so that their eyes met in the silvered frame. "Don't be ashamed. You're beautiful. You're the most honorable and decent woman I know. Free yourself from the past. Let yourself feel."

After a moment he took her wrists in one of his hands and held them firmly across her chest. Then his fingers began to move again, sliding against the still slick walls of her womanhood. The intensity of feeling rose quickly this time, not building slowly, but starting at a level that left her breathless. She lost herself to the feel, her hips undulating, her head thrown back against his shoulder, as a wave of soul-shattering intensity washed over her and she cried out.

He held her to him, his hand pressing against her quivering sex, his face buried in her hair. As her body relaxed, he lowered her with infinite care to the blanket and cradled her against his body. When finally her heart began to slow and she thought she might survive the world-shattering experience, she pressed her lips to his chest. His groan of pleasure made her bold and she took one nipple into her mouth.

"Damn," he growled, his body tensing.

Caroline cringed and looked up at him. "Have I done something wrong? Don't you want me anymore?"

Shane inhaled through his teeth and stared at her. Slowly, he took her hand and guided it to his hardness, proving his desire. "Yes, I want you, more than anything." He would have said more, but her fingers closed around him. He fell back, his eyes pressed closed as she stroked the length of him, tentatively at first, then with more assurance when he reached down and guided her hand.

They became frantic once again, rolling and grasping, panting, their hands roaming freely. He moved between her thighs and pushed her knees apart. "I can't wait any longer." He brought his burgeoning manhood up to her sweet opening. "This is going to hurt," he said with deep regret. But she only pulled him to her, his sex plunging deep inside. She stiffened and he held still. "The worst is over," he said, kissing her forehead and cheeks.

Gradually, he started to move within her, slowly at first as she became accustomed to his size, then faster, deeper, and she began to feel waves of sensation pulse through her body once again.

"Oh, Shane," she cried when she thought she could bear it no longer.

"Reach, Caroline, reach for it," he panted into her throat as he moved within her.

Her hands caught in the soft cambric of his shirt as she tried to pull him closer. But she paid it no mind when he pulled nearly out only to come into her again, hard, fast, deep, and she seemed to explode into tiny little pieces, her body alive with sensation.

He drove into her one last time and she felt him shudder with his release, whispering her name as he did. Caroline felt tears sting at her eyes, for in that moment she felt whole, complete—totally and utterly happy—proof that indeed she shared a life's bond with this man.

CHAPTER

✸

19

SHANE REINED IN at Ben Dowell's Saloon. He wanted a drink. He wanted to forget.

Sounds of music and merriment filtered to the street. When he pushed through the saloon door, several men shouted at him to join them. But he had no interest in camaraderie, only in the black void.

His long stride brought him to the bar.

"Evening, Shane," Ben Dowell called.

"Dowell," Shane said simply with a nod of his head.

"What will it be?"

"Whiskey, straight up."

Ben laughed as he found a new bottle. "Out here we don't serve it much any other way. Don't get much call for splashes of soda or water," he said, wiping the counter in front of Shane before he set down the bottle and a glass.

Shane poured a shot. "To your health," he said before he tossed the liquor back.

His eyes burned as the liquor seared a path down his throat to his belly. But still the scene in the deserted shack played itself unmercifully in his head. In his mind's eye he saw Caroline—fear, and determination not to show the fear, mingling in her eyes. He had come so close to . . . raping her.

He poured another shot and drank it down, willing the vision to cease. He caught sight of his face in the smoky mirror that lined the bar. Disgusted, he looked away.

Pouring another drink, he scanned the familiar faces reflected in the mirror. Suddenly his hand stilled. For a second Shane thought his mind was playing tricks on him. But the fancily clad man who stood at the back of the bar, his eyes open wide with astonishment, was all too real. With deadly calm, Shane swiveled on his stool until he faced the man.

"Well. Dean Fowler. We meet again."

Sweat beaded on the other man's forehead.

"What brings you to town?" Shane asked.

Dean flushed before a curtain of bravado came down and he strode toward the bar. "On my way to California. I've got a man anxious to run for governor out that way who wants my help. Met some people here, though." He shrugged his shoulders. "Ended up staying awhile. What about you? Last I heard, you were running from the law."

Shane's jaw tensed, and for a moment he thought he would take Dean Fowler in his hands and snap him in two. But he held back, forcing himself to remain calm. "Charges were dropped."

"Yeah." Dean grinned. "I guess I heard that." With a reckless disregard for his safety, he came up next to Shane at the bar. "Suspect you heard Whitley lost his bid for governor."

"I heard." Shane went back to the bottle, poured another shot, and drained the glass.

"You were engaged to his daughter, as I recall," Dean stated nonchalantly.

"You know damn well I was, Fowler. What game are you playing? You jealous of her past loves now that you're married to her?"

"Married? To Henrietta? Hell, no," he scoffed. "Thought about it for a while, but wised up to her ways. Her father took to drinking, and she had a shrew's own tongue."

"Spare me the details. I'm not interested."

"No, I suppose you're not. No hard feelings, I hope?"

Shane eyed him in the mirror, then took another drink to wash the bitterness away.

"What brings you out west?" Dean asked when he received no reply. "Could it have anything to do with the fact that one Miss Caroline Bromley is in town?"

Shane jerked up from his seat, amber liquid sloshing on the bar. In seconds he had Dean Fowler's lapels in his fists. "What do you know about Caroline?"

"Now, Rivers, don't get all riled up," Dean stammered, the bravado gone. "Just a fellow in here who I met that said she's a schoolteacher or something out at his place. No harm meant."

The man, Shane knew, could only be Diego. The realization sickened him and filled him with concern that Diego and Dean Fowler had discussed Caroline, perhaps had spoken of her past. And if it was true, he knew Diego would use the information against her. "What did you tell him?" he demanded.

"Nothing," Dean sputtered. "Nothing at all."

Shane eyed the other man, and knew that he lied. "Stay away from her, Fowler. Do you understand me? I don't even want to hear that you've mentioned her name. If you're smart, you'll head out of town at first light and continue on to California."

Dean was arched over the bar like a bow without an arrow. "You don't scare me, Rivers." He sneered, though his eyes were fearful as Shane tightened his hold.

"Señor! Señor Shane!"

Shane turned to the voice, the muscles twitching in his jaw. Esteban stood in the doorway, panting as if he had run the whole way from the hacienda.

"It is Miss Caroline! She is gone!"

"What are you talking about?" Shane demanded, dropping Dean to the floor. "What's happened to her?"

"She is gone, señor! I tell you she is gone. We looked everywhere."

Shane tossed Ben Dowell a silver coin, then ran from the bar, Esteban close at his heels. He barely noted the mule Esteban had ridden in on as he leaped onto his saddle and headed for the hacienda. All he could think about as the miles flew beneath him was that he had finally pushed her too far and she had fled. And who could blame her? But that didn't make it any easier to let her go. And he knew then that he couldn't.

He arrived at Cielo el Dorado to a scene of chaos. In the *sala* he found Henry trying to console Emma, Beth wailing, and Reina and Diego sitting calmly to the side.

"What's happened?" Shane demanded.

"She's gone, Shane," Henry said.

"She can't be far. I brought her back to the hacienda myself not more than an hour ago."

"The guards saw you and Caroline arrive, then saw you ride off again, but Caroline never came through the gate."

"Are you sure you've looked everywhere? What about the *acequia*? Or has anyone checked the depot?"

"Cousin, cousin," Diego said as he stood from a hard-backed chair. "You have mistaken the situation. Caroline has not simply left to go back to wherever she came from." He held up his hand to reveal a tomahawk with a lock of fiery red hair tied to the handle. "My guess is that your . . . family has come and taken her away."

Shane froze. He couldn't think.

"Shane!" Emma shrieked.

Slowly, he turned to her, his mind awash with dark images.

"They've taken her!" she cried as Henry took her into his arms. "They were here. Indians! I should have known. I should have felt their presence."

Diego glanced from Emma to Shane. "Your heathen *family*, I'm afraid, continually wreaks havoc on Grandmother's life."

It seemed impossible. Too difficult to take in. But the markings on the tomahawk and Caroline's red hair told the truth. Caroline was taken. By Black Bear, he was certain. The reason was clear.

To make him follow.

Riddled by despair, he thought of the scene in the deserted house, the reappearance of Dean Fowler, and now the capture of Caroline. How was he to keep her safe? Every time he turned around, it seemed he was itemizing all the ways he had caused Caroline pain.

"I'll find her and bring her back," he stated, his words a vehement promise. And though he knew he caused her nothing but grief, he also knew, as Emma had told him, that Caroline needed the safety and respectability of his name. "And when we return we will be married."

Diego sucked in his breath. Turning with fury in his eyes, Shane came to face his cousin.

"I'm afraid, cousin, that we are destined to come to a serious parting of the ways."

Diego lurched forward, but Emma hurriedly stepped between her grandsons. "You need only concern yourself with Caroline right now."

Shane's eyes bored into Diego for one last moment before he strode from the room without another word.

A slight breeze rustled through the courtyard, pushing dried leaves along in its path. Coiled like a spring, Shane made his way to his room and shut the door behind him. For a moment he leaned back against the hardwood plank, his eyes pressed closed, before he pushed away and walked to an old leather trunk that sat forgotten in the corner. He had cursed Emma when he found that she had brought the trunk with her in the move from East Texas. Now he was thankful.

The hinges protested when he pulled the lid free. Camphor tingled in his nose. Visions of long black braids wafted through his mind. He pulled a multicolored tightly woven blanket from the trunk. It smelled of sunshine long forgotten, reminding him of Indian war cries and laughter as he and Little Bear raced along the sandy path then leaped off the cliff, arms flailing, legs churning, to splash in the cool, deep waters below.

His mind drifted.

Beneath the blanket lay fine Indian clothing, well preserved. He pulled a breechclout from the depths, a simple length of leather made when he had still been certain that his father would come for him. Next, he found colored powders, moccasins, leggings, and a blue shirt of soft leather—all meant to have been presents for his father and his father's father upon Shane's return to the tribe. But no one had ever come, and the Indian trappings had been forgotten. Now, years later, he was forced to seek out the tribe on his own in the very garments that were meant to have been their gifts.

Shane stepped from his cambric shirt and snugly fitting trousers to fasten the leather around his lean hips. He pulled the soft blue shirt on over his head and belted it at the waist. It hung almost to his knees. A thick cluster of metal cones sewn to the long fringes of the dark blue leggings jingled as he tied the coverings on. When he stood, the sound was somehow both delicate and strong, masculine.

He found a beaten silver disk with a hole in the center and two eagle feathers attached. He worked the piece into a scalp lock in his hair before pulling on high moccasins with fringes at the calves.

He stood tall, his mind floating. He left behind the confines of the small adobe room. Strength and power built in his body as he found the small bags of colored powders. He took a pinch of red and spit into it, stirred it around, then ran three streaks across each cheek and two down his chin. One last search produced a necklace of eagle feathers similar to the ones in his hair.

You are an eagle, Fast As the Rivers. He remembered the words. *You fly fast and free, and soar into the heavens.*

He settled the feathers around his neck. His eyes darkened and the rise and fall of his chest slowed.

He had shed the white man's clothes and dressed as his father's people. And by doing so he stepped into a different place and time where the white man's reality no longer existed.

Long rays of the full moon glistened through the mullioned window. Silver light washed over him. He was both set free and enslaved by the path he suddenly found himself on. He was going to confront the tribe into which he was born. He would face the past—but only to save his sweet Caroline.

Shane Rivers was gone. A barely remembered Fast As the Rivers had returned in his place.

CHAPTER

✳

20

AT FIRST SHE was afraid. Scared to death might better have described her feelings, but Caroline refused to give in to the trembling that tried to rattle her brain. If ever she needed her wits about her, it was now.

She bounced along on her horse, her ankles secured by a rawhide strap that passed beneath her horse's belly. For the first time ever she was thankful for her practical black boots. To think, she thought dismally, when she had first arrived, she had been fearful that Mexican *bandidos* would swim across the river and murder her. Ha!

Though she had tried to turn a deaf ear to the tales of Indian savagery over the years, she couldn't help but hear a story or two about the gruesome and torturous deaths Indians inflicted upon their captives. The bandits, she mused unreasonably, would have proved a piece of cake compared with the fate she was afraid she was being served.

Under the bright night sky they rode for hours at a stomach-jolting trot on a road so narrow at points that her legs were scraped by the brush. Her Indian captor deftly guided his mount to avoid the woody branches, but Caroline, even under the best of circumstances, could not have managed her horse so well. As a result, her skirt snagged on thorns and brittle twigs, adding to her overall misery.

Her eyes bored into the bare, bronzed back of her captor. She recalled the gaudy red paint that slashed across the hawklike features of his cheeks and chin. His deep-set dark eyes had rings of black paint around them, giving him a startled appearance, though she knew all too well that she was the only one who had been surprised when he came upon her by the *acequia*. Even from this distance, when the breeze was just right, she could smell the smoke, tallow, leather, and something else she couldn't identify, that had nearly made her retch when he had manhandled her into the saddle.

His long black braids were wrapped in deerskin and beat against his back as they rode. He wore soft tan leggings that came to the top of his naked thighs. His dark blue breechclout fluttered like a flag behind him, giving Caroline the most unfortunate view of bare buttock. Naked thighs and bare buttock, her mind cried. Had this man no decency?

To keep her eyes from places they had no business going, she noted the lance with which he rode. Her head cocked to the side as she took in the deadly sharp flint head and the multicolored feathers that fluttered wildly in the breeze. Then she saw it. The bright yellow rising sun over three blue marks. The same sign that was on Shane's knife. The sight staggered her. This man who had captured her was from Shane's tribe.

Her discomfort and fear crystallized first into disbelief then into fury, leaving no room for caution.

"How—" The word caught in her dry and parched throat. She swallowed a few times, her eyes searing the Indian's back. "How dare you!"

She had not spoken since they had left the river, and the sound of her voice clearly startled the man. He jerked around and glared at her as if he had only just realized she was still there. And that made her all the angrier.

"How dare you, you . . . you . . . beast!"

His black eyes stared back at her, their horses still moving forward, until he turned away and continued pressing forward.

"Don't you dare ignore me!" she demanded. "You should be ashamed of yourself. One of Shane's own tribesmen capturing the woman whom . . . well . . ." She hesitated before she raised her chin. "Whom he has stated he will marry."

No response.

"I am speaking to you, sir! Have you nothing to say to me? Have you no shame? How could you capture someone dear to one of your own?" She realized she was pressing her luck in stating that she was dear to Shane. Just that second she was not altogether certain where she stood in the man's regard. He had been so silent and closed off from her when he had left her at the hacienda gate. But just then, accuracy didn't top her list of priorities. Survival did. And when the Indian still failed to respond, her anger redoubled, suppressing her fear.

"You are no gentleman, sir!" she stated only to shake her head in the next second. As if he cared. He had made it more than clear that gentlemanly behavior was not his forte. Flashing bare buttocks were proof enough of that fact.

"Have you no tongue in your mouth?" she harangued.

Suddenly she realized he might not speak English. Perhaps she should test him, she reasoned. "Fire!" she cried.

He failed to turn.

"Attack!"

Nothing.

"Your horse is a cow."

Still nothing.

"You are as ugly as a toad!"

Slowly, menacingly, he turned on the tightly woven blanket that served as a saddle. He still didn't say anything, but he provided her with a glare that would have cowed a lesser woman, or man for that matter. Certainly, her inclination was to shrink away. But she would not give in to such cowardice, she told herself as she straightened in her saddle.

"I'm thirsty," she stated, while at the same time bringing an imaginary cup to her lips.

He seemed to debate until finally he grunted, slowed, grabbed something that was attached to the rawhide surcingle that circled his mount, and tossed it to her.

Remarkably, she caught it, but then nearly dropped it when she realized it had once been the stomach of some unknown animal. Being a woman of medicine did nothing to alleviate the disgust she experienced upon discovering that the intestine was filled with water. Her imagination ran free with thoughts of all that had passed through the body part before it was removed from its unfortunate owner then filled with water.

For half a second she weighed her options. Grasping the fact that she had none unless she was willing to suffer from thirst, she closed her eyes, lifted the bag, and drank. Unaware that her Indian captor had stopped, she was startled when he snatched the drinking pouch from her after no more than a few measly drops had passed her lips.

"What are you doing? I'm still thirsty!" She reached for the bag.

With swift and easy movements he secured the bag back to the surcingle and urged his pinto forward. Her horse followed, and after no more than fifty feet, her stomach sloshing miserably, she conceded the wisdom of her captor.

They rode silently. The distant call of coyotes mocked her stupidity. What a fool she was for venturing to the *acequia* at night. How often had Shane told her it was not safe to venture out unprotected? He had asked her before if she hated him so much that she would put herself in danger just to thwart him. *Au contraire!* she thought miserably. It was the fact that she loved him so much and was afraid of that love that caused her to do such stupid things. And going to the river to think had certainly proved to be just that. Stupid!

When she could stand the direction of her thoughts no more, she started in once again on her captor.

"Shane isn't going to like this one bit once he finds I'm gone." She waited in vain for a response before she launched into a scathing lecture that lasted for a good long while. Just as the Indian groaned his frustration her mouth snapped shut. She became aware of faint sounds that echoed in the night.

She caught sight of a fire that glimmered in the distance. They moved steadily toward the orange glow until they came to a sea of horses pulling at tufts of grass. Soon the horses were behind them and Caroline took in the hide-covered conical tents. Lodges—the name came to her. She heard the gentle flow of the river as it snaked alongside the camp. A cool breeze rustled through the cottonwood trees. She took a deep breath, but still her fear began to resurface, pushing all traces of bravado away. What if they burned her at the stake? No, she reasoned, that only happened to witches in Salem, or so she hoped. Suddenly she wasn't sure. What she was sure of was that Indians were quick with a knife to the scalp. Her forehead tingled with foreboding.

They came to the largest lodge, which had a huge sun over three blue lines painted on its side, shining over the vast sea of similar, though smaller, conical tents. The largest man she had ever seen stood just outside the threshold of his home. He crossed his arms on his ponderous belly and ran his eyes over Caroline as if she were a piece of livestock, her mind raged indignantly. Her teeth clenched and her spine straightened, and she was certain that the man almost smiled.

He looked away and she made out his profile silhouetted against the orange backdrop of the raging fire. Her breath caught in her throat when for one mindboggling moment she thought it was Shane. Clarity came painfully when he turned back to her, and she realized with a start that this man was not only some sort of a chief, but a relative of Shane's as well.

"How dare you!" She spewed out the heated words without thinking.

Caroline launched into a diatribe that brought first a look of surprise then a look of impatience from the enormous man. He turned away from her and glared at her captor.

"I had no choice, Strong One," her captor stated with a shrug.

Caroline had no idea what they said since they weren't speaking English, but she watched and listened intently just the same.

"You had no choice, Black Bear?" the monument of a man continued, one dark brow raised quizzically.

Other warriors had started to gather around.

"My friend would not come. Hair Like Fire is his woman. Now he will follow."

Strong One flicked a glance at Caroline. "With a mouth like hers, my grandson might thank us for taking her off his hands."

The small group laughed. Caroline still failed to understand their words but their tone and disparaging looks were universal. She knew they were making fun of her. She snapped her mouth shut and threw the man a withering glare, before she launched into a new, more vigorous lecture.

Strong One hung his head, his thick gray braids falling forward. "Gag her to stop her incessant chatter. Then put her in Walks Many Miles's lodge. She will stay there until Fast As the Rivers comes."

And then she understood. Fast As the Rivers. The name Shane had told her he was called. She nearly fell from her mount when she realized that she was obviously being used as bait to lure Shane into their clutches.

Her sudden burst of kicks and screams didn't seem to faze the men as they dragged her from her horse, bound and gagged her, and carried her off. Part of her said to give in, but another part said she mustn't go down without a fight. And fight she did until they stopped at a lodge toward the edge of the encampment, opened the entrance flap, and unceremoniously dumped her inside.

The men left her bound, her face on the ground, choking on the dust. Her body ached and her bravado ebbed entirely. She lay immobile. A tear snuck out of the corner of her eye, streaking a wet path across her grimy face, then was lost to the ground. Squeezing her eyes firmly shut for half a second, she rolled over and stared up into the narrowing heights that ended in a perfectly round hole at the top. A cookie-cutter shape of stars glistened in the sky. She focused on them, refusing to think, and before long, exhaustion and anger and fear overwhelmed her and she lost herself to sleep.

Fright filled her.

Wrenched from a deep sleep, she couldn't catch her breath. She felt as though she were being pressed into the earth. When she tried to move, she couldn't. Her eyes blinked in the semidarkness as she tried to clear the sleep from her mind. When her sight adjusted, her heart seemed to stop as she realized that an Indian was lying half on top of her. She started to scream despite the gag, but was stopped by a large hand that covered her mouth. Her eyes grew wide with desperation.

Her body went into action, fighting, kicking, screaming silently into the rag.

"Caroline," her captor hissed through gritted teeth as he tried to subdue her.

At first her name failed to register in her mind.

"Caroline, it's me."

She stilled. Relief came slowly, but when it did, understanding left her weak. She would have cried out to him had she been able. Shane had come for her.

"Caroline," he whispered. He retrieved his ever-present knife and cut the rawhide strips from her ankles and wrists.

Blood surged through her limbs like a hundred pin-pricks of heat. Her hands and feet burned and itched, and she moaned into the gag. She started to sit, but Shane held her down.

"Hold still, Red. It's going to be all right."

He rubbed life back into her limbs, testing her fingers and toes. Voices sounded in the distance. He stretched out beside her to whisper in her ear. "Just lie still and don't make a sound."

He cut the gag from her mouth, and she had to resist the urge to cry out with thankfulness. She worked her lips until she remembered.

"Shane," she whispered furtively, her discomfort forgotten. "This is a trap. We have to get away from here."

Shane held her near. "I suspected as much. My grandfather gets what he wants. And it doesn't matter who gets hurt in the process."

"I knew it," she hissed. "I knew he was some relative of yours. But your grandfather? How could he be so cruel?"

"In his mind he is not being cruel. You simply are a means to an end. And I am that end."

"Why? What does he want from you?"

"I don't know, but I have no interest in staying around to find out."

"How are we going to sneak out of here? There are people all around."

"I made it in, didn't I?" Shane smiled boyishly, a flash of white teeth glimmering in the slice of moonlight.

"When you were by yourself and barely clothed, I might add. Not with a woman in long rustling skirts."

"We can take care of the skirts." His eyes grew serious.

"How?"

He gazed at her lips then leaned down to gently brush them with his own.

Caroline gasped. "Good God, how can you be thinking of kissing at a time like this? Shane!" She pushed at his shoulders. "Not now. The next time we make love," she began, red surging through her cheeks. "The next time will be special. Not like this."

Shane pulled back and looked into her eyes. "Will there be a next time, sweet Caroline?"

Her embarrassment intensified and her heart beat wildly out of control. She ran her fingers along his jaw, streaking through the smudges of paint. He took her finger and brought it up to her face and gently marked her cheekbone with color. When she failed to answer, he tightened his hold.

"I'm sorry," he whispered.

Confusion etched her brow.

"I'm sorry for what happened in the cabin."

Understanding dawned and she quickly shook her head. "Please don't be sorry." She took his finger and ran it through the colored streaks of paint. With infinite care, she guided his hand to her face and ran another line along her cheek. "I don't think I could bear it if you were sorry for what we shared. We're together— for the good and the bad."

He buried his face in her hair and held tight. She could feel his pain, and she desperately wanted to soothe him. But he pulled back and looked down into her eyes before she could speak.

"No matter what happens, Caroline, whether we manage to get away or not, know that I will gain your release. No matter what it takes."

"Shane—"

But her words were cut short when amber light flooded the lodge, catching them in its path. Shane leaped to his feet in one swift and easy motion, his knife held out before him, Caroline at his back.

"My grandson," Strong One said, his features hard and cold. "I have been expecting you."

CHAPTER

✳

21

WHEN CAROLINE WOKE again, she was alone. She saw no sign to confirm Shane's arrival during the night. Fear pricked at her heart. What if it had simply been a dream?

She caught sight of the cut and discarded rawhide strips that had bound and gagged her lying on the ground. She sighed her relief. It hadn't been a dream.

The flap to her tent flipped open, revealing not the much-hoped-for Shane, but a large woman who barely fit through the entryway. "I am Many Moons," she grumbled in stilted, but perfect, English, as she took in Caroline's disheveled appearance. She turned and eyed her surroundings. "I must apologize for this humble lodge. Walks Many Miles does not spend much time at the encampment, and when he is here, he eats with my family. With no woman, he has little need for niceties."

Caroline huddled beneath her blanket and stared at the woman, who walked in and started a conversation as if she and Caroline had not come together under less than ideal circumstances.

The woman toed the thin mattress on which Caroline lay, then snorted her obvious disgust. "Come, Hair

Like Fire. I will have Sunshine make this lodge comfortable for you. For now you come with me, and I will find you something to eat."

"Where is Shane?" Caroline croaked.

The woman considered for a moment. "Ah, you speak of Fast As the Rivers. He is with my brother, Strong One."

Caroline considered this piece of information and made a quick deduction. "Is Strong One his grandfather?"

"Of course," Many Moons stated with pride.

"Then you're Shane's great-aunt," Caroline said, finding it difficult to hide her shock.

Many Moons smiled, the gesture pulling her face into a web of many wrinkles. "Yes, he is the son of my nephew who has been to the Great Beyond for many years. I am glad Fast As the Rivers has returned." The smile faded. "Come, we eat."

Caroline wasn't sure if she wanted to go anywhere with this oversized great-aunt or not. The woman looked nothing like anyone she had ever met. But as was usual where Caroline was concerned, hunger and curiosity won out and she followed Many Moons. Besides, she reasoned, these people were Shane's family. Surely they wouldn't hurt her. She glanced uneasily at Many Moons. Surely.

In the light of day, the sea of lodges looked much larger than it had the night before. Women clustered together, laughing and sewing soft leather with what Caroline determined to be bone awls, pointed and polished from use. Racks of drying meat stood around the area. The sudden image of a young Shane racing along to snatch a slab of meat nearly made her laugh out loud. A dear, sweet, no doubt troublesome little Shane, she added. How she would have loved to have known him as a child.

Roaming dogs barked and followed children who ran and played. The women hesitated in their work to watch Caroline pass. While the newness intrigued her, all she could think about was finding Shane. But everywhere she looked, she saw no trace of him.

Many Moons led Caroline to the lodge with the bright yellow sun and three blue lines. Upon entering, she was amazed at the difference between the lodge she had slept in and this one. A small fire burned in the center of the floor. An old copper kettle hung on a tripod over the heat. The smell of roasting meat wafted through the lodge. On a small hide lay some sort of a bone obviously used to stir, a handcrafted wooden bowl, and a large butcher knife. The smoke spiraled up from the fire to escape through the cookie-cutter hole many hazy feet above.

Two raised bedsteads stood along the curved wall. Furs and buffalo robes appeared to serve as blankets. Rawhide boxes used for storage were stacked neatly underneath wooden pegs that were driven into the smooth tent poles from which tools, clothes, weapons, and ornaments hung.

Many Moons offered Caroline a meal of succulent meat that smelled of onions and herbs and a bowl of corn mush. As the woman busied herself about the lodge Caroline ate her surprisingly filling meal with relish.

It was several hours later when she finally caught sight of Shane in the distance. He sat with other men, talking and laughing, until his grandfather stood and he followed him away. Upon seeing Shane safe, her last bit of reserve melted away, and she relaxed and actually began to enjoy meeting the women and children of the tribe.

But her sense of safety began to crumble later that day when the sun sank on the horizon with no further sight of Shane. Late that night, Caroline finally fell into the newly cleaned lodge of Walks Many Miles, who thankfully was out walking many miles, and was nearly asleep when Shane ducked through the door. Instantly, she was wide-awake. He, however, looked exhausted.

He still wore his Indian garb, which somehow suited him in a way that his white man's clothes never had. Without a word he slipped beneath the blanket and pulled Caroline into his arms. He didn't speak, simply held her close.

Caroline's heart fluttered in her chest. He smelled of wood smoke and brisk winds, and she wondered if he would kiss her. Her heart pounded at the thought. But after no more than a few measly minutes, though she had never slept with another soul in her life, she recognized the deep even breathing of sleep. Shane Rivers was asleep. Apparently there would be no kisses.

She chastised herself for her wanton ways, but somehow the reprimand was lost on her. Suddenly kissing Shane no longer seemed so terribly wrong. He was a good man, a strong man. Pressed so closely to him, she could feel the strength of him through his soft shirt. But it wasn't simply the power of muscles she felt or that she could tell he was strong and aggressive and tough, that he could fight and protect. She could feel that there was an inner power to the man. He had courage. He had the courage to be kind and love and to hold his awesome physical strength at bay when need be. And this strength, this courage, was real. He was real, and they were finally together, not fighting, not at odds, but lying peacefully in each other's arms. Nothing else mattered. Not the past, not the future, only now.

With butterfly strokes, she caressed his brow. She thought about all that had passed between them and about all she had learned of his past. She lay in his arms as the moon passed through the heavens. And sometime around midnight, at just that moment when the new day begins, she pressed her hand to his chest and whispered a promise. "You saved me, Shane Rivers. Now I'm going to return the favor. I'm going to tear down your walls and heal your heart."

And then Caroline drifted off into a deep dreamless sleep, secure in the arms of the man she loved.

Days passed, all seeming much the same as the first. Many Moons and the women of the tribe taught Caroline the ways of the Comanche. Then, at night, Shane would slip into the lodge, pull her close, and they would drift off to sleep.

With each day that passed, Caroline experienced a growing sense of freedom. Once Shane had promised that as soon as he could he would send word to Emma so she could cease worrying, Caroline began to explore her surroundings and delve into adventures as never before. Needless to say, her exploits often led her into precarious positions that had Strong One and Many Moons shaking their heads in wonder that anyone could get into so much trouble and survive.

The People, as Caroline had come to learn Shane's tribe was called, lived in harmony with the land, and the rules and restrictions of the white man's world didn't apply. The People were kind and loving, making Caroline wonder if all the horrid stories she had heard about them were lies. She wondered if it was solely the white man who inflicted horrors on the native people. But it only took one look at some warrior's necklace of scalp hair to prove that there was at least a modicum of truth to the tales.

She came to know Black Bear and Strong One, who she learned had a soft heart despite his fearsome appearance. She also came to suspect Strong One had gout—a condition not usually associated with the People.

"Come, Hair Like Fire." Many Moons broke into her reverie. "The men have brought buffalo. We must clean the hides and prepare them for tanning."

"Me! But I don't know how."

"You will learn. Come."

Caroline halted abruptly when they came to a clearing. Pots of boiling water bubbled all around. Intestines and tripe were set to boil while the meat was hung on racks to dry. Women bent over the fresh hides. They talked and laughed, seemingly unaware of the stomach-churning stench that permeated the area. Many Moons motioned for Caroline to follow. With great reluctance she did.

Hides with flesh, muscle, and fur still attached were stretched out on the ground and staked down with small pegs around the edges. The women worked the better part of the day, Many Moons beside Caroline, relentlessly instructing. Kneeling over a small hide, Caroline learned to pare off the worst of the fat and muscle with an elk-horn-and-flint adz. Then it was scraping, back and forth, evenly and smoothly, shaving down the flesh a little with each stroke until the hide was revealed.

Sweat trickled down her face, leaving trails through the grit and grime. Caroline would have tossed her flesher aside and admitted defeat if she hadn't caught sight of Shane just then. He looked every inch the Indian warrior. Tall and lithe, sinewy muscles rippling as he walked alongside Black Bear. Their eyes met, and when he noted what she was doing, his face grew skeptical and he approached.

"Are you sure you should be handling such sharp objects?" he teased as he knelt before her.

Caroline was all too aware that her hair was stringy and dirty and that grime streaked across her face. Sweat soaked her clothes. She grumbled and turned back to her hide.

With a chuckle he stood. "This afternoon I'll take you to the river so you can clean up." Then he walked back to Black Bear and they disappeared among the sea of lodges.

The afternoon failed to arrive soon enough, but when Shane finally appeared, a sense of pride filled Caroline when he nodded his appreciation for the small hide that had been cleaned of flesh and fur.

They walked toward the river, a thick folded blanket underneath Shane's arm. He dropped the blanket on the ground and stretched out beside it.

"Aren't you going in?" she asked with a wanton twist of disappointment.

"Is that what you want? For me to get in with you?" he asked, his lips tilting devilishly, bringing a surge of red to Caroline's cheeks.

"Well, no . . . I mean . . ."

"Get in the water and wash up, Caroline. You're beginning to smell."

She started to balk, but he motioned her toward the stream. "Go on. I won't look."

Caroline hesitated, though not for long. She quickly stepped from her clothes and into the stream. The water felt heavenly.

"Did you bring any soap?" she called back after submerging herself, the cool water lapping at her chin.

"I didn't have to." He reached out onto the bank and grabbed a handful of sand. "Nature's cleaning agent."

"What am I going to do with that?"

Shane ambled over to the edge, dipped his fist into the water, then emptied the wet sand on her head.

"Ahhgh!"

"Close your mouth." With deft fingers he scrubbed her head with the sand.

Caroline quickly realized the logic to such a method. She took another handful of sand and rubbed it all over her body. She ducked beneath the surface to wash the sand free, and she felt tingly and clean and shiny.

"Come on. Time to go," Shane said.

With his back to her, Caroline climbed out of the water, hoping that he would kiss her. Disappointment creased her forehead when he merely handed back the length of woolen blanket.

"Dry off," he said. "I have a present for you."

Caroline harrumphed. "The last present you brought me wasn't much of a gift."

"Why, you ungrateful little baggage." He laughed. "That split skirt has served you well."

Caroline dried herself, and when she was through, Shane handed her what she soon realized was a brush made from porcupine tail stretched over a block of wood and a comb made of bone. She sat on a smooth, flat-topped boulder, the blanket wrapped around her, her legs crossed Indian style, as she worked the tangles slowly from her hair. When she was through, she reached for her clothes. Just the thought of putting the grimy garments back on made her cringe. But she couldn't traipse back to camp with nothing more on than a blanket.

Shane caught hold of her wrist. "Your present. From Many Moons."

He held out a small bundle. She found a rust-colored chamois dress. Her fingers caressed the baby-soft hide with awe. After a day of working with hides, she appreciated the hours that had gone into making such an exquisite piece of clothing. She held it out. "It's beautiful," she breathed. "Turn your back."

She slipped on the simple dress that slid against her skin like shimmery satin. The slit that formed the neckline was deep, angling down across her breasts, while the skirt clung to her narrow hips and hung down her long legs at the sides and scalloped up over her knees in front and back. The heavy fringe at the side seams swayed as she moved.

Caroline felt deliciously decadent. She swayed to feel the soft leather whisper across her bare skin. She loved it, but when she glanced down at her naked legs and the indecent amount of skin showing, her smile faltered.

"You're beautiful," Shane said softly.

His voice brought her around to face him. Her dry-ing heavy copper tresses curled about her breasts. He reached out and traced the red strands. "Not only are you beautiful, but you are brave and good." He said the words slowly and with great feeling. "You've come into this uncertain situation and rather than cower and curse the fates, you've taken to these people . . . and charmed them as well."

"Good heavens, they're your family. How could I not?"

"Many wouldn't have . . . most wouldn't have. I have learned that lesson many times over."

"Well, Many Moons is a dear, and Strong One is an old softy at heart." She looked into his eyes. "I wish I had known my grandparents or great-aunt."

Shane's hand came up to her face. "I think it's time we talk about your father."

Caroline stiffened. Things between her and Shane seemed so perfect. She didn't want to ruin it. "No," she stated stubbornly, then took a deep breath and softened her tone. "There is no need to discuss any of that. The past can't be changed. We can only deal with the present."

"Caroline, we can't pretend the issue isn't there. It will be like a deep wound that festers and grows, until one day it bursts or kills us. Either way it involves much pain. It's time." He took her hand.

"No!" she cried, jerking her hand free.

Hurriedly, she pulled on the moccasins that matched her new clothes, then slipped off through the trees toward camp.

CHAPTER

✳

22

AFTER HER SOJOURN in the stream, Caroline didn't see Shane the rest of the afternoon or during the evening. As she lay in her lodge that night she listened as the sounds of activity began to die down and the sounds of the night grew louder. And still he failed to come. Just when she was certain he would stay away altogether, she heard the now familiar jingle of metal cones before he slipped through the door.

He stepped from his clothes without speaking then lay down beside her as he always did. Wood spice and leather filled her senses, and she wondered how she ever could have doubted that he would come to her. Of course he would. For he was the other half of her whole.

And as if to prove her right, unlike other nights, this night he didn't simply hold her close. He dipped his head and kissed her eyelids. When he pulled back to look down at her, she sensed that something was wrong.

She reached up and touched his cheek. "What is it, Shane?"

He turned his head until his lips met the palm of her

hand. "Shhh," he said. "Not now."

She started to insist that he talk to her, but then his lips seared a path up her arm and she was lost. Her fingers trailed back into his hair, and he came down upon her. "Sweet, sweet, Caroline," he whispered into her hair.

He held her body close, tight, as if drawing her strength. They lay that way, quietly, reveling in the feel, until Shane captured her lips in a long, searing embrace. They kissed until their bodies would no longer be denied. He rolled her beneath his massive form, and trembled as he brushed his mouth against the pulse in her throat.

She wore nothing more than her newly washed, gossamer thin knee-length chemise. His hand ran up her leg and thigh, the sweet feel of her skin searing his palm. He continued his heated journey, brushing the curve of her hip, teasing her narrow waist, finally resting at her side, just under her arm, the heel of his hand pressing against the creamy swell of flesh. He watched as her back arched like the bough of a graceful willow, seeking more.

Her hands came up to caress him. Gently, with one strong hand, he pushed her arms back above her head, clasping her wrists between his fingers, then pushed the material aside and opened his mouth on the soft underswell of her breast.

"Shane," she gasped with pleasure, her head turning into the thin mattress.

Her naked leg lay between his thighs, and she could feel his short black leg hair against her skin. Unaware of what she was doing, Caroline brought her leg up, then down, slowly, again and again, bending her knee and sliding her foot along the mattress, loving the feel of her leg gliding between his thighs, her skin brushing against the soft hair.

Shane groaned and caught her partially raised leg between his thighs. And suddenly she became aware of the hard length of his desire. Her head jerked forward. "Oh, dear!"

"Oh, dear, is right. But rest assured, Red, I like it." He chuckled into her hair. "But if you continue, I'm afraid I'll turn into a schoolboy who can't control himself and spill my seed on your belly."

Caroline felt the blood singe her cheeks, but her embarrassment was soon forgotten when Shane moved her slightly, took one rosy nipple deep into his mouth, and brought his hand to the juncture between her thighs. His fingers slipped inside her, slowly at first, then deeper and faster, with maddening persistence. He let go of her wrists, and her hands came down to rake his arms, running up the taut muscles to his head, pressing him closer. She writhed with the feel, the ache and yearning that centered in the core of her womanhood.

His lips trailed down along her abdomen, sucking at the gentle swell of her stomach, his fingers still moving within her. Her hips mimicked his rhythm, and she cried out when he took his hand away. But she gasped and caught his head when his lips brushed against the tight curls between her legs.

Mortification filled her. "What are you doing?"

Shane rested on an elbow and looked at her with a teasing smile. "Our woman of medicine has to ask such a question?"

Caroline's mind quickly fled to the pages of *Dr. Mur-*

phy's Medical Book, wondering what else the man had left out of his worthless tome.

"Let me love you, Caroline," Shane demanded, his voice deep and low. He dipped his head once again.

Her legs pressed together. "Shane, no."

"Yes, Caroline." As he said the words his thumb found her damp cleft and stroked. "Open your legs for me."

Her limbs quivered, intense yearning washing over her. Her hips began to move again, thrusting forward of their own volition. "I don't think this is such a good idea, Shane," she whispered as she fell back to the mattress.

"I think you're wrong," he replied, moving between her thighs and bringing her to his lips.

The touch was like fire. Her body burned with a flame she was certain would consume her. She writhed with wanting, she reached and cried out. Just when she thought she could take it no longer as her body clenched and spasmed, Shane came up over her and plunged deep into her body, filling her. She wrapped her arms around his shoulders and held tight as he thrust into her until she breathed his name. He shuddered his release, then collapsed on top of her, pinning her beneath his weight.

Every inch of Caroline tingled. Some minutes passed, sounds of the night rustling in the distance, before she realized she was being crushed. "Ugghh," she grunted. "You're smashing me."

Shane's eyes snapped opened and he rolled, though he brought her with him, bringing her to rest on his chest. Then he smiled. "You liked that, didn't you?" His face came to life with boyish charm.

Caroline screwed up her lips in mock consideration. "Yes, you roll over with me attached quite well."

He growled and started to roll her back over. "Looks like I'll have to show you what I'm talking about."

"Stop, stop." She giggled. "Yes, I liked it. But I can't take any more."

"Oh, really? We'll see about that."

And sure enough they did, making love well into the early-morning hours.

They lay together, the camp quiet all around them, only the occasional muffled bark and scrabbling paws of dogs deep in dreams marking the silence.

"My grandfather thinks he's dying."

The words startled Caroline out of her languorous state. "What are you talking about?"

"Strong One thinks that his days are limited, and since my father was his only child, he is now without an heir."

"Isn't that unusual for an Indian, especially an Indian chief, to only have one child?"

"Yes, but my grandfather never took another wife other than Soaring Wings. And she was past childbearing age when my father was killed. It is thought to be inconsiderate for a man to have only one wife, for then all the burdens of the constant moving and of day-to-day life has to be borne by one woman."

Caroline felt Shane shrug.

"But Strong One loved Soaring Wings very much." Shane grinned in the semidarkness. "As a child I saw my grandfather help her often when they were in the confines of their lodge. Once he caught me watching.

Our eyes met and held. And somehow we both knew I would say nothing."

"Why would it matter?"

"Because a man, especially a great Comanche chief, would be demeaned by doing woman's work."

"Men," Caroline said with disgust.

"But *he* helped," he reminded her.

"True." Caroline sighed. "Then, other men!"

They both laughed, holding tight, Shane staring up to the top of the lodge, where he could see the sky.

"Where is Soaring Wings now?" Caroline asked.

Shane stroked her arm. "Strong One told me she died two years ago. And now Strong One seems to think that I am the only one who can continue his great line."

"Oh, Shane, that's wonderful!" Caroline rose to one elbow, long waves of red hair falling forward to frame her face. "Now you will be an Indian chief!"

Shane scowled as he absentmindedly wrapped a thick strand of hair around his finger. "Not a chief, but simply a half-breed who needs an Indian wife to produce an heir."

It took a moment for the words to register. "What about me?" she cried indignantly. But no sooner were the words out than she blushed with embarrassment. There had been no further mention of marriage—at least not marriage to her.

Shane pulled her back into his arms with a soft laugh. "I will have no one else but you, my sweet fiery Red."

She pressed close until she could feel the steady pounding of his heart against her cheek. They lay together, quietly, peacefully, until sometime later she asked, "So, tell me why he thinks he's dying?"

"His joints swell and stiffen, making it difficult to walk. His great toe especially gives him trouble."

"Hmmm."

"And he has difficulty passing urine. It has gotten worse over the years, convincing him that soon it will kill him."

"That's what I thought."

"What do you mean?"

"I have suspected that Strong One has gout."

"Gout?" Shane seemed incredulous. "An Indian?"

"Yes, but it can be helped, and I assure you he is not on the verge of dying."

The following morning when she met Many Moons, Caroline went to work on a shirt she was making for Shane with her bone needle and thin rawhide thread. The women worked quietly side by side.

"I have noticed," Caroline began carefully, "that Strong One has some discomfort at times."

Many Moons's hands stilled in their labor before she picked up her stitching once again. "What gives you this idea, Hair Like Fire?"

"His feet sometimes pain him and swell. You know I am considered a medicine woman by my own people."

"You? One so young?"

"I am six and twenty and have spent my life learning to heal."

Many Moons snorted. "Six and twenty. What could you have learned?"

"For one, that your brother has gout."

"Gout?" Many Moons probed, suddenly curious. "What is this?"

"A condition that can be helped, and one that is not going to kill him anytime soon."

Jerking around, Many Moons stared at Caroline. "What can be done?"

Caroline proceeded to tell Many Moons what was needed, and soon the older woman leaped to her feet and went in search of her brother.

That night Shane found his grandfather sitting in his tent in front of a small fire.

"Enter, Fast As the Rivers. Share my pipe."

Shane came to sit across from Strong One and took the long pipe. He inhaled then passed it back. The fire crackled softly.

"Many Moons has told me of Hair Like Fire's medicine. Is this true that your woman has powerful medicine?"

Shane thought of the way the People defined medicine. Great power—in Caroline's case, great power to heal. "Yes, Grandfather. She has strong medicine."

"Good," he said simply, and inhaled deeply of the smoke.

"I have given the matter great thought, Grandfather, and have come to the conclusion that I cannot stay with the tribe."

Piercing black eyes bored into Shane.

"I have missed the important years with the People," Shane added.

Strong One waved his hand as if to wave away Shane's argument.

"No, Grandfather, let me finish. I have never had my vision quest to become a brave. I am too old to do it now. And while the People have been wonderful to me, and I have learned a great deal that I did not know or perhaps had forgotten, I cannot stay here. They will never be totally comfortable with me because I have spent too much time with the white eyes."

Smoke spiraled up toward the hole at the top of the lodge. Strong One stared across the flame at his grandson, as if considering his words. Finally, he grunted and set the pipe aside.

"I find I must agree, Fast As the Rivers. You have grown to be a very wise man. And as long as I am not dying, I shall take a new wife and produce an heir. But know that as long as the People are on this earth, you are always welcome with us." Strong One pushed his ponderous weight up from the ground. "Come. I must choose a wife."

Shane followed his grandfather to the door. Just when the older man pushed open the flap, he turned partially back and said, "I think it wise that you marry your woman at the same time. An Indian ceremony will make your white woman even more accepted here than she already is."

CHAPTER

✳

23

"WHAT IS THIS?"

The venomous words brought Emma's head up from her sewing with a snap.

Diego crossed the *sala* floor with angry, pounding steps, a vein bulging in his forehead. He stopped at his grandmother's chair, his towering height seeming all the greater for his obvious displeasure. He shook a document in Emma's face. "What is this?" he demanded once again.

The sun lay low in the western sky. Emma sat next to the open window, a cool breeze rustling gently through the room, the soft calico and needle and thread lying forgotten in her lap. "Calm down, Diego. You're acting like a child. What are you going on about?"

"This!" He glanced at the sheet of parchment as if to prove to himself what he already knew. "This is a document transferring the winery and vineyards to Shane!"

With narrowing eyes Emma sat forward, her cotton shawl falling from her shoulders. "Where did you get that?"

"From the land office in town. Harvey Granger was

going to send it off to Austin whenever the next stage-coach arrived."

"You took it?" she demanded.

"Hell yes, I took it."

"Diego, besides the fact that you had no right to interfere with my business, taking such a document is a crime."

"It's a crime that you would give that bastard cousin of mine the winery and vineyard."

"Diego! You will not speak to me like this."

Emma started to push herself up from her chair, but Diego squatted down menacingly before her, blocking her path, so that they looked at one another eye to eye.

"It is about time I speak to you like this. Tell me why," he demanded quietly. "Why are you giving everything to Shane?" His words were steeped in venom, his quiet tone failing to hide his hatred.

Emma took a deep steadying breath and glanced helplessly at the doorway. "I am not giving him every-thing. I am simply giving the winery and vineyards to him as a wedding gift when he marries Caroline."

"Caroline." He sneered.

Emma cut him off, her courage growing. "Yes, mar-riage to Caroline. And need I remind you that more than once you have lamented the time you have been forced to spend dealing with the very land you are now making such a fuss about. You hate everything to do with the making of wine. You should rejoice that you no longer have to deal with it."

"Rejoice! Rejoice that some half-breed bastard walks back into our lives and takes what is mine! Mine!" he hissed, his hand crushing the document as he pushed himself up and away from his grandmother's chair.

"Yours?" A shiver of foreboding ran down her spine. She had seen her grandson's erratic behavior before, but never had it been turned against her. Emma glanced at the door once again and wondered where Henry was. But she knew. He was out on the range and would not be back for hours. Seeing no help for herself, she knew she must tread carefully. "The hacienda is not yours, Diego," she stated with a calm she did not feel. "It is mine. To do with as I please. Do you understand me?"

His face grew more fierce. The sharp features that when relaxed looked so handsome, became distorted and grotesque when filled with anger. "Yes, I understand you. I understand that you love Shane more. You have always loved Shane more. Always!"

"Diego, that is absurd."

"Don't lie to me!" Diego slammed his fist against the adobe wall, the force knocking small chips of paint and mud free. His face grew red and the veins in his neck bulged to match the one on his forehead. "You have loved Shane more since the day Grandfather dumped him at your feet after he recaptured Miriam."

Her head jerked back slightly, and her eyes burned when Diego's words dredged up the memory of Shane lying at her feet, scared and dirty. She closed her eyes to block the memory. But it would not be denied.

"Yes, Grandmother," she heard Diego add quietly from too close. "Remember that day. Remember how our lives changed."

And it was true. Their lives had changed. Irrevocably.

She had been working in the kitchen of the sprawling whitewashed house in East Texas with its many Orien-

tal rugs, fine china, and imported furniture, preparing
the evening meal. The long sharp knife she had been
using to dice the venison was still in her hand when
she came running out to the front porch at the sound
of all the commotion. Oliver had ridden up to her with
much the same look on his face that Diego's held now,
carrying a boy with a tangle of long black hair and a
foreign leather shirt. He dropped the youngster at her
feet with a thud and laughed. "Look what Miriam has
got us," he had said with a sneer.

She glanced from Oliver to the boy, trying to comprehend. It did not take long to realize he must be
Miriam's. Her heart had clenched and her mind
screamed denial at the thought of how her daughter
must have been used by the Indians. But all else
was quickly forgotten when she looked down to
see those strange slate-colored eyes staring at her
as if at any minute she would cut out his heart
with the long knife she clutched in her hand. Her
grandson. Defiance mixed with fear laced his eyes,
and in that moment she knew she was hopelessly lost
to the strange child.

Her love had only grown stronger with time. The boy
had taken what was doled out with quiet solemnity.
He worked harder and complained less than anyone
on that miserable farm. And for his efforts he had
received nothing but hate from his grandfather, mother, and young cousin—a young cousin he had futilely
tried to befriend.

With effort she turned her thoughts away. "I don't
have to explain anything to you, Diego. The hacienda
is mine to do with as I please. I came to this land and
bought Cielo el Dorado on my own."

"With Grandfather's money!"

"No!" she hissed, the calm replaced by her own anger. "No, Diego. With my money," she said, her fist coming to her chest. "It has always been my money, from my parents. Oliver Shelton married me for my money. Nothing more. And after he died, it was my money alone to do with as I pleased." She stood, no longer caring what Diego might do to her. "And it pleases me to gift Shane and Caroline with the winery and vineyards upon their marriage."

"Shane will not have what is mine," Diego whispered in Emma's ear as she passed so close. "That I promise."

Emma jerked around to face him.

"Emma!"

Emma and Diego turned quickly toward the door.

Diego sneered and stepped back. Tears came to Emma's eyes.

"Caroline, you're back." She opened her arms to the young woman, who ran into her embrace.

"Oh, Emma, what an adventure I've had."

Emma set her at arm's length and forced a smile. "From the looks of you, I'd say you truly had an experience."

Caroline glanced down at her beautiful rust-colored leather dress. "It was a gift from Many Moons, Shane's great-aunt."

Emma's eyes flickered with surprise and something else. Pain. Perhaps even jealousy. "Great-aunt?"

But Caroline had already pulled away and turned toward the door. She held her hand out to Shane, who stood quietly at the threshold. "My days with the People were a very special time that I will never forget."

Shane entered, his lips tilted in a half smile. "I'm sure your days there will not soon be forgotten by the People either."

Caroline blushed and blushed still further when Shane looked deep into her eyes and brushed her cheek with his knuckles before he stepped past her to approach his grandmother. "Emma." He leaned down and kissed her on the cheek. "Diego," he added with a nod of his head.

"How quaint." Diego strode toward Caroline. "Such a charming family reunion." He took a beaded piece of fringe that hung from her leather dress between his fingers. Inhaling through his teeth, he shrugged his shoulders. "I guess this means that your high collars and thick black boots were only for show."

Red surged stronger through Caroline's cheeks as her mind was well and truly forced from the Indian world back to the white man's. She became painfully aware of her bare legs.

"Stay away from my wife, Diego," Shane said in ominous tones.

Emma gasped.

"Your wife?" Diego said, his voice strangled.

Emma rushed forward. "When were you married?"

Shane looked at Caroline. "We were married by the People."

"The People," Diego hissed. "You were married by the People! Then you live in sin!"

Shane turned not to Diego but to Emma. "We plan to be married by a priest as well."

Emma's face tilted with a soft smile. "That will be nice. I have to admit that I'd be disappointed if I didn't get to give you a big church wedding. But of course you're married now. The other will simply be a formality."

"You say they're married now," Diego persisted. "Ha! I'd like to see what a priest says about that!"

"I warn you, Diego," Shane said slowly.

"You'll warn me what, cousin?" Diego swung around to face Shane. "You'll warn me to stay away from this woman you call wife. The woman who warmed your bed years ago in San Antonio. The woman whom decent San Antonio ladies purposely walked across the street to avoid being near."

Caroline moaned. Shane's body jerked slightly, and his eyes narrowed as he stared at Diego.

"Diego, that is enough!" Emma stated heatedly.

"No, it is not enough!" Diego screamed, his eyes bloodshot and wild. "This . . . this woman was turned away by every respectable citizen of San Antonio, Texas. But we open our arms to her, though only because she deceived us into thinking she was something she was not. Everyone wondered, including Henry, what such a seemingly intelligent woman was doing in a place like El Paso. Well, now we know. She was run out of a respectable town. They were only too happy when she fled. They wouldn't let her touch them with her healing, but we clamor after her skills. They wouldn't let her teach their children, but we bring her from across many miles to teach ours. Even her oldest and dearest friend no longer speaks to her. San Antonians spit in her face, but we kiss her cheek. And give her land!"

The story Diego related slowly penetrated Shane's

mind. Caroline had avoided telling him what her life had been like during those years. He had guessed it had been difficult, but had never dreamed how difficult. Guilt, pain, anger, and impotent rage surged through him. Why hadn't he gone back for her? he asked himself again. Why had he left?

"Did you know that, my dear grandmother?" Diego railed. "Did you know that you are giving your precious land to a *whore*!"

Shane's composure vanished with the simple though hateful word. He threw himself against Diego, both bodies crashing against the thick adobe wall.

"You lie!" he ground out.

"You wish!" Diego grunted.

Caroline stood to the side, her hand to her mouth.

"Stop it, you fools!" Emma cried.

But her words went unheeded when Diego flailed his arms against Shane, catching him in the jaw and back. Shane pinned his cousin to the wall, his breath ragged. "Caroline Bromley is no whore. She was the victim of hate, hate that should have been directed at me. But I was gone and there was no one left to punish—except Caroline. And punish her they did—for *my* crimes. She slept with no one," he ground out. "She suffered because people are cruel and take advantage of her goodness—people like you."

Diego tried to break free, but Shane held him secure. "I don't know what you're talking about when you speak of land, but I do know that you are filled with lies that I can only imagine you heard from Dean Fowler. Is that true?"

Kicking out, Diego tried to free himself. Shane slammed him against the wall once again. "I asked you a question. Did Dean Fowler tell you these lies?"

"Well, well, well."

The voice came from the door. Shane froze. Emma and Caroline turned to the sound. A woman Caroline had never seen before stood at the entryway. She was tall, with faded blond hair that was rapidly turning gray. Caroline knew with certainty that she had been a great beauty in her day. Long, billowing skirts flowed over still-slender hips. The bodice was cut low, revealing ample breasts. Her eyes were bluer than any eyes Caroline had ever seen, and just then they sparkled with mirth, and with what Caroline would have sworn was loathing.

The woman stepped into the room, snapping a fan shut against her hand. Her dress brushed against the tile floor, pulling slightly when it traveled over the finely woven woolen rug. "Shane, dear, is your cousin your latest victim?"

Shane's stiff shoulders slumped, his grip relaxing.

Diego quickly stepped away from the wall, straightening his coat and shirt, brushing at his trousers. Shane let him go. He didn't move at all. He stood still, facing the wall, tension playing across his well-muscled back.

"You always did have the most unfortunate habit of trying to kill people." The woman laughed. "But, once a savage always a savage, I suppose."

The words made Caroline gasp. How could anyone be so cruel? she wondered. And who could this woman be? But a sinking feeling crept through her body, making her weak. For she thought perhaps she knew.

Slowly, reluctantly, Shane turned to face the woman. "Mother," he said simply, his voice devoid of emotion, his hands held loosely at his side. "It's been a long time."

CHAPTER

✸

24

"IF YOU'LL EXCUSE me," Shane said tightly, moving toward the *sala* door. "I have things I need to see to after our absence."

No one tried to stop him, they simply let him go. Caroline watched the proceedings, shocked and grief-stricken. She followed Shane with her eyes and was surprised when he nodded to a man she had not seen enter.

"Davis," Shane said, passing the older man.

"Shane." The man took the hat from his head as he moved out of the way.

"Davis, there you are." Miriam Shelton Withers looked toward her husband, her son seemingly forgotten. "Have you unloaded my bags? I want a bath and fresh clothes. I'm covered in dust and am nearly death itself from heat exhaustion. I don't know why I continue to make this horrid trip."

Caroline wondered the same thing but kept her mouth shut.

When Miriam came to Caroline, she stopped. Her eyes traveled the length of Caroline's lithe body. "I suspect you must be the little schoolteacher Emma wrote me about. She didn't tell me you lusted after my son."

Caroline sucked in her breath.

"Don't play the innocent with me. I saw the way you looked at Shane." Miriam rolled her eyes.

"I'm not playing the innocent. I love your son and I care about his well-being. Which is more than I can say for you."

Miriam's eyes narrowed. But Caroline gave her no chance to reply. With a shake of her head, she slipped out the door to hurry after Shane.

She caught sight of him just as he made his way into the working side of the hacienda. "Shane!" she called out.

His step faltered, but only for a second. "Not now, Caroline," he said, his voice like steel.

"Shane, we need to talk!"

"No! Not now. I have work to do," he added, his tone softer, though he never missed a step.

She watched his receding back. A cold wave washed over her. During their days with the People, Shane had let down his defenses. They had shared a time of perfect accord. She thought he had begun to heal. But as she watched him disappear into the stable she knew his fortress walls had been resurrected.

She felt alone, on the outside of the massive structure. She remembered how Shane had never spoken of love—had only taken her body. She wondered suddenly if he was capable of love, and if he was not, could she stand a lifetime of that. She didn't know.

She headed toward her room, her steps heavy. She shut the door behind her. Carefully, and regretfully, she folded the soft leather dress away and pulled on one of the two remaining dresses she had brought with her from San Antonio.

She cringed at the thought of San Antonio and the things Diego had said about her. But somehow she found they didn't matter. While standing there taking in his hateful words, she noticed that neither Emma nor Shane looked at her with disgust. And now the truth was out. A weight was lifted from her shoulders. She felt free of her terrible secret. Truly, she was moving beyond the past.

But then she laughed harshly. Yes, she was finally free from the past and the worry that at any minute Emma would find out about her, but what did it matter if she had no future with Shane?

Caroline left her room and went to the schoolhouse. Despite her misery, she smiled when she opened the door to find her students. They slouched in their seats, talking in a low murmur.

"Hello, children."

Fifteen heads swung around. They took her in with excited eyes before jumping from their seats and racing to her side. "Miss Caroline, you are saved!"

Caroline was nearly felled from the surge of young bodies. "Of course, I'm saved," she said as she lovingly reached out to each child. "I was never in any danger."

"But Indians took you," Opal breathed.

"Nice Indians who took very good care of me until Mr. Rivers came to retrieve me. And now I am back safe and sound."

"Just in time for the fiesta!" Billy announced.

"Yes, so I've gathered." She looked around the room. "I suspect we'll have to perform our play another time. I hope you're not disappointed."

"We don't have to wait!" several shouted in unison. "We've been practicing!"

"And we are very good," added a voice from the front of the room.

Caroline glanced toward the sound and found Esteban lounging in her chair. "Are we, now?" she asked with a smile.

"Yes, we are very good," he repeated. "We have worked very hard so you would not be disappointed when you returned." He stood from the chair. "I knew you would return safely."

Her smile filled with love for these darling young boys and girls, with happiness for all that had come into her life when least she expected it. Tears threatened. If only she could find her way into Shane's heart.

The Fall Fiesta arrived with all the gaiety and excitement it had aroused in this part of the world for centuries. The day dawned bright and Caroline woke disoriented. It took a moment to realize she was not with the People but back at the hacienda. As everything started rushing back to her, she remembered searching for Shane last evening, but had not been able to find him, and had ended up sleeping alone in the little room she had used since her arrival.

Once she was up and dressed, Caroline walked through the hacienda, amazed by the transformation that she had failed to notice the day before. Boughs of pine, brought down from the mountains, were meticulously woven together to form a long rope, which was strung from post to post around the courtyard. From the roof beams hung tin lanterns pierced with holes that would let out the light of slowly burning candles at night. The courtyard was filled with rough-hewn tables covered with multicolored tablecloths.

In the kitchen she found loaves of bread piled high, next to cookies, cakes, and pastries. Emma stood at the huge stove, stirring a bubbling pot of beef, beans, and chilies.

"Good morning," Caroline said.

Emma half turned. "Good morning, dear. How are you?" She turned still further, her cooking momentarily forgotten. "I'm so sorry about Diego. He had no right to speak of you in such a way. And I'm sorry if those things he said about San Antonio were true. Know that we are not like that. And we love you no matter what."

Tears sprang to Caroline's eyes. "Thank you," she managed. What else could she say? How could she put into words how much Emma's statement meant to her?

"Now," Emma said crisply, turning back to her pot. "We have much work ahead of us before everyone starts arriving this afternoon."

"What can I do to help?" Caroline asked, taking a deep breath.

"You can go to the pantry. On the top shelf there is a package for you."

"A package?"

"Yes. Now go on and get it."

Caroline walked into the cool, dry storage room and found the brown-paper-wrapped parcel. When she returned, Emma stopped her from opening it.

"Not now, later, when you are getting ready for the party."

Caroline came up to Emma and gave her a quick hug. "Thank you."

"Bosh, you don't even know what it is."

"Thank you for whatever it is . . . and thank you for . . . everything you have done for me."

"Hogwash," the older woman murmured, tears glistening in her eyes. "Now out with you before I burn my *caldillo*."

Turning to go, Caroline hesitated. "Have you seen Shane? I've looked everywhere for him."

"No, dear, not lately. But he went out to work in the vineyard early this morning. I suspect he won't be back in for several hours."

Messengers had been sent far and wide to invite friends and neighbors to the grand fiesta. By late afternoon Cielo el Dorado began to fill with guests. Some would sleep within the walls; others would set up camp for themselves and their families in the surrounding area, well within sight of the promenade and *torreón*.

Caroline hurried to the bath house. Water was already heating in the corner on a small stove, and she had the copper bathtub filled in no time. After stripping away her clothes, she stepped into the water and sank down until the scented waves lapped at her chin. Her skin had taken on a golden glow from her time in the sun. Light streaks of gold wove throughout her hair, lightening her complexion, making her green eyes glow brighter.

She would have loved to soak for hours, but knew she had no time. Quickly and efficiently she scrubbed her hair and body before stepping out to dry with a large cotton towel. Once dried and ensconced in a thick wrapper, Caroline untied the strings of the package Emma had given her. She gasped with pleasure when she pulled a flowing dress of white silk lace from the paper—one of the free-flowing dresses she had coveted. Clasping the beautiful garment to her breast, she wondered if she dared wear it. But then she laughed when she thought how only the day before she had gallivanted across the land in attire that was far more revealing than this ever would be. Her smile grew luminous as she twirled about the small room, still clutching the dress tightly, and danced a few lively steps.

Once her hair was dried and brushed, she pulled on the dress that hung off her shoulders and accentuated her golden skin and riotous mass of red curls. The dress belted at the waist with a thin sash of matching lace, then fell to her ankles, where delicate white slippers of soft leather encased her feet. Standing before an old beveled mirror, Caroline could hardly believe that she was the woman in the glass.

Once in the courtyard, she caught sight of Emma in the distance. She hurried across to her and caught the older woman off guard when she threw her arms around her.

"Thank you, Emma."

Emma stepped back and took Caroline in. "It's perfect as I knew it would be. I'm glad you like it."

"I love it!" Caroline hesitated, searching for words. "Just as I have come to love you. I feel as though you're the mother I never had. Words will never adequately convey how much I appreciate all you've done for me."

Tears glimmered in both women's eyes. Emma hugged the younger woman quickly, though fiercely, then put her at arm's length. "You're beautiful, dear. Have you shown Shane?"

"No, not yet. I haven't seen him."

"I saw him ride in earlier." Emma glanced around. "But I haven't seen him in a while. Though I have seen the children, who are nervously awaiting their performance."

"The children!" Caroline cried, gathering her skirt. "I've got to hurry. The play should start within the hour, and I haven't checked on anything." She started away. "Thank you again, Emma."

"You are more than welcome. Now run along."

Caroline made her way to the schoolroom and found the stage set and the children ready. And indeed, within the hour, the small schoolhouse was crammed with family and guests attending the production. Excitement filled her. But then Reina walked in, and Caroline could hardly believe her eyes when she realized she was with Dean Fowler. She knew then that Shane had been correct when he had asked Diego about the man.

Just as Esteban walked to the center of the stage to begin, Caroline caught sight of Shane slipping through the door. Their eyes met, his hard and unyielding. Her heart stilled when she saw confirmation that he was not the same Shane Rivers who had been with her the last days with the People. She longed to go to him, to force him to talk to her. And she would, as soon as the play was over. She would be delayed no longer.

Shane walked to the side and Caroline saw him stiffen when he came face-to-face with Reina and Dean. She couldn't hear what was said, but knew heated words were exchanged. Surrounding guests turned to stare, and the room grew hushed. Dean glanced around, then cursed and pulled Reina from the room.

After the strained moment passed, the children performed to perfection in the flickering golden candlelight that filled the schoolhouse. Even Hortense the Hog acquitted herself famously.

The room filled with deafening applause when the youngsters took their final bows, then everyone hurried out in search of the food and fun the remainder of the fiesta promised. By the time Caroline reached the back of the room, Shane was gone.

Taking a candle with her, she stepped out into the courtyard and saw him. But he wasn't alone. His mother stood in front of him, Davis close by.

"So what brings you back to the hacienda?" Caroline heard his mother ask.

Shane merely stared at the woman.

"Need a little spoiling from Emma?" Miriam laughed. "That was always the way with you. A savage one minute, a babe in need of coddling the next."

"Miriam," Davis warned.

"What?" she snapped, her smile gone. "Are you going to defend this heathen next?"

Caroline gasped and started to step forward when Miriam's words stopped her.

"Defend him just like that little redheaded trollop did yesterday in the *sala*?"

Shane's eyes suddenly snapped with fury and he grabbed his mother's arms. "No more!" he raged. "No more of this, do you understand me?" But as soon as the words were out, his rage died.

He let go as if burned. He pressed his eyes shut when he caught sight of the angry red marks on his mother's arms where his fingers had grasped her. Every time he turned around, it seemed, he was losing control. In all the years of their verbal warfare, he had never laid a hand on his mother. It didn't matter that she was no mother in the true sense of the word. What mattered was that he had savagely used force against the woman who had brought him into the world—a woman, he had been taught as a very young child, he should honor no matter what.

"Take her away," he whispered hoarsely to Davis.

Shane turned on his heel and headed toward the other side of the hacienda. Caroline waited until Miriam and her husband had disappeared around the corner, then ran down the steps, cupping her hand around the candle flame to keep it from blowing out.

She was stopped when she entered the working side courtyard by Missy Surlock, who stepped out with her new baby.

"Miss Caroline," she said shyly. "I haven't had a chance to thank you for all you've done for me."

"I'm only glad I could help."

Caroline started to step away, but Missy reached out and caught her arm.

"I don't know what would have happened to Thaddeus and me if it weren't for you. I want you to know that we owe you."

Caroline sighed and tried to smile. "Missy, you owe me nothing more than taking care of Thaddeus."

"I *can* take care of him now that Mrs. Emma has given me work here at the hacienda."

This surprised Caroline at first, but then she realized she should have expected no less from the generous woman.

"She said Mr. Rivers suggested it, and I assumed he got the idea from you."

If her love for Shane could have grown more, just then it would have. The wonderful man never ceased to amaze her. "Thank Mr. Rivers, Missy. I'm sure it was his idea." Caroline squeezed Missy's arm and caressed little Thaddeus's cheek. "Now you'll have to excuse me. I have something to attend to."

In the distance, Caroline heard the mariachi band start up, filling the hacienda with music and singing. She imagined the children lined up around the ground that had been smoothed and cleared to form a dance floor, ready to show their new skills as dancers. She planned to be there with Shane within the half hour.

A weight pressed against her heart. The pain in Shane's eyes had been almost palpable. How could she ever begin to heal such hate and hurt within a man? she wondered. But that wasn't her problem just then. Finding him was first on her list.

She went directly to the stable. Whether day or night, Shane usually rode when he was upset. She pulled open the heavy door, just enough so she could slip inside. When the door fell closed behind her, she stood in a circle of light cast by her candle, the sounds from the party strangely muffled. She felt as if she were in a cocoon, disconnected from the outside world.

The smells of hay and leather wafted through the high-ceilinged space. Horses snuffled and nickered, their hooves rustling in the straw.

"Shane," she called.

Suddenly a burst of distant music flared behind her as the door was pulled open, then closed, shutting out the sound. Startled, she turned, and as she did so her candle wavered then flickered out.

Darkness.

"Shane?" she called, standing still.

No answer.

"Shane, Esteban, whoever is there, please light a lantern or simply open the door," she stated, forcing herself to be calm.

Still no answer. Panic started to build and swell, trying to take over.

"Shane!" she demanded.

She heard the footsteps move toward her, and she could hold her mind in the present no longer. Her mind jerked back in time, dredging up the past. No light, no sound, no lifeline to hold her to the present, to save her from the past.

The muffled voice from that fateful night so long ago filtered through her mind. *You been pleasuring that redskin?*

She turned her head in the darkness but could not quiet the voice. *Is he your lover boy?*

"No," she cried softly, "no." The useless candle and its holder fell from her grip. She pressed her hands to her ears. "No," she whimpered.

But the memories wouldn't stop. The voice that had seemed strangely familiar failed to cease its chatter in her head—deep and low, hoarse, muffled by some disguise.

Stay away from that damned redskin or you're gonna pay.

Tears streaked down her cheeks unchecked as she relived that night in the kitchen. It all rushed in on her with blinding clarity. She choked and gagged when in an agonizing rush of realization, she finally understood why the voice had sounded familiar.

"No!" she screamed, unwilling to believe.

A hand reached out of the dark and grabbed her arm.

"NO!" she screamed again, failing to realize the hand that grabbed her arm was real, not a memory from the past. "No, Papa. Please don't."

Laughter permeated the stable. Light flared. Shadows leaped to life, dancing with haunted laughter. Caroline staggered at the sight that met her eyes. Diego. Not her father. Confusion. Then she realized that she was no longer in that kitchen five years before. She was living a new nightmare that hatefully mimicked the old.

Diego laughed. "No, I'm not your father, but you'll be seeing him soon enough. The chariot of death rides at your shoulder, Caroline Bromley."

The flickering light twisted his features. He seemed to loom over her, larger than life, unconquerable. She wondered for a second if she had the strength to go on. The realization that it had been her father who had attacked her pressed in on her, making her sick with emptiness and betrayal. And she didn't know if she could take any more.

She relaxed, letting go, wanting to fade away, willing Diego to do his worst.

Diego's grip tightened on her arm, forcing her to stand. "No, no, no. Not until Shane arrives, which he will," he added with a crazed laugh. "He will come to save you. But when he comes, he will find he cannot help you or himself. He will die, just as you will, but not before he knows what it feels like to have the very thing he wants most taken away. He will not get you, nor will he get the land—my land!"

Diego pulled Caroline to him until she was forced

to look in his eyes. "He should have stayed away. But as long as he has come, I am glad you came, too. For you provide the means by which to have him destroyed."

"No!"

Diego laughed and tossed Caroline aside. "Yes, *Miss* Bromley." He sneered. "Shane Rivers will finally be destroyed."

CHAPTER

✳

25

SHANE, LIKE CAROLINE, had shed the trappings of the People when he returned to the hacienda. Soon after, he had thrown himself into work. He had come to Cielo el Dorado to forget. But he had done nothing but remember.

He had learned during the days he had stayed with his father's tribe that they were not savages. They were a people who lived in harmony with the land.

If the People were not savages as he had been led to believe, what could explain his own savage behavior? he wondered. He ran a hand through his hair as he walked toward his room, the night sky oddly peaceful, so unlike the turmoil in his mind.

How many times did he have to prove to himself he could not suppress his savage self, expunge it as he had sworn to do. He had failed. Yet again. He needed finally to admit that fact as it was only a matter of time before Caroline saw him for his true self.

He hardly knew how to explain why she hadn't seen him for his true self yet. But she hadn't, and he had no interest in seeing the day when realization dawned bright and painful on her perfect features.

Despair etched his face. All the reasons he had given to justify marriage to Caroline dimmed alongside the fact that he would cause her nothing but grief in the end. But what was he to do? he wondered. Leave her? He knew she wouldn't understand. How could he explain that he was a savage, unworthy of her love? She believed in him—she would deny his words until the day he proved her wrong.

Music played in the distance. Her students would be dancing, probably in the manner Caroline had taught them. He smiled at the thought that Caroline would be dancing, too. He wanted to be dancing with her, holding her in his arms, twirling her around the dusty floor, teaching her the intricate steps of the flamenco that he was certain would alternately shock and intrigue her.

He hesitated and started to turn back, damning all else. He wanted so desperately to hold her, to feel her warmth. But then he remembered that everything he had done was for her, not for him. During the time he had spent with Caroline and the People, he had almost forgotten that he couldn't love her. He couldn't forget that fact again.

His eyes narrowed and he continued on his way.

Entering his small room, he struck a match and lit the lamp before shutting the door. He leaned back against the doorframe, pressing his fingers to the bridge of his nose. When he opened his eyes, he saw a piece of crumpled buff-colored parchment hanging on his wall, stuck there by a thick, menacing stake.

He crossed the short distance to the opposite wall. His heart pounded as he carefully spread the sheet out against the adobe. It was a land-transfer title with his name on it, and beneath the spike, Caroline's name, skewered by the metal.

He quickly read over the deed. Emma was giving the winery and vineyards to him and Caroline as a wedding gift. His heart first leaped with joy then stilled in his chest when he realized Caroline was in trouble. He flew from the room, the slamming door ruffling the paper on the wall.

The working side of the hacienda was deserted, as all inhabitants were reveling at the fiesta. The main courtyard was packed, but everywhere he looked he found no sign of Caroline.

"Esteban," Shane called to the young boy, all slicked up and handsome, squiring young Beth around the dance floor. "Have you seen Miss Caroline?"

"No, señor, not since the play. Were we not superb?"

"Esteban," Beth reprimanded. "You shouldn't boast." She turned to Shane. "I haven't seen her either, Mr. Rivers."

"Me neither," Billy announced, from his position at the side of the dance floor.

Opal stood next to him, Hortense, still sporting mule ears, snuffling in the dirt. "I think she went looking for you."

Shane found Emma and Henry, neither of whom had seen Caroline. He raced to her room and found nothing. No sign of forced entry or of an altercation. The kitchen, empty. The chapel, deserted. Once convinced she was nowhere on the main side, he ran to the working side, fear racing in his heart when he acknowledged that not only was there no trace of Caroline, but none of Diego either.

He ran around the corner, through the archway that

took him to the other side. His slate-gray eyes scanned the surroundings as he leaped over low benches, throwing wide each and every door that opened off the courtyard. Chickens squawked and flew in every direction when Shane raced through the gaggle. The working kitchen, the tannery, the blacksmith shop. All empty and quiet.

Just as he came to the stable he heard it.

"No!"

The word echoed through the stable, seeping out into the night, penetrating his mind. The all-too-familiar rage washed over him. And he welcomed it. All his past and present congealed to form one mass of raging fury. He burst through the door, the hinges groaning under such a violent and unfamiliar motion, the heavy wooden door crashing against the adobe wall, then slowly fell closed.

Diego turned toward the flood of light with a jerk of surprise, but immediately composed himself, his lips pulling into a sneering mask. He held Caroline's arm tightly in his hand, forcing it forward as if in offering. "Ah, you've come for your woman. I wondered how long it would take you to arrive."

"Let her go." Shane's voice was like ice, hard and cold.

"I'm afraid I can't do that, cousin."

Shane's eyes flickered over Caroline, checking for injury. His eyes returned to the other man's before he stepped forward.

"Stay where you are." Diego stepped back, his smile wavering. "I don't want to hurt your pretty little paramour." Then he forced a laugh. "At least not yet."

The straw rustled beneath his booted foot as Shane took another step forward.

"I warn you." Diego's eyes widened, his grip tightening on Caroline's arm.

Still, Shane drew closer, his gaze deadly.

"I warn you!" Diego jerked Caroline to her feet. She groaned at the movement.

And then Shane lunged. He caught Diego off guard, causing him to release Caroline's arm to retain his balance. Shane and Diego came together, their finely honed bodies crashing, their combined weight tumbling them against the wall. They struggled against each other, their arms tangled together, each trying to gain control.

Caroline searched the area for some kind of weapon. She found nothing save bales of hay and her discarded candle and holder. When she turned back, Shane held Diego against the wall. Shane wrapped his hands around his cousin's neck, gradually extinguishing the life from his body. Diego stopped fighting, going limp. With halting movements, Shane loosened his hold. No sooner did he release the pressure than Diego burst into a fit of rage.

Shane pinned him by the neck to the wall once again. Diego's face rapidly turned red, veins bulging in his head. Caroline turned her head away. The scuffling receded again. Relief filled her. But her relief died an unmerciful death when a shot rang out.

The blast reverberated through the stable, bringing Caroline's head up with a snap. The dance of death had ceased, each man frozen in the other's arms.

"Oh, dear God," Caroline cried, running forward. "What happened?"

Diego sucked in a deep breath, gasping for air. Shane staggered back. Red stained both men, making it impossible to tell who the blood came from. And then Shane staggered again and dropped to the floor.

"No!" she screamed.

Diego caught her arm. She kicked and screamed, trying to break free.

"No!" she cried. "Look what you've done. You've killed him."

She jerked and clawed like a wild woman until Diego backhanded her across the face, dropping her to the ground.

"Better him than me," Diego said, his hand still rubbing his throat, his voice strained. "But he is not dead . . . yet. That would have been too easy. I only shot him in the thigh. He must watch as I wipe you from the face of the earth. Then he will know, just before I send him off close behind you, that I have won. After all these years of him taking my rightful place, I will finally win. No longer will he come and go as he pleases. And there will be no wedding with priests. He will not have what is mine."

Diego studied Caroline, then pulled her closer. "Though there will be no exchange of vows," he said thoughtfully, "perhaps there should be a bedding."

Once the meaning of his words became clear, revulsion racked her body.

Reading her thoughts all too well, Diego hissed. "You'd spread your legs for a bastard half-breed, but you turn your nose up at me. Well, not for long. I will show you what it is like to have a real man between your legs."

Her chin thrust forward. "You are no man. You are a weakling who can only achieve through killing and tormenting instead of hard work."

"Bitch," he bit out.

But Caroline wasn't daunted. "What makes you think you can possibly get away with such a scheme? If people haven't heard the commotion already, eventually they'll notice that Shane and I are gone—if not this evening, then tomorrow." She tried to reason with the crazed man, realizing with a sinking feeling that it might very well be tomorrow before anyone noticed their absence.

"You delude yourself, *Miss* Caroline, and I think you know it. These thick mud walls muffle a great deal, especially when the hacienda is filled with laughter and loud music. Everyone is too busy drinking and dancing to notice. And who do you think will question the disappearance of you and Shane? Emma? Perhaps, but she will not question for long. Shane always leaves, everyone knows that, many times without so much as a farewell. Emma will be disappointed, as always," he ground out, his hold tightening. "But she will get over it, and she will assume you went with him. So you see, my little schoolteacher, my plan is flawless."

Seeing the truth of his words, Caroline renewed her efforts to pull free, fighting for her life—and Shane's. Blood stained the hard-packed dirt floor scattered with straw. From the amount of blood, she concluded that no major artery had been hit. She had time. But not much. Shock would set in soon from loss of blood. Even if he didn't bleed to death infection was sure to set in if he was not seen to soon.

"Now, my cousin must be brought around," Diego said. "He must watch. He must know, he must feel, his defeat. Just as I have had to know and feel mine all these years. But in the end I will prove the victor."

Diego stepped closer to Shane and kicked him with

his boot. Caroline gasped and flailed her arms, catching Diego in the head.

"Damn you," he roared, knocking her to the ground with a brutal backhand.

She crashed to the floor, crying out in pain, bringing Shane up from the depths of semiconsciousness.

Memories filtered through Shane's clouded mind. He looked up and saw the towering man standing over him. Oliver Shelton. He shrank back, suddenly ten years old again. But then the vision cleared, and he saw not his grandfather, but Diego.

"So, cousin, you have come around. Good," Diego said, taking a step toward Caroline. "You will watch your paramour perform what she is obviously best at."

Shane felt as if every limb was carved from lead. His vision blurred. He had thought to save Caroline by marrying her. His mind cried out with the irony that he had only managed to make her life worse. He was not saving her. He was only getting her killed. And that he couldn't let happen.

His mind cleared. The pain receded. And without the need for thought or calculation, Shane moved like lightning. He grabbed the knife from his boot and hurled it through the air, striking with a force and sharpness that drove the blade to the hilt.

Diego's eyes narrowed with confusion as he stared down at the knife handle protruding from his chest. He seemed to study the yellow sun and three blue marks. His hands came up to the knife and gently touched the handle. His eyes traveled from the instrument of his impending death to his cousin. His breathing grew raspy, his head snapping back with each breath. His lips tilted in some semblance of a smile as he leaned back against the wall. "I guess," he gasped, "that I always . . . knew you . . . would win . . . in the end." Diego eyed the blood that seeped from Shane's leg. "Though per . . . haps . . . both of us . . . will lose."

Slowly, his knees gave way, and he sank to the floor. His hands dropped to his sides. His eyes fluttered closed.

The stable grew eerily quiet. Caroline stared at Diego. Gradually she turned toward Shane, her eyes wide and startled.

Shane watched as Caroline turned her luminous green eyes on him. He had prayed the day would never come that she was forced to see him as his true self. But he was foolish to think that it was possible to avoid. He saw the look on her face and read it as disgust. She had seen him for what he was, and like all those he had loved in his life, she was sickened by what he saw.

Sickened by what she saw. The words circled in his head. Caroline grew bleary. Her features grew hazy, distorted. He suddenly remembered the night she had thought him asleep and had promised that she would heal his heart. He had hoped she could. Now he knew that not only could she not heal his heart, but if he stayed with her, he would only succeed in destroying hers.

He closed his eyes, his head falling back to the ground. He couldn't take the pain any longer. Unwilling to witness any more of her revulsion, he lost himself to the misty plains of unconsciousness.

CHAPTER

✳

26

CAROLINE WRENCHED HERSELF from shock. She knew she had to work fast. Checking Shane's leg, she confirmed what she had only feared before. The bullet hadn't passed through, but was embedded in his thigh, hopefully not in bone. She gave small thanks that the bullet had not penetrated the femoral artery, which would have pumped Shane's life mercilessly out onto the straw-strewn ground in a few short minutes.

After ripping two wide strips from her beautiful new white dress, she wadded one up to stanch the flow of blood then tied the other around the thigh to hold the makeshift bandage in place.

"Hold on, love," she whispered, gently touching his forehead. "I'm going to get help."

Tripping and falling, she raced to the doorway, unaware of the blood that stained her dress. Outside, the courtyard was empty. The fiesta was obviously going on as if nothing had happened. Diego had been correct, she thought with a shudder. He could have killed them, then disposed of their bodies with no one the wiser. But there was no time for such musings now. After a glance back at Shane, she ran to the other side, where the fiesta was taking place.

"Shane is hurt," she called as she rounded the corner.

Heads turned at the sound, but laughter still rang out and music still played.

"Shane's been shot!" she cried louder.

Emma rose from her seat, her beatific smile faltering when she saw the splash of scarlet on Caroline's skirt. Uneasy murmurs began to mix with laughter and music as people began to take in, not Caroline's words or the distress that played across her face, but the blood. Visions of Indian raids and outlaw ambushes came to most every person's mind.

The music ground to a crazy halt, violins and trumpets ending on different notes.

Panting, Caroline rushed forward.

"You've been hurt," Emma said, trying to find the injury. "What happened?"

"Not me. It's Shane. He's been shot. He's in the stable. I need help to move him inside so I can tend the wound."

Emma's hand came to her chest. "Shot? How?"

Caroline realized then that Diego was in the stable as well. She looked from Emma to Henry. "Perhaps Emma should stay here."

"No! I'll not stay behind."

"Emma," Caroline began. "First I must tell you—"

"We don't have time to waste, Caroline," Emma said, cutting her off.

Henry and three guards raced toward the working side, Caroline and Emma following quickly behind. Once at the stable, Caroline rushed to Shane's side, forgetting about Diego until she heard Emma's gasping cry.

"Oh, dear Lord," she murmured.

Turning back, Caroline made out the pain in Emma's eyes. "Luz," she called to the serving woman who had followed. "Take Mrs. Shelton to her room."

Emma looked between Shane, who lay for all the world like a dead man, and Diego, who truly was dead. Crumpling to the ground, she began to wail. "It's all my fault. It's all my fault."

Henry came to her side and gathered her in his arms. "It's not your fault," he told her with force.

"Of course it is my fault!" She beat her fists against his chest as he lifted her. "If only I had done something. But I didn't. And now both Diego and Shane are dead."

"Shane isn't dead, Emma. He'll survive. He has Caroline to see that he does." Henry gathered her close, her racking sobs muffled by his chest, and led her toward the door. Glancing back at Caroline, he said, "I'll see to Emma, then I'll return."

"You take care of Emma. I have enough help here."

Under Caroline's direction, it took four good-sized men to carry Shane to Caroline's room. They carefully put him down, the bed looking absurdly small when his massive body was laid across it. Shane never woke throughout the move, and when Caroline felt his cheek, a shiver of fear raced through her. His body was like ice. He was going into shock.

"Build a fire," she demanded of the men, despite the warm weather. "And I'll need hot water and blankets."

Flames soon flickered in the small fireplace in the corner of the room. Over the heat, a large cast-iron kettle was placed on a small metal arm. By the time Caroline had pulled away Shane's shirt, cut away his pants, and covered him with blankets, the water was boiling. Pouring some of the hot water in a small pail of cooler water at her side, she wet a soft cloth, exposed the wound, and began to clean the dried blood away.

The small confines of the room quickly filled with heat, and gradually Shane's skin began to regain some of its natural warmth. It took some time, but eventually Caroline had the wound clean, and drops of fresh blood beaded to the surface.

"You'll need to hold him down now," she said to the men who stood back and watched.

Juan and Jorge looked on with wide eyes, but Paco stepped forward. "*Andale!*" he called. "Hurry, we must do what Señorita Caroline asks of us."

Caroline spread out her medical instruments then took a deep breath. She had dug out lead before, though never from someone whose pain was her own. But she knew there was no help for it, so she proceeded. Picking up the probe, she offered up a prayer then leaned close to Shane's ear. "Scream out if you want," she whispered.

When she received no response, she set about her task. Probing gingerly, she got nowhere. Knowing that her reluctance did him no good, Caroline probed deeper. Shane suddenly jerked against his captors' restraint, grumbling and moaning in his semiconscious state.

Deeper and deeper she went until finally she felt the solid hit of metal on metal. Beads of sweat glimmered on Shane's face as Caroline dug carefully about and pulled the bullet free. Further delving produced tiny shreds of material. When Caroline was satisfied the wound was free of foreign particles, she cleaned the gaping hole with vinegar and water and then mixed a thick poultice, which she spread on cheesecloth and applied to his leg.

When the bandage was secure, Caroline sagged, her dress soaked with sweat from her labor.

"Señorita, would you like me to call Luz to finish here?" Paco asked.

"Thank you, but no," she said, straightening on her small stool. "You all go on. I'll call if I need help." She forced a smile. "And thank you."

The men filed out of the room, shutting the door behind them. Shane lay still as death, his complexion gray beneath his bronzed skin. She felt for his pulse. Her breath came out in a rush when she found the faint but steady beat of his heart.

The fire crackled and popped. The music still played in the distance, but not with the exuberance it had held earlier. There was nothing Caroline could do now but pray and make certain the wound stayed clean.

Shadows flickered on the wall. Caroline watched as her own form swayed large and unfamiliar. Diego was dead. She saw as clearly as if they were still in the stable, the knife protruding from his chest, the yellow sun and blue marks blazing bright. Taking a deep breath, she sighed. Other memories threatened. Her initial reaction was to block them. She pushed the notion away. It was time. As if she had opened the floodgates, visions of her father and the years they had spent together came rushing in on her.

Her disastrous cooking, but his unwillingness to hire a cook. Her desire to go away to school, but his lecture on the impropriety of such an action. All the boyfriends and girlfriends that had disappeared from her life without explanation.

Caroline, I don't know what I'd do without you. Her father's familiar lament took on new meaning. And she realized now that he had gone to great lengths to see that he didn't have to do without her. She had been with him until he died.

Her throat clenched. She had accused Shane of planting a seed of hate in her mind to explain away his own abhorrent action of leaving her at the altar. She had accused Shane of betraying her, when all the while her father had been the betrayer.

"Why?" she whispered to the ceiling, choking back a sob. "Why, Papa?"

The tears could not be held back any longer. Silent sobs racked her body. Without realizing what she was doing, she lowered her head until her forehead rested against Shane's chest. Tears spilled over.

"Why, Papa?" she demanded again. "Why did you do this to me?"

She felt Shane's large hand against her head, and she realized with a start that he spoke. "He loved you," he whispered hoarsely, stroking her hair. "No matter what he did, he did it because he loved you."

"Love!"

"Shhh." He held her close, wrapping one arm around her shoulders. "Yes, he loved you."

His strength was gone, and she could have easily pulled away. But she didn't. She didn't want to; she only wanted to be held by this man she didn't know how she would ever live without. The thought left her paralyzed by loneliness. How would she go on without him when it was he who made her life whole? She had to have the opportunity to explain to him that she now knew that he hadn't lied.

He had to survive. She would see him through if she had to sit by his side every second to ensure that the wound stayed clean and his body regained all of its strength. If nothing else, her love and the bond she was certain they shared would keep him alive.

God give me strength and show me the way.

They slept. Sometime during the early-morning hours, when the sky was still dark, Caroline woke sitting on the stool, her head resting against Shane's chest. She checked the wound. It was red and healthy.

Once she had determined that his temperature was fine, she stretched out on a pile of blankets on the floor next to his bed.

Morning came and Shane rested peacefully. Caroline changed his bandage then cleaned up the room before setting out to find some broth for him and to check on Emma. The older woman, she found, had not fared so well.

"She's convinced that Shane is dying," Henry said when Caroline looked at him in question.

"Didn't you tell her otherwise?"

"Of course. But she doesn't believe me."

"Why?"

Henry stared across the room at the woman who suddenly looked older than the hills. "After all these years, I think she's giving up."

"Emma." Caroline sat next to the bed, her brow furrowed with concern. "Shane is going to be just fine."

"No, he's not," Emma stated defiantly. "Henry has made you say that."

"Good Lord," Caroline snapped, her patience running thin. "Why in the world would I tell you that? In a matter of days, if Shane were not up and walking around, how would I explain it? Diego is dead, yes.

There is nothing we can do about that. But you still have Shane. And he needs you, Emma."

Emma looked at her doubtfully. "Why does he need me?"

"Because he loves you. And if you were to give up on life so soon after Diego . . ." Caroline shrugged her shoulders. "He would blame himself for that, too."

A glimmer of recognition sparked in the older woman's eyes, but instead of replying she turned away.

"You won't lose Shane, Emma. See to it that Shane doesn't lose you either."

In the kitchen Caroline found a quick bite to eat for herself and some broth for Shane. She made up a pot of tea with sugar then took it back to her room on a tray. Just outside the door, Esteban, Beth, Billy, Opal, and Hortense waited silently.

"Will Señor Shane . . . be all right?" Esteban asked for the group.

Caroline sat on the bench next to Opal, the tray still in her hands. "Of course he will be all right. And soon you can come in to visit him. He will have difficulty getting around for a while, and I'm sure he'll need help. Perhaps you can provide some assistance when the time comes."

Esteban put his hands on his hips. "This is good. I will go now to make a crutch for the señor."

"I'll help," added Beth.

"Me, too," both Opal and Billy said at the same time, hurrying after the older children.

Caroline watched until they were out of sight then stood from the bench and entered the room. Shane still slept, but it was apparent he had moved, because the covers had fallen from his chest.

"Shane," she said as she laid out the broth and tea on the small table. "Shane, wake up."

His eyes fluttered open and he groaned. "I feel like hell."

Caroline smiled. "You look pretty much the same."

"Thank you," he grunted, raising himself on one elbow to take the broth.

His hand shook badly as he took the cup. Only with the help of Caroline's fingers wrapped around his own was he able to hold the cup to drink most of the soup and a few sips of tea before he sank back on the pillow. She smoothed his hair back from his temples and he sighed. His body relaxed.

"Red," he said weakly, without opening his eyes.

"I'm here."

His eyes opened and he stared at her for an eternity.

She felt awkward and uncomfortable under his scrutiny.

A knock sounded at the door.

"Well, Shane, I've seen you look better," Henry announced, stepping into the room.

Shane grunted some semblance of mirth. "I've felt better in my days, too." His face muscles tensed. "How's Emma?"

"Fine, Shane. She'll be in to see you soon enough."

"Good," Shane said simply, seeming relieved.

His eyelids grew heavy, and he turned to try to gain some comfort. He groaned at the movement.

"Be careful, Shane," Caroline said quickly.

She checked the wound, and when she turned back she found that Shane's breathing was slow and steady, his eyes closed. Caroline walked to the door with Henry.

"So you were telling it straight when you said he's not too bad," he stated in hushed tones.

"The wound isn't so bad. It's infection we have to worry about." Caroline shrugged. "But he's strong and the wound is clean. He'll be all right."

He started to pull the door open. Caroline glanced quickly back at Shane. He lay still.

"Where is Shane's mother?" she whispered, thinking that no matter what the woman's differences with her son might be, surely she would want at least to know about his condition.

"Gone. Back to St. Louis."

Her green eyes narrowed. "Before or after the shooting?"

Henry hesitated. "After."

"I see." Caroline sighed. Her thoughts ran in circles in her head, leaving her angry at a mother who could be so callous toward her son. She had never believed a child could hate his parent, though after witnessing Miriam's behavior toward her son, and after the revelation about her own parent, she saw things in a different light. "Perhaps she didn't realize. We could send a guard for her. They can't have gotten too far."

"No!"

Caroline and Henry turned quickly toward the bed. Shane's eyes were still firmly shut, but she could make out the tight line of his lips.

"No," Shane repeated with less force. Then despite the pain, he turned away from them, pulling the covers to his chin.

It was silent for a moment then Shane spoke again. "Henry, I want you to get a priest."

"Shane!" Caroline demanded softly. "You're going to be fine."

"I want a priest to marry us," he clarified. "Today."

"Shane, this is absurd. You need to rest. We're already married."

"No," he ground out, then sucked in his breath when pain seared his thigh. "We are going to be married in the eyes of *this* world as well as my father's. I want no doubt about the legitimacy of our marriage."

"There is plenty of time for that."

"No, Caroline. We will be married—today."

"I'll take care of it, Shane," Henry said, then left Shane and Caroline alone.

Caroline sank onto the stool beside Shane, but his breathing was even. He only woke again when Henry brought the priest into the room several hours later.

The ceremony was performed quickly and efficiently. When it was said and done, she saw Shane visibly ease—as if some weight had been taken from his shoulders.

Shane drifted off to sleep as the room emptied of the few wedding participants. Time drifted by and every few minutes Caroline checked on her patient to make certain he was still all right. It was hours before she drifted off.

Her sleep was filled with nightmares. Dark and relentless. She woke with a start much later to deep guttural screams. Fear coursed through her body. Her heart pounded in her chest.

It took a moment for Caroline to make sense of where she was and to still her heart enough to be of any use. Shane tossed on the mattress, the covers falling away. Feeling his arm, then his forehead, she found him burning up with fever.

How could it have happened? she demanded of herself. She had been so careful. But when she removed the bandage, she found the angry yellow pus of infection.

He thrashed about on the bed. She leaned over him to hold him still, hoping to calm him.

"Stay away from her, Fowler! Do you understand me?" The words came out in a sudden coherent burst. His eyes flew open, glossy with something Caroline could only describe as fear.

Shane and Caroline stared at each other, no more than a few inches apart, each a bit startled by the proximity. But Caroline quickly realized that while she saw the man she loved, he saw someone else entirely. Seconds passed before she could move. She came to understand that he was speaking of Dean Fowler.

"He's gone, Shane. He left and took Reina with him. They've gone to California."

Shane looked at her as if the words penetrated his glazed mind. His shoulders relaxed against her hands and he fell back into the murky depths of unconsciousness.

Years of practicality took over, giving her no time to think. She took boiling water and vinegar and began to clean the wound. Pressing the edges, she forced a pocket of pus from the depths. When she was satisfied she had extracted all she could and still found no missed bullet fragment or speck of material, she mixed a fresh poultice to draw out the poison that could kill him as surely as a bullet to the head.

Once the wound was tended to, she set out with a rag and basin of fresh, cool water to wipe his body, to bring his temperature down. She started with his head and neck, then went to his chest. Peeling back the covers, she carefully manhandled him onto his side. And when she did so, her hand flew to her mouth to stifle a cry.

"Oh, dear Lord," she gasped at the sight of the terrible scars on his back. She had made love to this man and never seen the scarred flesh that slashed across his back. She realized with a start that he had always kept his shirt on. Her fingers traced the lines. Shane tensed in his sleep.

"Who did this to you?" she whispered into the quiet. She wondered if the whipping had occurred while he was in the army. But years as a healer told her the scars were much too old and faded to be from the war. She remembered Emma telling her that Shane's life had been different. Was this what she had meant? That Shane had been beaten? If so, by whom? His Indian family? Her mind wandered back to their days with the People. No, she reasoned, not the People.

Her heart clenched at the thought that the hatred Shane held for his mother and the scars on his back were somehow tied together. How could a mother do this to a child? Or how could she not prevent it?

She finished washing his limbs, then called Paco to help her pull a nightshirt on Shane and change the sheets. Once Paco was gone, she could do nothing more than sit back and wait. She stared at Shane and willed him to get better. She had changed the bandage, eaten her meal, and was straightening his covers for the night when he began to moan and writhe again. His eyes fluttered open, the depths fathomless and haunted.

"Where is Diego?" he demanded of her.

Caroline didn't know how to answer. Did she tell him? Did she wait until he was stronger? But her silence, apparently, was answer enough. Shane pressed his eyes closed and groaned.

Emma walked in then, looking tired but resolute. Shane glanced up at her, a light sheen covering his face. "I'd like to speak to Emma," he said with effort. He turned to Caroline. "Could you bring me some . . . soup?"

"You run along, dear," Emma said. "I'll see to him until you return."

Caroline slipped from the room, not wanting to leave, but knowing she could do nothing else. Hurrying to the kitchen, she found a bowl of broth and more tea before she hastened back to her room. Emma stood when she entered. Shane was propped up against the headboard. Everything looked so normal, and for a moment Caroline wondered if she had dreamed that Shane was so ill.

Emma left the room, and as Caroline shut the door she caught sight of herself in the mirror. Her hair was tangled about her face and her dress was creased with wear.

"Red," he said, his stormy eyes filled with that look she had been afraid she would never see again.

Self-consciously, her hand came to her hair. Shane's lips twisted, somewhere between a smile and grimace.

"You look lovely," he said.

Blood rushed to her cheeks. "Hardly. I look a mess. The sight, I'm certain, is enough to scare the strongest of hearts away." She set the tray down and started to move away. "I should clean up."

"No."

"Do you need something?"

He took her arm. "I want to talk." He moved slightly and stiffened.

"Careful of that leg, Shane. Lie still. Let me look at it."

"No, Caroline. Listen to me." He pulled her down onto the stool. "You are my wife," he began simply, the effort visibly tiring him. "As my wife you are entitled to all that is mine. If anything were ever to happen to me, Emma will see that you receive what is rightfully yours."

Caroline flinched. "What are you talking about? Nothing is going to happen to you."

Shane looked at Caroline for a long time. "If not my name, then my inheritance will make you secure. Just as it has done for Emma all these years, money will make you beholden to no one. Remember that, Caroline Rivers. Beholden to no one."

"Shane," she said with forced calm, not liking the direction she was afraid this conversation was taking. "You are going to be fine. I'm in no danger of becoming a widow." She smiled down on him, her voice tight with unshed tears. "Do you hear me?"

"Let me hold you," he said softly, as if she had not spoken at all. "I just want to feel you, feel your warmth."

She hesitated, not because she didn't want to be held by him, but because somehow it didn't seem right to crawl in bed with a man so seriously ill.

At her hesitation, the dark, haunted look returned to Shane's eyes. He nearly turned away but stopped.

"Please," he whispered instead, his throat tight. "Just for a little while."

Failing to notice the desperation in his eyes, Caroline glanced about as if someone could see them, then crawled in beside him. No sooner had she wrapped her arms around him than he sighed.

"I love you, Caroline," he whispered, already half-asleep. "Always remember that."

Her heart surged with joy. All her doubts and worried fled. He loved her. He had finally said what she was afraid was only a figment of her imagination. And now she felt certain they could get beyond anything.

She brushed the hair from his forehead and looked down at the man in her arms. A smile curved on her lips. He was asleep.

"Rest, my sweet, and heal so I can show you how much I love you, too."

CHAPTER

✳

27

"THIRSTY."

The single word woke Caroline from a deep, dreamless sleep.

During the night, she had carefully extracted herself from Shane's arms to check his wound. Unwilling to risk waking him, she had fallen back asleep on her blankets on the floor.

"I'm thirsty," he called again, his voice oddly tight.

As her mind cleared she was encouraged by the sign of recovery. She pushed up from the blankets and retrieved a bit of water. "Shane," she said gently, drawing near.

In a flash, he reached out with surprising speed and grabbed her arm, sending the cup flying from her hand.

"I will not beg, damn you!" The words burst forth in a sudden poisonous rush, unmercifully dashing all hope that he was recovering.

His eyes were wild. Black streaks of hair stuck to his face with sweat. "Whip me all you like, Grandfather, but I will not beg."

He released her arm with disdain and fell back into the covers.

Caroline stood breathless, her arm aching where his grip had been. He began to moan and writhe, mumbling words she couldn't make out. "Are you fighting your demons?" she whispered, her voice strained. "What are they, my love? How can I heal you if I don't know what it is you battle?"

But slowly and painfully she was coming to understand what he fought. She had seen his mother and she had seen his scars.

Shaking and unsure, she took the cloth and cool water and began to bathe his body, stroking and whispering words of love and kindness, having no idea what else to do.

Days passed and his condition only worsened. Caroline checked the wound and found no reason for the infection—no bullet fragments missed or pieces of material unfound. But still his fever raged. She mopped his brow and had Paco and Juan lower him into a tub of cool water when his skin became virtually untouchable. Nothing, however, broke the fever.

Emma and Henry came and went, bringing the supplies and medicinal herbs Caroline asked for. Even the children stuck their heads in, Esteban holding out the rough-hewn crutch he had made for "Señor Shane." But nothing seemed to penetrate Shane's tormented nightmares and fitful sleep. Caroline had promised Shane, Emma, and herself that he would live—and he should have been recovering . . . but something stood in the way.

She had lost count of the times she had scoured *Dr. Murphy's Medical Book* for the answer. Each time she opened the leather cover, she thought that perhaps the last time she had missed something, anything, some tidbit of information that held the answer to why Shane was not getting better. But each time she looked, she found nothing, leading her to the conclusion that the answer lay within himself. And the only answer she could come up with was that he had no will to live. But why? her mind raged. Because he had killed his cousin? His cousin had nearly killed her. She shivered at the thought of what would have happened had Shane not come to her rescue.

But no matter how often she whispered those very words into his ear, he failed to respond. And that made her angry. She alternately pleaded and cajoled, then taunted and berated him, all in an attempt to penetrate his mind.

"Fight, damn you," she cried as exhaustion took hold. "You can't die! We've come so far! Don't throw it all away!"

No response. No movement.

Her voice grew frantic. "I've known you to be many things, but I've never thought of you as a coward!" Her eyes were wild and mad. "Did you hear me, Shane Rivers! You're a coward!"

His sudden movement sent her flying from her stool. His arm snaked out with unexpected speed and strength and grabbed her.

"No more, Mother!" he raged, his eyes furious, his nostrils flaring, his fury seeming to shake the very walls. "No more!"

Caroline tried to pull away, a shiver of fear racing through her. He was sick and delirious, but still strong as an ox and perfectly capable of doing her harm. But then his voice softened, his face seeming to melt like wax. He reached for her hand and began to stroke it, staring at it with fever-glazed eyes, unwilling to meet her gaze, his voice suddenly young, unrecognizable. "I promise I won't be a savage anymore." His grasp loosened, and his eyes fluttered closed as he fell back onto the mattress, his body tense. "I promise, Mother," he whispered. "Please say you love me."

The world grew silent. Her heart seemed to stop in her chest. Her throat tightened and tears stung at her eyes. Instinctively, with no thought for his earlier ravings, she moved to the bed and pulled him into her lap, cradling his body to her breast.

"I love you, Shane Rivers," she whispered, holding him tight, stroking the black hair at his temples. "I love you very much."

He calmed then. Caroline had no idea who he thought said she loved him, but it didn't matter. His mother or her, it failed to signify. He deserved his mother's love and he had hers.

The words that his mother had spoken when she entered the *sala* came to mind. *Once a savage always a savage, I suppose.* She realized then that Shane thought himself a savage—unworthy of anyone's love. Five years ago he had said she didn't know him when she had tried to say she loved him. She realized now that while her words were true, his past wouldn't allow him to believe it.

Pain seared her. "Oh, dear Lord," she murmured, taking a deep breath. She wondered how to fight such an impossible battle. She could clean his wounds, make sure he ate, and even love him, but she could never provide him with the love of his mother.

She had come to accept that he hated the woman, when all the while he only wanted desperately to be loved by her. How could she possibly heal such a wound? And she realized with a painful start that she couldn't.

If she hadn't hated his mother already, she would have come to hate her then. His mother had made him believe he was a savage when it was she alone who deserved such an appellation.

Tears streaked down Caroline's cheeks as she clasped Shane to her breast. She nearly laughed out loud at what a fool she had been. The bond they shared would heal him, she had said. How wrong could she have been? There was no bond, only the silly dreams of an overimaginative spinster.

She rocked his motionless body, murmuring sweet words in his ear. "I love you," she whispered through her tears. "No matter what, Shane Rivers, I love you so very much."

CHAPTER

✸

28

HE WOKE IN the night. His eyes focused on the beams in the ceiling. He felt the heat from the fireplace and the brush of soft wool against his skin. His body ached, and when he moved his head to look around, he had to grit his teeth to keep from giving in to unconsciousness.

Glancing about the room, Shane noticed the basins of water, the rags that were hung up to dry, and the vials and pouches of herbs and concoctions. He forced himself up onto one elbow. And then he found her.

She lay on the floor, partially covered by thick blankets. Her hair was pulled back in a loose braid and dark circles shadowed her eyes. He could hardly believe it. She was there.

He fell back onto the mattress as it all came rushing back. First his mother, then Diego. He had killed Diego. He cringed when he recalled that Caroline had witnessed the savage act—but still she was there. Yes, she was still there. And he knew then that he had not been dreaming. She had cared for him when he had wanted nothing more than to be left alone. She had fought for him when he was certain he was not worth fighting for. And she had told him she loved him even though he was unworthy of her love. And somehow he knew, though he didn't understand how, that indeed she did love him, despite witnessing his savagery.

He forced his feet over the side, his head swimming from the effort. He took a deep steadying breath. He would not be defeated in his purpose. Once his vision cleared, he lowered himself to the floor. He stretched out beside Caroline, and still she slept.

He stared at her, the glow of the fire washing her with golden light. Tracing her cheek with a shaking finger, he willed her to wake. She moaned and turned her face into his hand, but her eyes remained shut.

He wanted to kiss her, but couldn't. Not until he saw her eyes, saw her reaction, until he verified what he was afraid to believe was true.

"Caroline," he said, his voice hoarse, the word sticking in his throat. "Caroline."

Her eyes fluttered, then opened with a snap. "Shane," she gasped, coming awake like a soldier.

When she took in the sight of him on the floor, confusion etched her brow. "Did you fall?" she asked crazily. "Are you all right?" Her hands checked over him until she saw that his eyes were clear.

"The question is, are you all right?"

"Shane," she cried. She pressed her forearm to his cheek. "No fever," she breathed. "No fever!"

"It looks like I'll survive," he offered with a crooked smile.

She cried then, the tears and sobs flowing fast and loud. Shane pulled her into his arms, absorbing her tears.

"I thought you were going to die," she wailed. "I thought I couldn't save you."

He held her tight to his heart. "You did save me. Though I didn't realize it until now."

They woke in the morning, entwined on the hard floor, the sun bright and shining as it ascended in the cloudless sky. The madness was gone, along with the rage and hurting. Peace and love filled the sun-drenched room—feelings Shane could hardly fathom.

With strong though barely steady hands, he reached down to pull Caroline up. He looked into her eyes for a long moment and found once again the unmistakable glow of love and caring he had been afraid was only a dream of his tortured mind.

She reached out to him and touched his lips, softly, with infinite gentleness. "I love you, Shane Rivers."

His throat tightened. From the ashes of his life he had found her love. Even now, after seeing her, after confirming the love in her eyes, it was hard to believe such love could come his way. He closed his eyes and pulled her tight. "I love you, Caroline. I love you as I've never dreamed possible. My worst fear came to pass—but you're still here by my side. You saved me, have given me a life I didn't believe I could have. You looked beyond the savage and found someone you could love."

Caroline sighed. With infinite care she reached up and traced his brow as if etching the feel on her mind.

"The savage was only in your mind, put there by a hate-filled woman." Her fingers trailed down to his jaw. "But it's over now."

He took a deep breath and then pressed his lips to her forehead. "No, sweet Caroline, we're only just beginning."

FREE
Romance
(a $4.50 value)

Send in the Coupon Below

To get your FREE historical romance and start saving, fill out the coupon below and mail it today. As soon as we receive it we'll send you your FREE Book along with your first month's selections.

Mail To: **True Value Home Subscription Services, Inc. P.O. Box 5235**
120 Brighton Road, Clifton, New Jersey 07015-5235

YES! I want to start previewing the very best historical romances being published today. Send me my FREE book along with the first month's selections. I understand that I may look them over FREE for 10 days. If I'm not absolutely delighted I may return them and owe nothing. Otherwise I will pay the low price of just $4.00 each: a total $16.00 (at *least* an $18.00 value) and save at least $2.00. Then each month I will receive four brand new novels to preview as soon as they are published for the same low price. I can always return a shipment and I may cancel this subscription at any time with no obligation to buy even a single book. In any event the FREE book is mine to keep regardless.

Name _____

Street Address _____ Apt. No. _____

City _____ State _____ Zip Code _____

Telephone _____

Signature _____
(if under 18 parent or guardian must sign)

Terms and prices subject to change. Orders subject
to acceptance by True Value Home Subscription
Services, Inc.

0007-7